MURDER
MOST
MELLOW

JAQUELINE GIRDNER

DIAMOND BOOKS, NEW YORK

MURDER MOST MELLOW

A Diamond Book / published by arrangement with
the author

PRINTING HISTORY
Diamond edition / June 1992

ISBN: 1-55773-721-5

Diamond Books are published by The Berkley Publishing Group,
200 Madison Avenue, New York, New York 10016.
The name "DIAMOND" and its logo are trademarks
belonging to Charter Communications, Inc.

PRINTED IN THE UNITED STATES OF AMERICA

10 9 8 7 6 5 4 3 2 1

IRRECONCILABLE DIFFERENCES

"I've got to find out who killed Sarah," I said from inside Wayne's arms.

He put his hands on my shoulders and glared down into my eyes. "Don't do it," he said.

I stepped backwards, away from his hands. "Is this what it will be like if we get married?" I demanded. I could feel my face heating up in anger. "Will you be telling me what I can and can't do?"

"Kate," he whispered, a plea appearing for a moment in his eyes. But he sighed and turned away before I could respond. "Can't force you," he muttered.

I wondered if he meant he couldn't force me to forget Sarah's murder, or couldn't force me to get married. But he walked out the door before I could ask him.

MURDER MOST MELLOW
A KATE JASPER MYSTERY

Don't miss Kate Jasper's
other exciting adventures . . .

THE LAST RESORT

When Kate muscles her way into a ritzy health club to blow the whistle on a murder case, she finds that detective work may be hazardous—to her life!

ADJUSTED TO DEATH

A visit to the chiropractor—who has a corpse on the examining table—teaches Kate a valuable lesson: A pain in the neck may be pure murder!

"A FUNNY, FUNNY BOOK!"
    —SUSAN DUNLAP, author of
        PIOUS DECEPTIONS

KATE JASPER MYSTERIES by Jaqueline Girdner

ADJUSTED TO DEATH
THE LAST RESORT
MURDER MOST MELLOW

I'd like to thank the "critters": Terry Shames, Merrill Sanders, Annie Reasoner, Lynne Murray, Judy Koretsky, Marjory Harris, Virginia Crowder, Susan Cox and Janis Bradley, for their thoughtful critiques; the proofers, Eileen Ostrow-Feldman and Greg Booi, for their unerring eyes; my editor, Hillary Cige, for her manuscript-saving edits; and my agent, Sandra Watt, for believing in Kate Jasper.

I couldn't have done it without you all!

Thank you.

– One –

I watched through the steam as a drop of sweat rolled slowly down Peter's long, thin nose and into the churning waters of the hot tub, then let my own hand float down through the hot, hot water to touch the molded fiberglass bench lovingly. This was my own hot tub on my very own back deck, financed by my recent divorce settlement. And I loved it unconditionally, from its rough redwood exterior to its smooth fiberglass heart. Soaking in the hot water could be so sensuous, so relaxing, so mellow. At least it could be when there weren't a lot of other people there to share the experience with you.

But there were other people in the tub with me that cool Sunday in October, four other people in fact, all there to discuss human potential. I wasn't feeling very sensuous, relaxed or mellow. Tense, troubled and angry was more like it. And it wasn't just the others in the tub. It was the one person who wasn't in the tub who had me upset, my sweetie, Wayne. I brought my wet hand back out of the water to wipe the perspiration from my forehead and tried to force my mind back to what Peter was saying. But my mind just couldn't digest one more lecture on the meaning of being human.

I slid deeper into the tub, slowly surveying the others as a jet of hot water massaged my tight shoulders. Were they really interested in what Peter was saying? Sarah sat next to me, her moist Howdy Doody face alert and smiling at Peter through the steam. She seemed to be listening. On my other side however, Tony was staring vacantly at the patterns his hands were generating in the bubbling water. I wondered what he was thinking about. I'd have bet it wasn't Peter's lecture. Linda's head was turned toward Peter, but her brown face was expressionless. Of course, this was nothing new. In the six months since Linda had joined our group, I had never seen her face do anything more athletic than lifting an eyebrow.

"Self-esteem goes hand in hand with responsibility," Peter was insisting.

Peter Stromberg habitually insisted, argued or contended, rarely satisfied with merely making a statement. His contentious nature may have made him an effective career attorney, but he could certainly be a wearing conversationalist. I turned my eyes back to his long, pinched face with a sigh. His body was long and lean too, but somehow he looked elderly at forty-six years rather than fit. He waved his nearly empty Perrier bottle in the steam as he continued his lecture.

"Personal responsibility isn't limited to our own lives," he declared. "We have a responsibility to help others who are less fortunate."

Sarah bent forward, grazing me with her elbow as she did. My new hot tub was a tight fit for five people.

"It isn't up to us to tamper with the lives of other people," she countered, her voice loud and clear with confidence. "They have their own karma, their own lessons to learn from the universe."

Peter opened his mouth to disagree, but Sarah kept on talking. "You label these folks 'less fortunate.' But you're forgetting that they create their own fortune, good or bad. The most humane thing you can do is to leave them alone and let them do their own——"

"Sarah!" Peter objected. He sat bolt upright, sending a wave across the hot tub to splash over the side, spraying our faces in the process.

"It's true," she said, then giggled at the outraged look on Peter's face. "My sister was like that. Bad grades in school, in a shitload of trouble most of the time. I tried to help her out. A lot of good that did!" Sarah shook her head. "But the minute I left home, she got her act together. Without my help!"

"That's not the point," Peter corrected her.

"Isn't it?" replied Sarah, tilting her head to the side and grinning. Sarah Quinn was the only person I knew who liked to argue even more than Peter did. Not that Peter would ever admit that he enjoyed arguing.

"No," he snapped. "The point is our own responsibility. . . ."

My mind shut down. I couldn't listen anymore. I looked out over everyone's heads, over the log pile against my redwood fence, and over my neighbor's shingled rooftop to Mount Tamalpais in the blue distance. I wondered what it would be like to be Sarah, to be that confident, that positive. If I were Sarah, would I be having problems with Wayne?

Sarah didn't have problems. She had "learning experiences." But then, Sarah was positive in everything she did. She even claimed to be immortal, to be "youthing" instead of aging. Sometimes I wondered if she really was getting younger. She had been forty-five when I had first met her, and she had looked it. Now, a few years later, she looked about forty. She was a tall blond woman with a big bosom which had been gradually unsagging, and a clear face which had been unwrinkling ever since I had met her. I suspected exercise, maybe even surgery, but I wasn't certain. I turned my eyes in her direction, squinting at her face, examining her intense hazel eyes, heavy brows and wide Howdy Doody mouth. If she had undergone surgery, there were no scars to prove it.

I let out another sigh as Sarah leaned forward again, happily sparring with Peter. Being forty years old and short, dark and A-line myself, I envied Sarah not only her self-assurance but her height and bust measurement.

I closed my eyes to better brood over my deteriorating relationship with Wayne. I had thought that finally divorcing my husband, Craig, would free me to have the relationship I wanted with Wayne. Wayne was a passionate, kind and intelligent man, but as far as I was concerned, *he* thought *I* was the one being unreasonable lately. Of course, *he* thought *I* was the one being unreasonable.

I felt a hand on my shoulder. Startled, I opened my eyes and found Tony peering into my face anxiously.

"Are you feeling okay?" he asked softly as Peter ranted on.

I smiled at him. Tony Olberti was such a kind man. He was easy to smile at. And he was certainly easy on the eyes. Thirtyish, compact and muscular, his cinnamon-colored hair, round blue eyes and open Irish face belied his Italian ancestry. Tony was also unashamedly gay, but again he belied the stereotypes. He was earnest and slow-speaking, rarely witty, and never biting in his comments.

"I'm fine," I whispered back to him.

His eyes remained round with concern. Tony was kind, but he wasn't stupid. He squeezed my shoulder gently.

"Let me know if you feel like talking," he said and turned his face away, allowing me my privacy.

I pulled myself up straight in the hot tub, exposing my wet

shoulders to the cool October air. Sarah was speaking again. I tuned in.

"You create your own reality," she said.

I tuned back out hastily. I didn't need to hear any more of this particular sermon. The first time I had heard Sarah say, "You create your own reality," the concept had seemed profound. But after a few hundred too many repetitions, it had begun to sound more like the metaphysical equivalent of "so's your old man" to me.

One look at Peter's face told me he didn't want to hear the phrase again either. The skin on his dripping face was so tight as he glared at Sarah that it looked as if his cheekbones were ready to slice through.

Then Linda caught my eye. She was staring at me, with no more expression than usual, but staring all the same. Damn. Why was she looking at me like that? Linda Zatara, I thought, woman of mystery. Linda was a brown-skinned woman with long, prematurely grey hair and matching grey eyes. The combination was chilling, especially when combined with her emotionless face. Six months ago, Sarah had introduced Linda to our group. I still didn't know much about her. Her job, her hobbies, her ethnicity, even her marital status, remained a mystery. As for her opinions, she was as reticent as a Supreme Court nominee. The woman even sweated unobtrusively! But the real mystery was why she bothered to come to our group meetings.

None of us was really comfortable with Linda. She had to know that. But every time one of us questioned Linda's presence in the group, Sarah had shouted the questioner down. She had even outshouted Peter. And after a while Linda had just seemed to melt into the smooth inner surface of the hot tub. Except for her eyes, which were now unblinkingly fixed on mine. I crossed my arms uncomfortably.

Suddenly I noticed that Linda wasn't the only one with her eyes on me. Peter and Sarah had stopped arguing and were looking at me curiously, too. What were they looking at? A scarlet A on my chest, spinach between my teeth?

"Kate, you're awfully quiet today," said Sarah. "Is there anything you want to share with the group?"

Out of the corner of my eye I saw Tony turn my way again. That made it unanimous. The pressure was on. Should I tell the group about my troubles with Wayne?

"I'm all right," I muttered. I needed time to think about the offer. The group in the hot tub were not really my closest friends. I had met Peter, Sarah and Tony a few years back at a Human Potential in Business seminar that my then husband, Craig, had dragged me to. After the seminar, which had turned out to be unexpectedly useful as well as fun, the five of us who lived in Marin County had decided to continue the exercise in a study-group format. Somehow we usually ended up at my house, where we discussed whatever new business, success and personal-growth techniques were floating around. Then we generally alternated griping or bragging about our businesses. Craig had dropped out of the group when the two of us had separated. And Linda had dropped in. Now it looked like the only way Linda would ever leave the group was on a stretcher.

I leaned back against the tub's edge and sighed.

"There you go again," Peter remarked peevishly. "You've been sighing all day, for God's sake. What is the matter with you?"

No, they weren't my closest friends, but they sure felt like family, if family means a bunch of people who jointly and individually drive you mad half the time and are there to support you the other half. I even shared Sarah's gardener and cleaning lady. When my workload had gone over sixty hours a week, she had taken me in hand, convinced me that I would ultimately save money if someone else did the housework and gardening, and arranged everything for me.

I looked at the sweating, staring faces one more time.

"All right, all right," I muttered ungraciously. I took a breath. "Wayne wants to marry me," I confessed.

The hot tub went silent except for the whoosh and gurgle of the circulating water. The faces around me didn't look particularly enlightened by my confession. Even Sarah's ever-present smile held a hint of uncertainty.

"That's it?" asked Peter incredulously, breaking the silence. "Wayne wants to marry you and you're upset!"

Tony put a wet hand on my shoulder. "Take your time, Kate," he said gently.

I took another breath and explained. "You see, he wants to get married, but I don't. Now he's refusing to see me at all if I won't agree to marry him, and—"

"Then why don't you agree to marry him?" Peter demanded.

Damn. I knew I shouldn't have opened up. Did I have to explain how I felt about marriage, only a year after my divorce from Craig?

"I just don't want to, all right?" I said finally.

"Of course, it's all right," murmured Tony, squeezing my shoulder. "You need to do things at your own pace."

"What you really ought to ask yourself," advised Sarah enthusiastically, "is why you created this separation with Wayne."

I turned to her, my pulse suddenly pounding furiously. "I did not 'create' this separation! Wayne's the one who won't see me—"

"Kate, Kate," sighed Sarah, shaking her head. "Of course you created this separation. You have to be honest with yourself."

"I did not—" I began again.

Sarah blithely ran me over. "Everyone creates their own reality. Everyone, Kate! And then they complain." She shook her head again, her smile sad but tolerant. "When that gardener of ours, Jerry, complains that he's not making the bucks he was when he was an attorney, I ask him, 'If you really want to be a lawyer, why did you quit?' "

Sarah tilted her head at me, as if to ask if I got the point.

"Listen, Sarah—" I started.

"What Jerry does or doesn't do is irrelevant to this discussion," Peter interrupted. "The real issue is one of commitment—"

"The real issue," Sarah corrected him, "is acknowledging our own karma. We can't learn what the universe has to teach us unless we're honest with ourselves. Take my cleaning lady, for instance. She fancies herself a computer programmer, but she's still a cleaning lady. She blames others for her failures—"

"Your cleaning lady's problems are irrelevant!" Peter asserted loudly. The water in the tub shivered nervously. We all knew Peter wanted to be a judge some day. He was already good at rulings.

"The issue here is Kate's commitment to Wayne," he finished, his volume lowered but his tone still righteous.

Sarah wasn't impressed. "Kate has to meditate on what she really wants," she insisted. "We all have freedom of choice in our actions, in our reactions. I got a weird phone call last night on my answering machine. The voice said I was an 'arrogant, unfeeling hag.' And that my money wouldn't do me any good when I was dead. Huh!" she snorted. "I could have let it upset me, but I didn't—"

"You ought to take that kind of call more seriously," Peter told her, shaking his Perrier bottle sternly. "As an attorney, I receive my share of abusive calls, and let me assure you, I take them very seriously. Right now, I'm dealing with one disgruntled client—"

"You missed the point, Peter," interrupted Sarah. "My intuition told me it was a wrong number. If I'd believed the call was for me, I would've flipped. But I take a positive world-view. You see, you really can create your own reality."

Peter twisted his thumbs around the neck of his Perrier bottle. "Sarah," he threatened. "If you say 'you create your own reality' one more time, I'm going to strangle you!"

"Kate," Tony interjected softly. "Relationships can feel—"

"You can strangle me, but you can't kill me," Sarah teased Peter. She stuck out her tongue, then leaned back against the tub's wall, grinning. "I'm immortal, remember?"

I turned to Tony. "Go on," I prompted. Tony opened his mouth again, but Peter was faster.

"First of all, you are not going to live forever any more than I am," he told Sarah. "Secondly . . ."

Tony shrugged. There was no way either of us was going to get a word in edgewise, now that Peter and Sarah were off and running. I rolled my eyes for Tony's benefit, patted his knee, then slid down in the hot water again. At least Linda wasn't watching me anymore. Her head was turned toward Peter again. I let my eyelids drop and resumed brooding. Peter's words came breaking into my thoughts a few minutes later.

"Kate, I'm talking to you," he scolded. I opened my eyes reluctantly and focused on Peter's pinched, frowning face.

"I'm concerned about you," he told me.

"Thank you, Peter," I replied cautiously. But he wasn't finished.

"Your attitude towards marriage indicates a profound lack of commitment. And commitment and responsibility are what make us human."

"And love," added Tony. "But don't worry, Kate. This kind of mix-up happens in relationships, even in caring ones. Lovers always test each other. But if it's the right relationship, it'll weather the storm." He smiled warmly at me.

I returned his smile. Clichéd or not, his words had the ring of truth. And more importantly, it was a truth that I wanted to believe.

"But marriage—" began Peter.

"Can we talk about something else?" I requested hastily. I had received enough advice for the day.

"Dammit, Kate, you brought the subject up!" Peter objected.

"I did," I agreed quickly. "And I appreciate everyone's suggestions," I assured him, with the silent amendment that sometimes I actually appreciated Linda's silence more than his suggestions. "But I need some time to think about what everyone's said."

Sarah nodded and gave my arm a friendly pat. "You know what they say . . ." she prodded me.

"No, what do they say?" I asked impatiently. I wasn't in the mood for jokes.

"When you ask for free advice," she replied, "you get exactly what you pay for."

I had to laugh. Even Peter's face relaxed momentarily into a rueful smile. As Tony chuckled, I felt a warm moment of companionship with the others in the tub. I glanced at Linda's face, wanting to include her. She stared back, her grey eyes cold and dead. The moment ended.

"Anyway, I'll be glad to change the subject," Sarah went on. "I'm working on this far-out new computer program. It models the genius of the very best stockbrokers. And I'm almost done. All I have to do now is come up with a name for it."

"Broker In A Box," I suggested.

Sarah giggled appreciatively.

"Does it go in a robot?" asked Tony slowly, his face reflecting his confusion. Sarah mostly programmed personal robots for robotics firms.

"No, no," she said. "I'm branching out in a whole new direction. . . ."

I leaned back, relieved, as the conversation went on to business. We were all small-business owners, with the possible exception of Linda Zatara. I had no idea what she did for a living. Peter Stromberg had his law practice. Tony Olberti owned and cooked for his own vegetarian restaurant, The Elegant Vegetable. His cooking was inspired, so good that even the major San Francisco reviewers had praised him unanimously. Sarah Quinn made big money designing software for computer games, personal robots and whatever else caught her attention. And I was the sole proprietor of Jest Gifts, a mail-order gag-gift company.

My cat, C.C., came skulking around the tub just as Peter launched into a tirade about that rarest of commodities, ethics in the legal profession.

I dangled a wet hand over the edge of the tub to keep C.C. company. She sniffed it, then yowled her objection to the chlorinated water that dripped from my fingers. Peter stopped mid-sentence to glare at her. Was he going to overrule her objection?

Before he had a chance to, Sarah began to serenade the cat. "Sing the blues, honey," she caroled, blissfully off-key.

C.C. obliged with a long, mournful meow. C.C. was hungry. C.C. was always hungry.

I was hungry, too. I hadn't had any breakfast. I was saving room for one of Tony's spectacular meals.

"Isn't it about time for lunch?" I asked him hopefully.

Tony nodded and stood carefully, barely disturbing the surface of the water. "I've got medallions of tofu, shitake mushrooms and greens in a lemon-herb sauce . . ." he began.

I hustled recklessly out of the tub into the cold air, leaving a small tidal wave behind me.

"And avocado-stuffed zucchini," he continued as he stepped out onto the deck. Peter and Sarah scrambled out after him.

"And spiced oatmeal-raisin bread . . ."

Even Linda was out of the tub and drying off by the time Tony got to the apricot-and-currant crêpes with whipped tofu-carob topping. We all threw on dry clothes as fast as we could, mostly sweat suits except for Sarah's orange and purple caftan. Tony's meals were worth hurrying for.

Once inside, I set the kitchen table as Tony pulled the elements of our lunch from my refrigerator. He even had something for C.C., a cooked corncob, the only vegetarian dish she would eat. He squatted down and held it out to her. She inspected it suspiciously, then clamped her teeth around it and pulled it rudely from his hand. Tony was smiling dreamily as he straightened up.

Sarah sidled up to him with a mischievous grin on her face and sniffed. "I know your secret," she stage-whispered.

The dreamy smile left Tony's face. A pink tide rose slowly up his neck and into his cheeks.

"But I won't tell," promised Sarah, winking. "I like your cooking too much."

Tony made no verbal response to her words. He turned back to the refrigerator and pulled out the rest of his covered dishes in silence. Sarah giggled as she walked to the kitchen table.

Peter and I looked at each other and shrugged simultaneously. What was Sarah teasing Tony about? We all knew he was gay. That was no secret.

I watched Tony as he put the finishing touches on the zucchini. His skin color had returned from pink, passed through normal and settled into pale. So what was the big secret?

"Tony—?" I started to ask.

He turned and handed me a fragrant loaf of bread. I could smell cinnamon for sure, maybe nutmeg. "Kate, will you slice this for me?" he asked quietly.

I opened my mouth to pry.

"Please?" he said.

I sighed, shut my mouth and sliced the bread.

We devoured Tony's feast with the quiet focus of gluttony, only speaking to one another to claim more food. Once the last dollop of whipped tofu-carob topping had been licked from the serving bowl, we waddled into the living room, past the pinball machines—relics of a defunct business as well as a defunct marriage—to sit in comfort. C.C. claimed Tony's lap as he flopped into one of the swinging chairs suspended from the redwood beam ceiling. Sarah grabbed the other swinging chair, and Peter and Linda sat down on the homemade wood-and-denim couch. I lowered myself carefully onto a large pillow on the floor, one hand on my too full stomach.

"If no one else has anything pressing," Peter began, "I'd like to discuss a potential client—"

"Excuse me for a moment," Sarah interrupted, rising from her chair. Ignoring Peter's scowl, she promised, "I'll be right back," and walked out the front door.

Peter sighed, but continued with his story. "A man came in yesterday who wanted to sue his therapist for unlawful touching because the poor woman hugged him. Do you believe it?"

Tony shook his head in commiseration. Linda merely stared as usual.

"So what did you do?" I asked.

Peter opened his mouth to answer, but the ring of the doorbell cut him off.

Sarah? Or another visitor? I pulled my overfed body from my pillow with an effort, walked back past the pinball machines and opened the front door. A four-foot-tall aluminum robot wearing a curly red wig and padded bra stood on my doorstep.

– Two –

"I HAVE GONE beyond bodily limitations," the robot announced in a choppy, metallic voice. Then it laughed. "Ha-ha-ha." Each "ha" was a distinct syllable.

I couldn't help smiling. For all its metallic mannerisms, the robot was clearly Sarah's child. Peter, Linda and Tony joined me at the door. Tony was chuckling softly.

"Watch," commanded the robot. It executed a neat quarter turn on its fat tires, rolled across the front porch to an electrical outlet, pried it open with clicking metal pincers, and plugged itself in for a battery recharge.

"Ahhh," it sighed. "I needed that."

Tony burst out laughing. But Peter just glared. Linda watched without expression, as usual.

Sarah walked up the stairs and took a bow.

"Pretty neat, huh?" she asked, once Tony and I had finished applauding.

"Pretty neat," I agreed. It was a lot better than some of the robot jokes we had endured at *her* house. Robots popping out of closets like jack-in-the-boxes, giving you the Bronx cheer or joining you in the bathroom. Sarah was big on practical jokes. Luckily, we didn't go to her house that often.

Peter wasn't amused. "I was talking, Sarah," he said through clenched teeth.

"About a client whose case you didn't want?" she asked, turning toward him.

"Right," he snapped.

"Well, did you take the case?" she demanded.

"No, but somebody will," he shot back. "And then I look picky because I didn't."

"Well, aren't you picky?" she asked cheerfully.

"Yes, but—"

"If you are picky, look picky, and sound picky, then you must be creating your own reality most effectively." Her mouth stretched into a wide Howdy Doody grin.

"Sarah!" Peter yelped, his voice rising from misunderstood to outraged in one word.

Sarah jumped forward and hugged him violently. Then she kissed Tony and me on our respective cheeks, nodded at Linda, shouted "The universe doth provide," and was on her way down the porch stairs before you could say "transpolitical ecological awareness."

Sarah's robot whirred and clacked dutifully down the stairs behind her on its hydraulic lifters, then joined her in her new BMW.

We watched the back of the car as it shot out of the driveway, popping gravel. The license plate read ILOVEME and a bumper sticker affirmed "Too Hip, Gotta Go."

Peter snarled, "I could strangle that woman," once more for the road, and our Sunday discussion group broke up for the day.

I couldn't sleep that night. I wish I could claim it was because of my precognition of death. But it wasn't. I was worrying about a lot of things that Sunday night, but mostly I was worrying about Wayne.

I popped out of bed, dislodging C.C. from her comfortable position on my chest. She scolded me as I began to pace the length of the bedroom. *My lover Wayne,* I said to myself sadly as I reached one wall. I turned. Some lover. I stomped angrily toward the other wall. We hadn't made love in three months!

I stopped pacing to pick up C.C. She was a small black cat with white spots, one shaped like a goatee on her chin and another like a beret balanced rakishly over her right ear. I buried my face in her fur and hugged her. She squirmed impatiently out of my arms. Damn. My cat didn't even love me anymore.

I sighed and wandered into the living room, struggling with my wide-awake mind. Wayne and I had been blissful lovers for almost a year when my divorce from my husband Craig had been declared final.

And then the fertilizer had hit the proverbial fan. Wayne wanted to marry me. A simple enough desire. Except that I didn't want to be married.

I sat in one of the canvas chairs that hung from the beams of the ceiling, remembering Wayne sitting in the chair when we had met two years ago. He had been so shy, so . . . so unassertive.

I let out a deep, martyr's sigh. Our relationship had been everything *I* wanted. At least until the prospect of marriage had reared its ugly head. I pushed off with my feet and let my chair swing slowly back and forth.

Wayne was a man of such contradictions. A gentle man with a black belt in karate. A man with a scarred and battered face on top of a gorgeous body. A man with a law degree who had spent most of his adult years as a bodyguard and companion to a wealthy manic-depressive. An articulate writer whose speech was brusque, often to the point of unintelligibility. And a kind and loving man who was as stubborn as I was.

For many months Wayne had gone along with my hesitation about marriage. But finally he got fed up. Then, three months ago, he became militant. Either we were married or we were "just friends," he insisted. He wouldn't make love to me until I agreed to marry him. Coy maidenhood from a six-foot-two, muscular body-guard?

I got up from the swinging chair and walked over to the Texan, one of the pinball machines in the living room. If we got married, would we share expenses? That's how I would want it. I had been down the road of financial dependency before and it had turned into a dead end. But how do you share expenses with a man who owns a mansion, a Jaguar and a restaurant empire?

I switched on the pinball machine and watched the game light up. The Texan on the backglass gave me a broad, toothy smile that always reminded me of my ex-husband Craig's. Craig and I had actually managed to have a warm, platonic friendship once we had finally separated. But after his girlfriend's death, he had begun to think of me romantically again. And as little as I wanted to marry Wayne, I wanted even less to be romantically involved with Craig.

I shot a ball listlessly. It hit a thumper-bumper and careened across the playfield. Bells rang. God, I missed Wayne. Was it time to give up my illusion of independence and marry him? I shook my head. Surrender couldn't be a good basis for marriage. The ball came plummeting down the playfield. I pressed the flipper button a second too late. The ball touched the flipper's tip, wobbled uncertainly, then dribbled down the drain hole. I turned off the machine and went back to bed.

I had just fallen asleep with a little help from NatuRest, the "natural" sleeping pill, when the phone rang. Had I forgotten to set my answering machine? The second ring answered the question. I *had* forgotten. I pulled myself out of bed and looked at the clock. It was almost two in the morning.

Groggily, I ran down the hall to the phone in my office. C.C. was ahead of me all the way. I flopped down into my comfy old Naugahyde chair and picked up the receiver. Sarah's greeting came singing over the line. I grunted in return.

"I've got a problem for you, Ms. Detective," she announced cheerfully as C.C. jumped into my lap.

"I'm not a detective," I groaned. "Do you realize what time it is?" C.C. began ecstatically purring and clawing my thigh through my pajamas. That hurt! I hadn't trimmed her claws for weeks.

Sarah's voice became more serious. "I really need someone to help me figure this out," she said.

"Figure out what?" I demanded. I was beginning to wake up. I plucked C.C.'s claws from my thigh and held her paws in my hand.

Sarah didn't answer me right away. "Come on over and we'll talk about it," she said finally. C.C. loosened a paw and dug in again. I unceremoniously dumped her on the floor.

"You mean right now?" I asked Sarah incredulously.

"Sure, why not?" she answered, her tone cheerful again. "You're up, aren't you?"

"No, not tonight, Sarah," I told her firmly.

"Just for a few—" she began.

"Tell me about it now, over the phone," I interrupted. But Sarah wasn't going to let me off that easily.

"I want you here in person," she insisted. "Can you come over tomorrow morning?"

"No, I can't come over tomorrow!" I exploded. Sarah was as imperious as ever and I just wasn't in the mood for it. After ten more minutes of her badgering, I ungraciously agreed to visit her on Thursday evening.

I slammed down the phone just as C.C. jumped into my lap for another try at my thighs.

"You'd better watch it, cat, or I'll have you de-clawed permanently," I threatened, with a glare I wished I could have turned on Sarah. C.C. looked at me unblinkingly and sank her claws in again. I dumped her on the floor once more, set my answering machine and went back to bed. Tomorrow, I promised myself. Tomorrow I'll trim her nails.

The next morning I overslept. It was after ten, and I had a NatuRest hangover. So much for "natural." I was lying in bed when I heard a sound in the house. I jerked awake. Was it only C.C.? No, there it was again. A human being was definitely in the house, creeping around. Actually, whoever it was seemed to be *banging* around. A loud burglar? I wondered drowsily.

Still half-asleep, I pulled my robe around me and crept out the bedroom door. I nearly collided with my quarry. I jumped. She jumped higher.

"God, you scared me," I told her.

"Well, you scared the crap out of me! What the fuck are you doing sneaking up on me like that? And not even dressed yet," she growled, shaking a handful of wet paper towels at me.

My mysterious burglar was none other than my cleaning lady, Vivian, here as usual on Monday morning to clean house. Vivian was close to my age but she certainly didn't look it. Especially that morning with her muscles rippling under her Liz Claiborne jumpsuit, her pretty, tan face registering shock, disgust and, finally, amusement. The amusement was one reason I counted my cleaning lady as a friend. The other was that we were born within a few days of each other, under the same sign. The sign was gossip. We both loved talking about other people's business.

"Wanna do tea?" she asked, pointing her spray cleaner toward the kitchen.

"Yeah, but let me get some clothes on," I answered, yawning.

"I suppose you want herbal," she grumbled, her throaty smoker's voice loaded with disapproval. She had learned to carry her own Lipton tea bags when she came to my house. And on occasion, her own whisky as well.

I stifled another yawn, nodded and shuffled back into my bedroom.

"Hey, you got a shitload of calls on your answering machine!" she yelled behind me.

Monday morning. I brushed my teeth, washed my face and dressed in a hurry. I'd shower later. I didn't want to miss a good talk with Vivian.

I cooked some Rice 'n' Shine brown rice cereal while Vivian made tea for both of us. C.C. came slinking into the kitchen, eyeing Vivian warily. She knew who ran the vacuum cleaner, and she didn't like her. I gave C.C. some KalKan as a consolation prize and joined Vivian at the kitchen table. Vivian handed me my tea, ran her hand through her bleached curls and started in.

"I don't see how you can eat that crap without milk or sugar," she said, rolling her eyes heavenward.

"Sugar and dairy will rot your teeth and your mind," I mumbled incoherently. The cereal was gumming up my mouth. A healthy vegetarian lifestyle has its own hazards.

"You look great," I told her after I managed to swallow. "Are you still pumping iron?"

"You better believe it. I'm not going to give up these biceps," she bragged, flexing as she spoke. "Maybe some guy will appreciate them some day."

"If you'd pick someone for his brains instead of his body, you'd have a better chance," I reminded her. Vivian, according to her own account, had divorced three husbands. Each one had been incredibly handsome and incredibly stupid. She would fall in love with them at first sight and fail to notice their oafishness until about the time the minister said "I pronounce you . . ."

"Yeah, I know," Vivian answered. "Maybe a writer or an artist," she whispered with a faraway look in her hazel eyes. Then she shook her head and grinned sheepishly.

"Anyway, the muscles make me feel strong," she went on in a normal voice. "I could take anyone on. Not like your airy-fairy tai chi. It wouldn't work worth shit against a real mugger."

"I don't know," I said diplomatically. I didn't tell her how tai chi had once helped save me from being murdered. I didn't like to think about that incident.

"I've heard some amazing stories of tai chi used in self-defense," I told her instead. "And I've seen a movie of the master taking on the Marines. He was fifty-three or fifty-four in the movie, a little tiny man. First, four Marines all tried to push him over. They couldn't budge him. Then one by one, they punched him in the stomach. He just smiled—"

"It was probably trick photography," Vivian cut in.

I didn't argue. I practiced tai chi for the exercise, and for the serenity and clarity of mind that followed a good session. I wasn't in it for the martial arts aspect.

"It's a trick," she repeated, narrowing her eyes. She pulled a pint of J&B whisky out of her purse. "Like this prosperity-consciousness bullshit. Imagine yourself rich and, poof, you will be. Huh! I can imagine being rich. I clean for rich people all day long." She poured a good dollop of whisky into her tea and tasted it.

She looked at me sadly. "You're the only one who treats me like a friend. Other people treat me like dirt because I'm not as rich as they are. Is that fair?"

I shook my head sympathetically and took a sip of my own, herbal tea.

She continued, "And no one will give me a programming job. They say I'm a self-taught hacker." She paused for a long swig from her cup.

Vivian was not in a good mood. I wondered what she'd had to drink *before* she'd arrived.

"And meditation, now there's a joke," she muttered angrily. "I've tried to meditate. What good does it do?"

Time to derail the woman, I thought.

"What's the latest on Sarah?" I asked. If anyone would know what was going on in Sarah's mind, Vivian would.

Vivian shrugged her shoulders, but said nothing. Too bad. I had hoped she would know why Sarah wanted detective assistance.

"Come on," I prodded, still hoping. "There's always something new on Sarah."

"Well, you know her house," Vivian offered. She smiled a little as she got up to make herself more tea.

I did know Sarah's house. It was a huge redwood Gothic castle complete with turrets—plus solar panels and skylights. And it was a mess inside. Orange decor dominated the huge rooms, each of which was equipped with a computer terminal. Even the bathrooms were wired. Pictures of gurus, saints and billionaires lined the walls. And piles of computer printouts, dirty laundry, self-help books, leftover food and miscellaneous junk covered the floors. Outside, it was just as bad. A sunken hot tub was surrounded by more debris, in various states of mildew and rust. Sarah paid Vivian double to spend a full day each week carefully dusting and replacing anything not actively rotting.

"Sarah wants to be more 'open to the universe,' " Vivian mimicked, sticking her nose in the air. It was actually a fair imitation. "So she's taken down all of her curtains. Now all the neighbors will get to see the mess, too. I'll tell you, she's not a good advertisement for my cleaning services." Vivian shook her head. "And the neighbors are still screaming about her dog, Freedom. The local kids call the dog 'Dumb' for short. He's still crapping all over the neighborhood. And she won't put him on a leash."

"I guess you can't put Freedom on a leash," I joked. "It would be a contradiction in terms."

"That's just what Sarah said." Vivian looked at me suspiciously for a moment. Then she laughed. " 'Freedom on a leash,' I get it." She sat back down at the table. "But the biggie is—" She paused dramatically.

"What? Tell me," I prompted.

"I finally saw her boyfriend!"

"Really?" I asked in amazement. This was news. None of the group had ever seen Sarah's boyfriend. I had often suspected he was a figment of her positive-thinking imagination. He was a sculptor and a recluse, according to Sarah. She said he never left his own house. She had to visit him there.

"I just caught a glance of him," said Vivian, her husky voice gaining speed. "Sarah sent me over with some groceries. I rang his doorbell but he didn't answer. So I left them on the doorstep. I saw him, though, looking out the window as I was leaving."

"Wow! What does he look like? Where does he live?" I demanded.

"He lives in San Anselmo," she answered.

"That far away? I always imagined he lived around the block." I looked Vivian in the eye. "So what'd he look like? Is he a frog or a prince?"

The teakettle began to shriek before she could answer me.

Vivian shrugged and got up to take care of the kettle.

"That reminds me," she said when she sat back down. "You know that crazy beautician I clean for, the one who calls herself an 'esthetician'? Her husband's been running around on her. Well, I saw *her* out the other day, and you'll never guess who with. . . ."

And so it went until we finished our tea. I never did get any more information out of Vivian about Sarah. Or about Sarah's boyfriend. But I hoped I had cheered her up a little.

While Vivian vacuumed the living room, I played back the messages on my answering machine. My ad copy for Christmas ornaments had been mangled and would need redoing. The manufacturers had run out of red cloth for the attorneys' shark ties and wanted me to consider green. An enthusiastic voice wanted to sell me a new retirement plan. A less enthusiastic voice wanted to sell me a course in shamanism and cosmic power. It was definitely Monday morning. There was no time to trim C.C's nails. I had to get to work.

* * *

I was dead tired by the time I came home from the Jest Gifts warehouse on Thursday. I had spent the whole day there straightening out messes. True, I owned the messes, but that fact didn't comfort me.

It was a little past six o'clock, early for me to knock off work. But I had promised to visit Sarah. What I really wanted was a nice bowl of leftover potato-leek soup and a soak in the hot tub. But I put the fantasies of relaxation on hold, ignored my blinking answering machine, and got back in my Toyota to drive to Sarah's. I dutifully put on my new glasses before starting up the car. I needed glasses to drive now, according to my eye doctor. Damn. I had thought we were supposed to get more farsighted as we got older.

Sarah and I both lived in that unincorporated area of Mill Valley under the shadow of Mount Tamalpais, which the locals called "Tam Valley." Here, modest, older wood-frame and stucco homes sat side by side with the newer, skylighted, sun-paneled, upwardly mobile residences. Architectural styles ran rampant. I passed, among others, a Swiss chalet, some ranch houses, a few redwood cottages like my own, and what looked like a Moroccan castle as I drove toward Sarah's. Buildings sat on anything from standard quarter-acre lots to three-acre parcels. And the landscaping was as mixed as the architecture.

Sarah's redwood Gothic habitat sat in the back corner of a hilly, full-acre lot overlooking a stream. Her yard was surrounded by tall hedges, some trimmed into whimsical fish shapes.

As I turned onto Sarah's street and sighted the fish hedges, a Marin County Sheriff's Department car came gliding toward me. It turned before passing me, however—into Sarah's yard. My shoulders tightened. I pulled my own car in on the sheriff's tail. Once inside the hedges I could see a half-dozen vehicles jammed into Sarah's circular driveway. The scene might have been festive except that most of the vehicles belonged to the county. My pulse began pounding noisily in my head. What kind of surprise did Sarah have for me this time?

– Three –

I PARKED MY Toyota behind one of the sheriff's cruisers and reached for the door latch. But before I had a chance to get my door open, a man in uniform marched up to my Toyota and held up his hand in a warning to stop.

I rolled down my window. The sheriff was tall, with a mustache, mirrored sunglasses and no discernible expression. I couldn't see his eyes at all. My stomach tightened.

"May I see some I.D., ma'am?" he asked without preamble. His voice was as soulless as his face.

"What's going on—" I began.

"The I.D., ma'am," he repeated.

Obediently, I fished in my purse for my driver's license, but my mind continued its questions. What was the sheriff doing here? Had Sarah done something criminal?

I handed him the license. "Are you going to give me a ticket?" I joked nervously.

"No, ma'am," he answered seriously. I clenched and unclenched my hands. I didn't like this at all. What *had* Sarah done?

The sheriff jotted something down in his notebook and handed my license back. Then he asked me what business I had there.

"I'm a friend of Sarah Quinn's," I answered.

"No visitors today, ma'am," he said, his voice thawing for a moment. "But the Sheriff's Department will contact you later if you'll give me your phone number." He held his pencil over his notebook expectantly.

"Why?" I asked. I could hear the shrillness in my own voice. I lowered my pitch. "What's happened here?"

"Couldn't say," he responded. Whatever warmth had been in his voice was gone again. "Your phone number?" he requested once more.

"But I have an appointment with Sarah," I insisted. Suddenly I felt very cold. Had something happened *to* Sarah? The sheriff angled his mirrored eyeglasses down at me. I rattled off my phone number. He wrote it down and closed his notebook.

"You have no further business here," he told me in a voice that could freeze fire. "You'll have to back out the driveway."

I wanted to argue, but it's hard to argue with a man who has no eyes. I put my Toyota in reverse under his unreadable gaze and began to roll back.

Then Sarah's door burst open. Men and women came buzzing out and around the entrance like bees around a hive. The back of one man emerged into the center of the activity. His gloved hands were holding the end of a stretcher. As the whole stretcher came into view I saw what was on top of it. A long, zippered plastic bag.

I jammed on the brake and leapt from my car. The sheriff with the mirrored glasses rushed back toward me.

"No!" I shouted. My body went rigid with fear. "That's not Sarah, is it?" It couldn't be, I told myself. Not Sarah! Sarah was immortal.

The sheriff blocked my way and said nothing. I looked over his shoulder and watched the stretcher being loaded into a county van.

"Tell me—" I began.

"What the hell are you doing here?" boomed a voice from behind me.

I turned and saw a familiar face, Sergeant Tom Feiffer's of the Marin County Sheriff's Department. He didn't look much different than he had two years ago, still tall and muscular with curly blond hair and blue eyes. Only now he had maybe ten more pounds on his frame and a very angry expression on his face. When he jerked his head in dismissal, the sheriff with no eyes left us.

The rigidity flowed out of my body into the ground, leaving my muscles weak and rubbery.

"Sarah . . ." I began, then faltered under Feiffer's angry glare. "I had an appointment . . . that's not her, is it?"

He didn't answer me. Damn.

"Why are you here?" I demanded shrilly.

"This area is outside city limits, under county jurisdiction," he answered briefly.

I heard the doors of the county van slam shut.

"Is that Sarah's body?" I asked again, struggling to keep my voice level. I looked into Sergeant Feiffer's eyes. I saw the anger go out of them.

He nodded and turned his face away. Sarah dead? I couldn't take it in. The air shimmered around me. Was I going to keel over?

Feiffer turned his face back to me. "How come every time there's a mysterious death in Marin you show up?" he asked. His suspicious tone knocked the dizziness out of me.

"Mysterious!" I repeated sharply. "What do you mean 'mysterious'? Was Sarah murdered?"

"I don't know," Feiffer answered, his blue eyes glued to mine. "Was she?"

"How should I know?" I shot back. I backed up a step. I didn't like the sound of his question.

Feiffer sighed. He looked back at the buzz of activity behind him. Then he returned his eyes to mine. "Come with me," he said evenly.

I followed him through the gaggle of men and women at Sarah's door into her house and down the dimly lit hall to her living room. Feiffer cautioned me not to touch anything, then motioned me to an orange velvet love seat, the only clear surface in the room. Every thing else was covered in the refuse of Sarah's life. Feiffer removed a stack of computer printouts from an easy chair, then sat down himself. I looked around the room at the litter of books, dishes, magazines, laundry and computer paper. Everything was in its normal place. Whatever had happened to Sarah, it must have happened in another room.

Sergeant Feiffer asked me why I had come to Sarah Quinn's house. I explained that we were in a discussion group together and told him how she had called wanting to talk about a "problem" four nights earlier.

"That's it?" he pressed. "She didn't tell you what the problem was?"

"No," I answered numbly. "She was . . . she was enigmatic." I still couldn't comprehend her death. I expected her to pop out the door any moment, yelling "Surprise!"

I looked into Feiffer's serious eyes and let the expectation die. I straightened my shoulders.

"Now, *you* tell *me*," I ordered. "How did she die?"

"Whoa!" he answered, putting up a hand to ward off my questions. "We don't know yet. We're in the process of investigating."

"Was she murdered?" I pressed.

"We don't know," Fieffer repeated, through clenched teeth this time. "We're in the process of investigating."

"But—" I objected.

"But nothing," he interrupted. Then he stood up.

"Just tell me—" I tried again.

"I'll talk to you again, later," he told me firmly. He took my elbow and steered me out the front door. "Be available," he ordered and turned me over to the sheriff with the mirrored sunglasses.

I let the sheriff lead me to my car. I looked back briefly at the men and women in front of Sarah's house, then backed out of her driveway.

On the way home I kept thinking of Sarah. Sarah the enigmatic. Sarah the immortal. I saw her smug smile in my mind and my eyes teared up. "I'm sorry," I whispered.

I shuffled into my house, trying not to cry. C.C. twined around my legs and yowled. I picked her up and squeezed her to my chest. For once she was willing to console me. She purred and even reached her paw up to tap my nose gently, as if to say, "there, there." Together we sat down in my comfy Naugahyde chair. I saw my answering machine light flashing through a filter of tears.

I pushed the playback button and listened absently. First there was a hang-up. Then a sales pitch. Then a message from Peter asking to speak to me. Another hang-up and a call from a ceramics firm followed. On the final message I heard a voice I barely recognized as Vivian's.

Vivian's speech was usually raucous. This voice was a shrunken version, small and lifeless.

It said softly, "Sarah's dead. Call me. Please, call me."

I began to shiver as I dialed the phone. By the time Vivian came on the line, I was shaking so violently that C.C. abandoned ship, leaping from my lap to the floor.

"I found her. I found her body," Vivian said in a zombie's voice.

The finality of Sarah's death bore down on me with Vivian's words. I swallowed, then asked her, "What exactly happened?"

"I went there to clean today." She took a rasping breath. "I finished the house and then I went out back. She was in the hot tub. So was one of her robots."

My mind created a comfortingly cozy picture of Sarah and a robot chatting over tea. I shook it off impatiently.

"Was she already dead?" I asked softly.

"Of course she was!" Vivian bawled. At least her voice was getting back some life, even if it was hysterical.

"All right, it's all right," I soothed her. "What was the robot doing in the tub?"

"I don't know. How should I know?" She was wailing now.

"But what—?" I began.

"She . . . Sarah . . . the body looked terrible," Vivian stammered. "And the police, they questioned me for over an hour before they let me go. And I called you, but you weren't there." She paused and her voice became very small. "Don't ask me any more questions, please." Her last plea shook me into sensitivity.

"I'm sorry, Vivian," I said gently. Should I tell her I had seen Sarah's remains in a body bag, myself? No. She didn't need to hear that. "What can I do for you?" I asked instead. She didn't answer me.

Suddenly I wanted to help her. To help anyone. It was too late to help Sarah. "Do you want me to come over?" I asked.

"No, don't worry about it," she answered, her voice apathetic again. She made an effort to speak. "My son Billy came over. He's going to spend the night with me. I'll be okay."

I said goodbye and hung up. I wanted to call somebody, to talk to somebody. To talk to Wayne. But my body seemed wooden and my mind sluggish. From a great distance I realized I must be in shock. I slowly walked into the bathroom, where I swallowed four NatuRest capsules. Then I put on my pajamas and went to bed.

Sleep pulled me down and my thoughts went again and again to Sarah. Pictures of Sarah pontificating, laughing and telling stories flickered through my mind. I could even hear the tone of her strident voice. And feel the array of emotions she had generated in me—anger, affection, amusement, frustration and admiration. As I finally dropped off, I saw in my mind's eye her bumper sticker proclaiming, "Too Hip, Gotta Go."

Early the next morning I awoke from a nightmare with tears on my face. I couldn't remember what it was about, only that I had been saying "I'm sorry" over and over again. My sheets were soaked with sweat. Looking around the familiar room with growing recognition, I felt the relief of consciousness spill over me. But that relief was quickly displaced by the memory of Sarah's death. And the questions. How had she died? Why had she died?

I struggled out of bed and down the hallway in my pajamas. I wanted answers, but I didn't know who to call. Wayne? I dismissed that sentimental thought, and its accompanying twinge of self-pity, with irritation. Then I thought of Tony. As I dialed his phone number I realized that he probably didn't know that Sarah was dead at all. Was *I* going to have to break the news to *him*?

I shouldn't have worried. All I got were the gentle and loving tones of his answering machine. I banged down the receiver and threw myself into my comfy chair, where I sat shivering in sweat-soaked pajamas. Damn it, I needed to talk!

I could have called Peter. After all, he had called me. But I didn't want to be the one to tell him about Sarah. I considered my friend Barbara. But she was probably sleeping. She was not an early riser. And she hadn't ever met Sarah. I let out a sigh and decided to call Vivian.

Vivian answered after seven rings with a sleep-saturated "Hello."

"How are you feeling?" I asked her.

"God, my head hurts," she replied. Her words were slurred. "I took a couple of sleeping pills. I was going to sleep in this morning, but you called," she said. There was a note of irritation in her tone. It was better than the apathy of the night before.

"I'm sorry. I didn't realize. What time is it, anyway?" I asked.

"It's five-thirty. Don't you ever look at your clock?" The note of irritation had swelled to a full measure.

"Look, Vivian, I wanted to talk to you—"

"Why?" she interrupted.

"Because I want to know what happened to Sarah!"

"Sarah died in a hot tub," she mumbled.

"You know what I mean," I pressed. "How did she die? Why? What's going on?" There was no response from Vivian. I asked, "Aren't you curious? Don't you want to talk?"

There was another moment of silence, and then she replied slowly, "Maybe . . . but I don't know any more than I told you."

"I just want to understand what happened," I explained. "And about Sarah, I really did like her, weird as she was. I mean . . . Oh, I don't know what I mean!" Suddenly I felt angry. "Do you know Sarah's boyfriend's name?" I demanded.

"Why do you want to know?" she asked suspiciously.

"I want to talk to someone who cared about Sarah," I told her. "Maybe he did."

After a moment of silence, Vivian spoke.

"His name is Nick Taos. It's a 'spiritual name.' That means he made it up." Vivian's voice was friendlier now. Probably because she had some exclusive information to share. "I think Taos is supposed to have to do with Chinese philosophy, or maybe he's named after that town in New Mexico," she went on. "But it won't do you any good to call. He won't talk to you. He doesn't talk to anyone."

I waited for more, but she only said, "Listen, I'm going back to bed. I bet you have a stack of papers on your desk gathering dust. You usually do. Why don't you go deal with it?"

"Vivian, come and see me for lunch today, all right?" I asked. "Just to talk."

"I know what kinda stuff you eat for lunch. I think I'll pass," she said. Harsh words, but there was a hint of affection in her tone.

"I'll make chili," I offered. "You like my chili."

"Okay, okay! I'll see you for lunch, but I gotta go back to sleep now. Good night, or good morning, or whatever!" she finished, and the line went dead.

I knew I needed to take a shower eventually and begin my paperwork for the day, but I sat rooted in my comfy chair for hours thinking of Sarah and how I had failed her. Then I remembered Sergeant Feiffer. The Sheriff's Department had to know by now how Sarah had died. I picked up the phone and dialed.

Ten minutes and three transfers later I got the sergeant. But he wasn't very informative. He told me three things. One, Sarah Quinn was dead. Two, they were indeed investigating the death. And three, he wanted to talk to me again. That was it. All my attempts to elicit additional details were stolidly met with "We're in the process of gathering information now," the key word being "gathering" as opposed to disseminating. I agreed to be interviewed at my house at one o'clock.

Only then did I shower and sit down to my Jest Gifts paperwork. My mind was still churning with questions. I worked on my Saw-and-Bones Christmas ad for the medical magazines and wondered. Had Sarah succumbed to a heart attack? Wouldn't she have shown some sign if she'd had a heart problem? I called the ceramics firm that was supplying the shrunken-head mugs for the psychiatrists. Had she drowned? Can you drown in a hot tub? I checked work orders. Of all people, how could Sarah die? And the worst question of all, would she have died if I had agreed to go and talk to her Sunday night?

Sarah was special. I had actually begun to believe she was headed for an impressive old age, if not actual immortality. I slogged through vouchers, accounts, bills, registers, freight charges, invoices and tax forms. Then I remembered the answering machine message that Sarah had talked about at our last group.

Damn. How the hell had I forgotten that? I stopped breathing. Hadn't the message said something about Sarah's death?

That was too spooky to even think about. Suddenly I needed to be with people. Warm living human beings to shield me from the apprehension of death. I pushed myself out of my chair, put on my driving glasses and tore out the door to the shelter of my old brown Toyota. As the engine turned over I even thought up an excuse for leaving the house. I had promised Vivian chili and I didn't have the time, or the heart, to make homemade. I could pick up canned vegetarian chili at the health-food store downtown and claim it as my own.

I was pulling up to the stop sign at the end of my narrow street when a white Volvo came whipping around the corner into my lane. It screamed to a stop a few inches from my front bumper. My heart went berserk, crashing erratically against my ribs. I rolled down my window to yell at the driver. Then I saw who was behind the wheel. It was Linda Zatara.

She backed up and drove around me without looking me in the face. Had she even recognized me? I rolled up my window and turned unsteadily onto the main drag. What was Linda doing in my neighborhood? On my street? The third or fourth time that I asked myself these questions, and received no answers, I realized I was driving the wrong way. I was driving toward Sarah's house.

I took a deep breath, made a U-turn, drove downtown and parked.

Walking along to the health-food store, my eyes absently skimmed the headlines of the newspapers in the vending machines. The afternoon *Marin Independent Journal* stopped me cold in my tracks. POLICE INVESTIGATE BIZARRE HOT TUB DEATH, it announced in thick black letters.

I reached into my purse for change with icy hands. There is something mind-altering about seeing a part of your life in print. I felt drugged as I pulled out a paper, walked slowly to the bus stop, and sat down, my eyes on the newsprint.

"Local Marin resident and computer programmer, Sarah Quinn, was found dead in her hot tub yesterday. With her in the tub was a robot still plugged into the outdoor electrical outlet. Death was caused by electrocution." Oh, God! "Chief Deputy Sheriff Horace May would not reveal how the robot came to be in the hot tub. However, reliable sources disclosed that in the past the robot had been programmed to plug itself into the outdoor electrical outlets in order to recharge its batteries." I remembered the cute little robot with the curly red wig and padded bra. Was that the killer? "It is believed that upon this last occasion the robot was additionally programmed to maneuver itself into Quinn's hot tub, thereby electrocuting her."

My horror in imagining death by electrocution was interrupted by a flash of indignation. Sergeant Fieffer had known this the whole time he was talking to me and had never let on. I wondered whether he had seen the *I.J.* yet.

I read further. "May, who is in charge of the Sheriff's detective bureau, would not comment when asked if the death was being treated as an accident, suicide or murder." Murder. There it was. "Sheriff's Sgt. Tom Fieffer commented that they have some key pieces of the puzzle but haven't yet been able to assemble them."

I wondered what key pieces they had. Whatever they were, Fieffer wasn't going to share them. That was clear. I thought again about Sarah's answering machine message. I looked up from the paper. How had she described the message? Something about her money not doing her any good when she was dead. Had that message been a death threat? Had the mysterious caller carried out the threat? I looked back down. The paper went on to discuss Sarah's illustrious career.

"Sarah Quinn came to Marin in 1978. She established a word-processing business, Word Inc., with partner Myra Klein at that time. In 1981 Quinn left the word-processing business to start her own computer software company. This company, Quinn Unlimited, had been quite successful, according to Steve Barnard, local Chamber of Commerce leader. Most recently, Quinn had been engaged in programming domestic robots. It was one of these robots that was found in the tub with her."

Murder? Or, just maybe, the ultimate practical joke gone awry? The article concluded by listing Sarah's civic activities: the Marin Business Exchange, the Marin Ecology Club, and Citizens for a Nuclear Free Marin. There was a picture of Sarah staring out at the camera from the Citizens for a Nuclear Free Marin campaign headquarters. It didn't capture her spirit. Maybe that was because the picture was motionless. Sarah had always been in motion.

I tucked the paper into my purse, bought my chili, found my car and drove slowly back home. During my drive I considered the possibilities: accident, suicide or murder. And in my mind's eye the word "murder" was repeatedly circled in red ink. Suicide was unthinkable in respect to Sarah, and she had loved life far too much to fail to guard against accidents. Even from my dazed point of view,

I could see that murder was the only reasonable answer to the question of "how" someone like Sarah could die. And I might have prevented it.

"Why?" remained unanswered. And I had a new question, "Who?"

– Four –

THE "WHO?" QUESTION didn't go away as I drove home. If Sarah had been murdered, the murderer had been no random street killer, no interrupted burglar. Whoever had killed Sarah must have been someone familiar with her house, hot tub and computerized robots. How else could they have programmed the robot? I knew Sarah had opened her home to only a few select people. Peter, Tony, Craig, Linda and I had qualified to visit as group members. Vivian had been there to clean, and Jerry to garden. Maybe Sarah's boyfriend, sister, neighbors or business associates had been invited. I might be able to find out.

But even among those who had been in Sarah's house, how many knew how to use her computer system? How to program her robots? I tapped my fingers on the steering wheel impatiently. Of course, she did tend to show off that computer system.

As I pulled into my driveway I could hear an internal voice whispering insistently, "It's someone you know." The tone and tempo of that voice were my grandmother's. She had always prided herself on a fierce pessimism disguised as practicality. I shook my head emphatically. It was not anyone I knew! But still . . .

Once I opened my door, I hurried to my desk, made a foot-square clearing in its forest of paperwork, and set my telephone in the exact center.

I phoned Peter first. As I punched out the numbers, I considered briefly just what I could say to him. He might not even know that Sarah was dead. Her death had seemed so all-encompassing a reality for me that I had forgotten how little time had actually elapsed.

"Law office," the voice at the other end of the line said. I had also forgotten the lioness at the gate. I told her my name and asked to speak to Peter.

"And what is this concerning?" the voice inquired politely.

"Uh, Sarah Quinn."

"I'll see if Mr. Strauss can speak to you now," the voice said and put me on orchestral hold. Piped music poured relentlessly from the telephone receiver. Holding it as far away from my ear as I could and still be alert for the change to a human voice, I stared at the old photos, postcards, aphorisms, articles and shipping schedules that were tacked haphazardly to my bulletin board.

The voice came back. "Mr. Strauss is in conference right now. May he return your call?" The "conference" probably consisted of Peter and some files. This, on top of the piped music, fueled my annoyance.

"Tell him it's important," I said in a tone which I hoped conveyed fury just held in check. "Tell him I have to talk to him *now*."

"Please hold," the voice said and the orchestra filled my ear once more.

"Dammit, Kate, I'm busy," Peter announced, mercifully cutting short a violin-heavy rendition of "Maria."

"Listen, Peter," I said. "You called *me* last night, remember?" Now that I had him on the line I wasn't sure how to tell him about Sarah. And I did want to know why he had called me.

"Oh, right. I called you," he said with some contrition. Then his tone went shrill. "It's about Sarah." My stomach constricted. Did he know? "She's not following the rules of the group," he complained. "Our group is a serious discussion group, not some latter-day fraternity party. These practical jokes have got to stop. Someone has to talk to her and—"

"Peter," I interrupted softly.

"What?" he snapped.

"Sarah's dead," I said.

There was silence at the other end of the line, and finally, "I don't believe it."

"Then go get a copy of the afternoon *I.J.*!"

"But she can't be dead, she's . . . she's immortal," he sputtered.

"Oh, Peter," I whispered softly, hearing Sarah's "youthing" speech in my mind. I shook off the reverie and continued, rattling off facts quickly to get them over with. "Sarah is dead. I saw them bring her out in a body bag. And I know what killed her. One of her robots crawled in her hot tub and electrocuted her."

There was a long silence before Peter replied.

"Is this a joke?" he asked, his voice tremulous. "Because, if it is, you can tell Sarah I don't think it's funny! This is even more tasteless than the robot in the bathroom. I didn't think you would stoop to being a party to Sarah's jokes—"

"It's not a joke, Peter," I said. Something in my tone must have gotten through to him. He didn't reply. "The *I.J.* wouldn't print a joke like this, would they?" I pressed.

I heard him tell someone to go out and find a copy of the newspaper. Then he was back to me.

"What exactly did you mean when you said a robot crawled in the tub with her?" he asked, his voice deeper and steadier now.

"A robot was found in the hot tub, still plugged into the outlet," I told him. "They think someone programmed it to electrocute Sarah."

"Good God, do you mean she was murdered?" Peter asked in a whisper.

"I think so," I answered. "I mean, can you imagine Sarah committing suicide?"

"No."

"And she was a competent programmer," I pressed on. "So I don't think it was an accident."

"No, not an accident," Peter answered thoughtfully. "Unless . . . unless it was an unfortunate joke that backfired." His voice picked up speed. "Even then, it would have to be programmed exactly to do what it did. But, good God, we can't be talking about murder!"

"Why not?" I asked. "You have criminal clients. People do kill each other sometimes."

"But not people like Sarah," Peter insisted. "People like us! Dammit, I can't believe this!" He was shouting now.

"Listen," I said softly, soothingly. "I need to talk to you about this thing in person. When can you see me?"

"I, I don't know . . ." Peter's voice wavered. "I've got a heavy schedule for the next week. I still can't believe . . ."

"Are you okay?" I asked, belatedly remembering my own shock and recognizing the symptoms in Peter.

"Of course I am." He drew a breath and steadied his voice. "Next Thursday for lunch."

"Next Thursday?" I repeated incredulously. Sarah was dead and he was putting me off for a week! "No, tonight," I insisted. "We can talk over dinner."

"But I have work to do," he whined, like a child who knows that punishment is inevitable but still tries to avoid it.

"I have work to do, too," I snapped. Then I softened my tone. "Come talk to me, Peter," I cajoled.

He sighed dramatically. "Okay, tonight," he said, giving in. "Seven-thirty at the Safari Café."

"All right, I'll be there," I said. "And Peter, I know it's weird," I added. "I'm shook up, too. That's why we need to talk."

"I can't believe it," he repeated and hung up.

I sat in my easy chair feeling queasy after he hung up. Was my queasiness due to being the bearer of bad news? Or something else? Unbidden, more questions forced their way into my mind. How would my conversation with Peter have gone if I had been speaking to a murderer? Would it have been any different? I felt my skin tighten. Could Peter act that well? All good trial attorneys have to be actors, I answered myself.

The sound of wheels crunching the gravel in my driveway startled me back into the present. Through the window I could see Jerry Gold's van pulling up with its gold-on-green legend: GOLD'S GARDENING. A little visual pun, he had explained to me once.

It was not his day to do my yard. Was he here to talk me into paying for additional unnecessary work? Sarah had once told me that all those extra trim jobs, pest sprays and fertilizations were not necessary for my garden but essential for Jerry's cash flow. She had been amused at my gullibility. He hadn't conned her into any extra work.

He got out of his van, a squat, leathery man who looked like one of his own gardening gloves. He stared at the house but didn't move toward the front door. It occurred to me that he might be here to talk about Sarah. But why was he hesitating?

The phone rang. I turned away from the window to answer it. It was Tony. Sweet, kind Tony. He had read the *Marin Independent Journal* article. As he spoke, I could hear the sound of Jerry's van backing out of my driveway.

Tony said we needed to "get in touch with our feelings" about Sarah. I wondered, Would Tony and I better digest the indigestible news by "getting in touch with our feelings"? Did talking about Sarah's death help to make it real, or help distance it?

"Her death is really troubling to me," Tony said with typical understatement, his quiet voice sounding sincerely troubled. Uneasily, I remembered all those *National Enquirer* murderers of whom the neighbors always say, "he was such a nice man," after the fact.

We agreed to meet at The Elegant Vegetable for lunch the next day. At least I'd get a good meal.

My next move had to be a call to Nick Taos. I was looking up his number in the phone book when I heard another car crunch the driveway gravel.

I went to the window and peered out. A white Volvo was parked under my apple tree. Linda Zatara's white Volvo. My heart began to beat erratically. I had almost forgotten the Volvo's near crash into my Toyota this morning. Here, on my street. And here was Linda again. I told my heart to settle down as I watched her get out of her car, look to both sides and climb the stairs to my front door.

I was at my door before she pushed the bell. What did she want from me? Her face was as expressionless as usual when I opened up. She surveyed me with cool grey eyes, as if from a distance.

"Sarah," she whispered.

I moved from my position blocking the doorway and motioned her into the living room. She walked slowly past the pinball machines to sit on the couch.

"Did you read about it in the *I.J.*?" I asked, flopping down into one of the swinging chairs.

She nodded.

"God," I said, shaking my head. "It had to be murder. But who would murder Sarah? She called me the other night—"

I saw a flicker in the grey eyes. I stopped mid-babble.

"She called you," Linda prompted.

"Nothing," I said uneasily. "It was nothing." I didn't like the grey ice in her eyes any more than usual. I shivered, feeling physically chilled by her coolness. Why was she here?

I rubbed my hands together to combat the cold. "Were you coming to see me earlier?" I asked.

She nodded.

"About Sarah," I prompted.

She nodded again. Damn. How could I get her to talk? An inner voice asked me if I really wanted to get her to talk. What if—

"Can I get you some tea?" I asked, cutting off the voice.

She shook her head.

"Water?" I offered desperately.

She nodded.

Linda followed me into the kitchen. The sun shone into the room, bouncing cheerfully off the cream-colored walls. But I felt trapped by Linda's dark, silent presence.

Then C.C. came skidding around the corner into the kitchen as if summoned. The atmosphere seemed to lighten. C.C. issued an interrogatory yowl for food. I told her it wasn't lunch time yet. She dropped onto the floor and began industriously licking between her back legs. I chuckled and glanced at Linda to share a smile. Linda stared back without a change in expression. Not a cat person, I remembered, stiffening. Not a human person either.

I walked to the refrigerator and pulled out a bottle of Calistoga water. Then I turned. Linda was right behind me. I jumped. I hadn't heard her following on my heels.

"What did Sarah talk to you about?" she asked, pushing her face close to mine. Up close her grey eyes didn't seem totally lifeless. There was a pinpoint of light in her pupils, like a light at the end of a long tunnel.

I was trembling as I handed her the Calistoga. I stepped sideways and around her to sit at the kitchen table, where I nervously straightened papers and books. Then I took some deep breaths. The woman wasn't going to attack me in my own home, I chided myself. She sat down across from me.

"What did Sarah say?" she repeated in a monotone.

"Nothing much," my voice squeaked. I took another breath to get my voice under control. "Where did you meet Sarah?" I asked.

"A group," she answered. This was progress. A two-word reply. But before I could congratulate myself, she threw another question at me. "Do you know Tony's secret?" she asked.

Tony's secret. Damn. Another little mystery I had managed to forget. I shook my head.

"Do you know who left the death threat on Sarah's answering machine?" Linda pressed.

I shook my head again, wondering if I was looking at the person who had. My mouth felt very dry. Why had Linda been so quick to label the message a "death threat"?

"Why do you want to know?" I demanded.

Linda smiled a rare smile, her lips drawing back tightly from sharp, gleaming white teeth. She made no reply.

"I don't know anything," I said, suddenly tired of this game. "She's dead, murdered! I don't know who did it. It could have been any one of us who had access to her computer. I saw them take her away—"

I shut my mouth and clamped my lips together. I was babbling again. Was that what Linda wanted?

I stood up. I wanted her out of my house. I centered myself in a tai chi posture. "I have to get back to work," I told her firmly.

Linda shrugged and left. It was only after she was gone that I thought of all the questions I could have asked her. Should have asked her. I sighed. She probably would have avoided them anyway. Especially the important questions. Had she murdered Sarah Quinn? And if so, why? I didn't have a clue.

I did a little more deep breathing, then resumed my search for Nick Taos's number in the Marin County phone book. I hadn't really expected to find him listed, but there was his name and number at the beginning of the T's in black and white. I was surprised. I hadn't thought recluses had telephones, much less listed phone numbers. I was further surprised when he answered my call. His "Hello" was high-pitched and loud.

"Nick, my name is Kate Jasper," I began.

"Oh, you're the one in the group who got a divorce and doesn't want to get married again," he bawled in my ear. If this was his idea of social skill, it was no wonder Sarah had kept him locked away.

"Yeah, well, anyway," I said impatiently. "Do you know about Sarah?"

"Uh-huh, the police have been here," he said loudly enough that I had to hold the telephone receiver away from my ear. Was he deaf? No, he had heard my question. I opened my mouth to ask another, but he cut me off before I could speak.

"What will I do?" he wailed. "Sarah takes care of me! She takes care of everything! She gets my groceries! She buys my clothes! She's the only one who knows how to take care of me! And she's gone!" I held the phone further away from my ear. "What am I gonna do? I haven't been to a grocery store in years! She kept saying we'd go together one day! Oh God, whatamIgonnado?" he bellowed. He was clearly not a verbal recluse.

"How old are you?" I asked, truly curious.

The question stopped his wailing. "I'm twenty-eight," he mumbled. Then his voice got loud again, and defiant. "I'm an artist, you know. Sarah says I'm a genius. She moved me out from my parents' to this house eight years ago so I could work in seclusion."

"Do you need me to bring anything over?" I asked slyly.

"Would you really bring some stuff over?" he cried.

"How about this afternoon?" I pressed. The fish had taken the bait. Now all I had to do was reel him in.

"Oh, this afternoon'd be great," he yelled. I pulled the phone away from my ear again. "I need hamburger and Mallomars and root beer and lots of stuff," he told me.

"Sarah let you eat that junk?" I asked without thinking.

"Uh-huh." His voice filled my ear. "Sarah used to try to make me eat brown rice and stuff, but finally she said it was like 'trying to pound sand' and gave up," he explained. Sadly, I imagined Sarah saying that.

"Now I eat anything I want," Nick clamored on. "And I'm as healthy as she is . . . was—" His voice rose perilously.

"Listen," I said, cutting off the threat of hysterics. "I'll see you in a few hours, all right?"

"Uh-huh," he answered and gave me a long, loud order of toxic substances to be delivered. He didn't offer to reimburse me.

After I hung up, I picked up the phone book again and found Word Inc., Sarah's former word-processing business, in the Yellow Pages. I briefly considered the ethics of pumping Myra for information under the guise of looking for word-processing help. Being in business myself, however, I didn't like to con someone into believing they were going to make money off a nonexistent deal. Then I had an idea. I could really use some word-processing help. I had stacks of letters to write. I could act in good faith, recruiting some secretarial assistance at the same time that I examined Myra's attitude toward Sarah. Feeling myself to be a woman of integrity once again, I rang up Word Inc.

A friendly female voice answered.

"This is Kate Jasper," I told her. "I'd like to speak to Myra Klein."

"Were you interested in our word-processing services?" she asked politely.

"Yes, I am," I lied. Well, partially lied.

"Then maybe I can help you. I'm Susan. What kind of services do you need?"

I didn't answer. I had clearly bungled my introduction. Damn. How was I going to extricate myself?

"Hello, are you still there?" Susan asked.

"Actually . . ." I said slowly, "I also wanted to talk to Myra about a mutual friend, Sarah Quinn."

"Oh," said Susan in a cooler tone. Either she knew Sarah, knew of her, or knew of her recent death. In any case, the name alone seemed enough to lower her temperature. Or else Susan was just belatedly deciding I was more trouble than I was worth. She put me on hold.

At least there was no piped music on their line. I tapped my fingers on the teak surface of my desk and looked at the bulletin board again. My eyes settled on a rare photo of Wayne that my friend

Barbara had taken. His eyes were just visible under his low brows. I pulled the picture down from the board as a new voice came through the receiver.

"This is Myra Klein," the voice enunciated carefully. "What is it that you wanted?"

I was beginning to think I was too embarrassment-prone for effective sleuthing. My cheeks were hot as I opened my mouth to speak.

"I wanted to talk to you about Sarah," I told her.

"Are you a reporter?" she asked. Was it the telephone connection or was her voice trembling?

"No, I'm a friend," I assured her.

She sighed, then spoke in a breathy rush. "As you may know, I haven't been a friend of Sarah's for some time. I've got some very mixed feelings about her right now."

"Did you know she was dead?" I asked.

"Yes, a reporter called," she answered quickly, then paused. "Look," she finally said, her voice eager. "I do need to talk to someone about Sarah. Can we meet? I have this afternoon, after four o'clock, free."

"I'll be there at four," I told her. As I hung up, I felt perversely discomforted by her easy acquiescence. Why hadn't she needed more convincing?

I leaned back in my comfy chair and thought of all the work hours I was going to lose while pursuing the questions surrounding Sarah's death. I picked up Wayne's picture again as if to ask him what to do. Should I cancel all the appointments I had just made? Then, with a lurch of my stomach, I remembered. Sarah might still be alive if I hadn't refused to visit her that night. I had to investigate. I had to know what my refusal had cost.

The doorbell rang. Wayne? I wondered hopefully. I ran to the door and opened it. My ex-husband was on my doorstep.

– Five –

"HEY, LADY, YA wanna buy a good set of encyclopedias?" Craig asked in his former New Jersey accent.

I rolled my eyes toward the ceiling.

He grinned. "No? Then how about some rug cleaner? Aura cleaner? Healing crystals? Herbal laxatives?"

"Not funny," I said, but a small smile tugged at the corners of my mouth.

"How about a little support and comfort, then?" he suggested, his accent returning to California. The grin left his face. "I heard about Sarah."

My ex-husband, Craig, looked good as he stood there framed in the redwood doorway. He had left his suit jacket in the car. The white sleeves of his shirt billowed out from his grey pinstripe vest, hinting at hidden muscles. He brushed a few errant brown strands back into his groomed-for-success hair and surveyed me with puppy-dog eyes.

I wished for a moment that we had our old post-separation friendship back. But that had passed when he lost his girlfriend. Now his brown eyes held that Why-can't-you-fall-in-love-with-me-again? look.

I crossed my arms over my chest and tried to look forbidding.

He put up his hand as if to ward off my anger. "Just passing by," he assured me. "Thought you might have a cup of herbal tea for a thirsty man." He cocked his head and smiled a little-boy smile.

Then I remembered that my ex-husband was something besides a pain in the rear. He was a computer expert! I stuck Wayne's photo in my back pocket and silently ushered Craig in.

At the kitchen table five minutes later I handed him his favorite mint tea, taking care not to touch his fingers. "How much do you know about Sarah's death?" I asked him.

"Just what I read in the paper," he answered, shrugging. "Something about her being electrocuted in the hot tub. It's been a long time since I've seen her, but it's still a shock." He made a wry mouth and laughed. "Sorry, wrong word."

Then he looked into my eyes. "I thought of you, Kate," he murmured softly.

The tenderness of his expression almost snared me, until I noticed that familiar smirk lurking around his mouth. Was he setting me up for seduction? I averted my eyes from his face and reminded myself that the man was merely a good source of information.

"Just how difficult would it be to program her robot to land in the hot tub?" I demanded. I kept my voice steady and hard. "How much experience would you need to pull it off?"

He cocked his head again. "Are you sure you've really considered the advantages of owning an encyclopedia?" he asked.

"Still not funny," I told him. "Answer the question."

"It would depend," he temporized. He shot me a sharp look. "Do you really need to know this?"

"Yes," I answered brusquely.

He sighed and put down his cup, the tea untasted. "The robot is probably pretty easy to run, even to program, given that you'd seen it done before," he admitted.

"But would it show that you were the one who did it?" I pressed.

"Not necessarily," he said slowly, thinking. "All you'd have to do is delete any references if it did. You could just type in a different name and time for that matter, if those things were even required to get on the system."

"I've been thinking about it," I told him, my thoughts crystallizing as I spoke. "For all her eccentricities, Sarah was a creature of habit. She meditated in the hot tub every evening around the same time. And she went into a pretty deep trance." I looked at Craig for confirmation. He nodded.

I went on. "Then there's her sunken tub, and her robots that can plug themselves into the outdoor electrical outlets. What if . . ." I felt suddenly lightheaded. I took a breath and continued. "What if someone—someone who had the coordinates of the setup outside—programmed one of her robots to plug itself in, traverse the necessary distance, and plop itself into the hot tub at the given time? Could it have happened that way?" I asked him. I could feel my pulse pounding.

"Yeah, maybe," he replied reluctantly. He shrugged his shoulders and continued. "I guess it'd be possible. But only if the robot was programmed to override any signals it got to stop at the edge of the tub." He stared off into space for a moment, thinking. "It probably would've been easy enough to program, though whoever programmed it would have needed to know about Sarah's house. And about her habits and robots and computers." His eyes widened. I could see he'd finally thought it through.

"Holy shit, Kate! This means it must have been someone who knew Sarah," he whispered urgently. He stared into my eyes. "Messing around with this could be risky."

"Yes," I agreed simply. I glared back at him. "Well?" I pressed. "Will you help?"

He was silent for a moment. I continued to glare at him.

"Okay, okay," he said finally. "I'll help." He smiled weakly at me. "Knowing you, I'll bet you already have a theory. And you're going to ask questions till you find out if it's right. But Kate"—his voice deepened—"this isn't product research we're talking about here." He reached his hand across the table to touch mine.

I removed my hand quickly. "You think it was murder, too," I said.

"I didn't say that," he squawked.

"You know computers," I insisted. "Could it have been an accident?"

He took a huge gulp of his mint tea before answering. "If I talk to you about this, will you lay off asking other people questions?"

"Probably not, but at least I won't have to ask someone else these particular questions," I answered honestly. Then I leaned forward and burned my eyes into his. "You know more about computers than anyone I know. Help me understand what happened."

He squirmed in his chair.

"Could it have been an accident?" I demanded.

This time he raised *both* hands in surrender. Then he spoke quickly, probably to get it over with. "I wish I could say for sure it was an accident. If the robot plugged itself in, it might have gotten an electrical glitch that caused it to behave erratically. Or maybe Sarah programmed the robot to come up to the edge of the tub, and miscalculated so that it went a little too far. But then it should've stopped anyway, unless it was programmed to override the sensors." He frowned before continuing.

"I'll be honest with you," he said. His voice was high with tension now. "I doubt if it was an accident. And if it wasn't, you ought to be careful."

"If it was murder, and murder by someone close to Sarah—maybe someone close to me—I want to know about it," I said steadily, ignoring my racing pulse. "I don't want to wonder for the rest of my life if someone I know is a murderer."

"How about the police?" he asked.

My mouth dropped open. Craig certainly hadn't trusted the police before. Not when they had suspected *him* of murdering his girlfriend.

He saw my look and threw up both hands again. "Okay, okay," he grumbled. "You win." Then he cocked his head at me. "But what *are* the police doing?"

I shrugged. "Whatever they're doing, they're not telling me about it," I said.

He nodded gravely, then suddenly grinned. "Kate Jasper to the rescue!" he sang out. "Powered only by tofu, she leaps tall buildings—"

"Sarah was talking about some way she was going to make a fortune," I cut in quickly. "Something involving the stock market and computers." His grin faded.

"Her and everyone else," he said, shaking his head. "Everybody and their roommate's dog thinks they have the stock market computer program that's going to make a fortune. But there are just too many variables and unknowns in the market. Stuff that can't be programmed in. It just doesn't work."

"Thanks for answering my questions," I said softly.

"Got any more?" he asked with a smile.

I shook my head and smiled back, basking in the good will of the moment.

"How about I move in for a while?" Craig asked slyly. "Built-in security guard, dish washer—"

"Cut that out," I said. Would the man ever quit trying?

The doorbell rang before he could try any more. Craig rose from the kitchen table as I went to answer the door. Another visitor. Just what I needed. How the hell was I supposed to get anything done?

I jerked the door open angrily.

Then I saw Wayne. He was hunched over the doorbell, ready to ring again. My eyes moved quickly up his long, well-muscled body, over his thick neck to his battered face. After a short stop at his cauliflower nose, I looked into what I could see of his eyes.

They were mostly hidden under his dark heavy brows, as usual. But what peeked out looked warm and concerned.

"Wayne," I whispered.

"Kate," he growled softly.

He opened his arms and leaned forward to hold me.

But his body tensed just as we touched. I looked up. He was staring over my head. And his face was suddenly dead. Craig. I had forgotten Craig.

Wayne straightened up and stood absolutely still. I turned to Craig.

"Well, I guess I'll be going," Craig said in a suddenly high voice. "Two's company and all of that." He smiled weakly.

"See you later," I said in a shaky imitation of nonchalance.

"Not if I see you first," he replied with a braying laugh. Always the joker. Never the straight man.

Craig edged his way out the door around Wayne.

Once Craig was gone, I asked Wayne, "Where were we?" in the most seductive tone I could muster.

But Wayne's face was still devoid of feeling.

I put my arms around his waist and laid my head against his chest. I sank into his warmth and heartbeat. Slowly his arms came around me and tightened. We stood there breathing in rhythm for a few moments of bliss. Then he broke away.

He held me out at arm's length and looked into my eyes. "You okay?" he asked. His voice was gravelly. I wanted to rub up against its rough texture.

I nodded my head violently.

"Sarah died," I said softly.

"I know," he growled. He pulled me to him again.

"I've got to find out who killed her," I said from inside his arms. He sighed deep in his chest.

I ignored the sigh. "Want some tea?" I asked him.

He didn't answer.

"Are you hungry—?"

He broke away again, dropping his arms this time.

"I'm not here for tea, not for crackers," he rumbled. "I'm here because you're going to involve yourself in something dangerous." He put his hands on my shoulders and glared down into my eyes. "Don't do it," he said.

I stepped backwards, away from his hands. "Is this what it will be like if we get married?" I shrilled. I could feel my face heating up in anger. "Will you be telling me what I can and can't do?"

"Kate," he whispered, a plea appearing for a moment in his eyes. But he sighed and turned away from me before I could respond. "Can't force you," he muttered.

I wondered if he meant he couldn't force me to forget Sarah's murder, or couldn't force me to get married. But he walked out the door before I could ask him. I watched miserably as he climbed into his bottle-green Jaguar and drove away.

I sat down at my desk, hoping to quell my misery with work. I removed the telephone and brought out my new necktie design for orthopedic surgeons (navy blue with neat rows of little pink feet). All the design needed was a few more details and I'd send it to the manufacturers.

I worked on it for all of two minutes before the doorbell rang again. Damn! Who was it now? I'd need traffic cops here before long.

I opened the door more cautiously this time. I sighed in relief when I saw who was on my doorstep. It was my friend Barbara Chu. She looked as trim and elegant as ever, even in her khaki electrician's jumpsuit. Of course the lightning-bolt earrings helped. And the new asymmetrical cut of her black hair contrasted attractively with her smooth Oriental features.

She peered at me for an instant, then exploded into the room, talking and hugging me at the same time.

"Are you all right, kiddo?" she asked, anxiety and interest evident in those all too scrutable eyes.

"You saw the paper?" I guessed wearily.

"No, no. Not the paper," she said, releasing me from her embrace. Her face became even more animated. "I was at work when I had this flash of violence. Then I saw your face. I asked my spirit guide and she said you were safe, but I couldn't shake it off." She peered at me again. "You haven't beat someone up or something?"

"No, but Sarah . . ." I hesitated.

"Someone died?" she asked, her voice low and spooky.

I nodded, then shivered. Sometimes Barbara's psychic abilities were too much for me.

"Murdered?" she pressed.

"Are you sure you didn't see the paper?" I asked, feeling queasy. She shook her head.

We sat on the couch, and I told her about Sarah's death in detail. My tale was punctuated by Barbara's frequent outbursts of "Wow" and "I knew it!" When I was finished, I leaned forward eagerly to hear her appraisal.

"So how's Wayne?" she asked with a sly smile.

Damn.

"How'd you know I saw Wayne?" I demanded. "More psychic flashes?"

"I passed his car on the road," she admitted.

I leaned back and laughed. It felt good to have something to laugh about. Then I told her about Wayne's visit.

"Don't worry," she said cheerfully. "You're soulmates. You'll always be together."

Sometimes Barbara's pearls of wisdom were as aggravating as Sarah's. It was too bad they hadn't ever met. They might have enjoyed each other. Maybe they could still meet, I thought suddenly. Barbara was psychic, wasn't she?

"Do you think you could communicate with Sarah's spirit?" I asked. I felt foolish the moment the words left my mouth but I figured it was worth a shot.

"Like a seance?" Barbara asked thoughtfully.

I nodded. Even if she wasn't able to contact Sarah in the ether, it sure would be interesting to see how the other group members responded to such a possibility.

Barbara closed her eyes for a few moments to commune with her spirit guides. When she opened her eyes she said "Yes," and put her arm around my shoulders.

"Thanks," I said. She was a good friend even if she was a wacko. I squeezed her hand. "I'll get together what's left of the study group," I told her. "We can meet here."

But before I could arrange any more seance details, Barbara stood up from the couch and looked down at me with serious eyes. Damn. I was beginning to recognize that look. I got ready for the inevitable lecture.

"Kate," she said softly. "I know you'll be safe physically, but I'm worried about you emotionally. You need to ground yourself better." She let her gaze travel around the outline of my body. "Your aura is black around the edges. Are you sure you want to get into this?"

"I have to," I told her. "I have to know whether Sarah's death was my fault."

She reached down and gave me another hug. "It's not your fault, Kate. But I know you'll have to find that out for yourself. And you will."

"Are you into prophecy too, now?" I asked.

"Could be," she chuckled.

She planted a kiss on my cheek and whizzed out the door with a "Take care, kiddo," as fast as she had come in.

Once Barbara had left, I sat on the couch brooding over Sarah. And mulling over all those who had known her. At least Wayne hadn't known her, I thought. I felt in my back pocket and pulled out his picture. I passed my eyes over it quickly, then walked back into my office and shoved it in a drawer.

By the time I looked at the clock, it was nearly twelve. I had ten minutes left to produce "homemade" chili for Vivian. And then I realized I had never set a date for the seance.

As I clattered an iron skillet onto the stove, yet another realization came to me. Craig had been a member of our study group, too.

My heart hiccuped in my chest. I dumped two cans of chili into the skillet and told myself that he hadn't come to the group for a long time. But still . . . I sliced into an onion impatiently. The acrid fumes wafted upwards to sting my eyes.

– Six –

AT LEAST VIVIAN didn't ring my doorbell. She didn't bother. She just dragged herself through the back door into the kitchen and sat down heavily in her customary chair. I glanced at her over my shoulder. She didn't look well.

I turned from the chili I was stirring and examined her more closely. Her usually glowing tan was tinted grey, and there were hollows under her eyes. Were they the result of shock or grief? Or too much alcohol? Then I wondered if I looked as sick as she did. I shook off the thought and asked her how she was doing.

She grunted in reply.

How was I going to get her to talk about Sarah? I considered asking her if she had read the *I.J.* article. No good, I decided. Vivian knew everything about everyone. It would probably insult her dignity to imply that she resorted to such prosaic sources of information as newspapers. But I couldn't just jump in and ask her about finding Sarah electrocuted in the hot tub. That thought brought up a sudden surge of pity in me. I knew what it was like to find a dead body.

"Are you all right?" I asked her gently.

"Oh, I can handle it," she replied, her voice wooden. She sat staring at her lap without expression. Her uncharacteristic reticence was beginning to worry me as much as her appearance. Perhaps this wasn't the time to pump her about Sarah.

"Maybe you should talk to a therapist," I suggested, taking a seat across from her. "You've been through a horrible experience."

"Naah," she said. She lifted her head to look at me. The whites of her eyes were marbled with red. "I mean, thanks for sharing and all of that, but I'm really fine. Let's just eat, okay?"

It was a quiet meal until I tempted Vivian with some purposely inaccurate bits of gossip concerning a prominent city councilman. She stopped mid-bite and corrected me with a touch of her usual spirit. The man was not into cocaine but gin, she assured me, and then she told me just who the real druggies were on the council. This led to a story about the trials and tribulations of one pot-smoking man she cleaned for, whose daughter had become a policewoman, of all things. And so it went until Vivian regained at least a ghost of her former delight in the foibles of the human race. A healthy swig from her J&B bottle didn't seem to hurt her mood either.

"What's going on now with Sarah's demise?" I asked lightly, having primed the pump to my satisfaction.

"I dunno," she said, her voice gone wooden again. She returned her gaze to her lap.

"Vivian, is that you?" I demanded. "*You* must know the latest scoop. Did her sister ever come to town?"

"Yeah," she answered, brightening a little. "The sister did show up. Her name is Ellen. She *claims* she flew in today." Vivian lifted her head to give me a knowing look. I let out my held breath. Vivian was going to be all right.

"Sarah was supposed to meet her at the airport," she continued, her voice gaining life and speed. "But she didn't, so the sister snagged a rent-a-car and drove out to Sarah's house and, of course, no one was there. She talked to the neighbors, and one of them is one of my ladies I do house for, so she gave Ellen my number. So Ellen calls me like I'm Information Central—"

"You *are* Information Central," I interrupted affectionately. Vivian shot me a look. "Sorry," I said. I waved her on. "Go ahead, tell me about Ellen. What's she like?"

Vivian moistened her mouth with another sip of J&B before continuing. "Ellen was pretty upset about Sarah, but not *real* upset," she told me. She raised an eyebrow and tilted her head slyly. "If you know what I mean."

I nodded wisely.

She bent forward to tell me more. "And she wasn't in a big hurry to call the cops either. She wanted to ask *me* all the questions. Then she asked for Nick Taos's address. It sounds like she knows she splits the estate with him," Vivian finished in a low voice.

"You mean Sarah had a will?" I asked eagerly. I had figured Vivian would be a gold mine once she started talking. I was right.

"Yeah," Vivian answered, with a self-satisfied smile. "Half to the sister and half to Nick."

"Wow," I breathed. Then I thought out loud. "Pretty strange for an immortalist to have a will, isn't it?" Had Sarah known she was going to die? My pulse began to pound audibly.

"I think maybe she made it before she decided she was living forever," Vivian said thoughtfully. "Anyway, she didn't leave anything to her mom."

I looked at Vivian for more.

But she just said, "I don't know why," and shook her head before going on. "Her mom's in an old folks' home in New Jersey. And her dad's dead. And the sister, Ellen, she was supposedly the black sheep of the family."

"Yeah?" I prompted eagerly. A gold mine, all right.

"I'm not sure what Ellen did wrong exactly," Vivian mused. "But that's how Sarah talked about her."

"What about Nick?" I asked.

"He probably needs the money," Vivian offered. "He hangs out in his house, never goes anywhere. He's never even been to Sarah's. She took him over his groceries and stuff." Her voice softened. "He'll need someone to take care of him now."

"I'm going to visit Nick this afternoon," I announced proudly. "It's a matter of food. He needs a chocolate fix."

"I don't believe it!" Vivian protested. She sat straight up in her chair and stared at me.

"It's true," I said, keeping my tone light. "That man will do anything for junk food."

"Shit," she muttered. She glared down at her empty plate. It was clear that I had made a tactical error in mentioning my own visit.

"Maybe you should go see him and find out if he needs a little cleaning," I suggested softly.

"Yeah, maybe." Her words were noncommittal but she looked up and smiled. "Anyway, you know Sarah's mutt, Freedom?" she went on, picking up her bowl and carrying it to the sink.

"Sure," I answered.

"Well, this guy Peter is taking care of him." She turned on the water.

"Not my Peter?" I asked, gazing at Vivian's backside in wonder. "You mean Peter Stromberg?"

"Yeah, him," she threw over her shoulder. "He took Freedom out of the pound right after the cops put him in."

I picked up my own bowl and joined Vivian at the sink. "But Peter always said he hated dogs," I told her. "And Freedom in particular. I wonder if he feels guilty for arguing with Sarah all these years or . . ." I let my words drift off. Could Peter be feeling guilty of something far worse?

"Or what?" Vivian demanded. She swiveled her head toward me as she turned off the water. "You'd better keep your nose outa this!"

I kept my sigh internal. That made five people today who didn't want me to investigate. Time to change the subject. "Do you know who Sarah's attorney and accountant were?" I asked quietly.

I saw the struggle in Vivian's face. It was a good bet that she wouldn't be able to resist showing off her inside information in spite of her disapproval of my investigative efforts.

"Yeah, I do," she said finally, her voice sullen. "Her attorney was this lady, Janice Jackson, neat lady. And her accountant is a weird little guy, Donald Simpson."

"What do you mean 'weird'?" I pounced on her words.

Vivian tapped her head meaningfully. "He's one of these 'there are aliens among us' guys," she explained. She was into her story now, no longer sullen. She wiped her wet hands on a towel. "He says there have been beings from other planets living here for years and they're infiltrating all walks of life. He says you can tell who they are because they don't blink."

"I never noticed whether Sarah blinked, did you?" I asked thoughtfully.

"Jesus, I was never crazy enough to check!" Vivian exploded. "Don't tell me you buy that crap?"

"No, no," I assured her. But Linda Zatara popped into my mind suddenly. If anyone was an alien . . . I shook off the thought. "I was just thinking that if Simpson *thought* Sarah was from another planet . . ." Vivian was glaring at me again. "Did he ever go to Sarah's?" I asked.

"I don't know," she muttered.

"I can't believe there's something you don't know," I flattered cagily. "How do you find out all of this stuff, anyway?"

"I have my sources," she replied with dignity, and returned to her chair.

"How about Sarah's hotshot computer program that was supposed to make her a fortune?" I asked, following her back to the table.

"What about it?" Vivian responded, her voice sulky once more.

"Sarah must have told you something about it," I pressed, unwilling to believe I had lost her again.

"Sarah didn't tell me anything any more," Vivian muttered. "I was just hired help to her."

"Aw, come on—" I ventured.

"What do you wanna know all this crap for anyway?" she demanded, cutting me off. "Are you gonna play amateur detective? Huh? That's a good way to get killed, you know."

"How about helping me?" I asked. I sat down across from her and looked beseechingly into her eyes. "You could get state secrets out of the KGB, for God's sake! We'll make a great team."

She didn't even deign to answer that one. She just set her jaw and looked deliberately out over my head. The phone rang. I signaled Vivian to stay put while I answered, but she turned a blind eye to my gesture. She got up, thanked me in a hasty whisper for the meal, and went clattering down the back stairs as I said "Hello."

My friend Ann Rivera was on the phone. Her cheery voice asked me where we were going to eat next Tuesday. My mind shifted gears slowly to respond to her simple question. She was the first person I had spoken to all day who knew nothing of Sarah's death. The sudden return to normalcy felt like swimming up from the murky realms underwater to pop through to the air and sunshine. What a relief. We chatted about nothing in particular and decided to meet at The Elegant Vegetable the following week.

The ease of the light conversation shook my resolve to investigate Sarah's death. Maybe everyone was right. Maybe I should just ignore it. I went to the sink to wash the remaining dishes. But by the time I had put the last spoon in the drainer, I had convinced myself once more that I couldn't endure never finding out if the "who" was possibly someone I knew. I dried my hands and reached for my phone book.

I found Janice Jackson listed in the Yellow Pages under "Attorneys." She had a small advertisement, listing her specialties as business and family law, and offering free half-hour consultations. Would she talk to me about Sarah? About Sarah's will? A knock on my front door interrupted my thoughts.

I looked out the window and saw Sergeant Feiffer. I put on a friendly face as I opened the door.

Feiffer's face wasn't friendly, though. His blue eyes were cool and serious. "Ms. Jasper," he said. "I'd like to ask you a few questions about Sarah Quinn." My muscles tensed when I heard the formality in his tone.

"Come on in," I said, hoping I was speaking as the spider to the fly, not the fly to the spider. I could ask questions too, I reminded myself.

As I led him into the living room, he gazed at the pinball machines longingly.

"Hayburners, Hot Line, Texan," he murmured. "God, you're lucky."

"Would you like to play a few games?" I asked and turned on the machines.

His eyes lit up along with the pinballs. His hands reached out to the sides of Hayburners as if of their own free will. I had forgotten he was an addict. But he stopped himself as he reached for the plunger. He straightened up and glared.

"Thanks, but I'm not here to play pinball," he said. He forced his eyes away from the machine and back to me. My stomach flip-flopped.

"A chair?" I offered nervously.

"Thank you," he said and sat down on the couch. All traces of lightness had disappeared from his face. He took a small notebook out of his pocket. Then he looked up at me and frowned. My stomach did another somersault.

"Tea?" I blathered.

"No," he replied sternly. "Please sit down."

I sat. He continued frowning at me as I plopped into my swinging chair. Purposeful intimidation, I decided. Well, I wasn't going to fall for that. I'd conduct my own investigation.

"What have you guys found out about Sarah's death?" I demanded as if I had the authority. "Was it murder?"

"Whoa," he said. I thought I saw a smile pull at his mouth for a moment. Then he leaned forward seriously. "What makes you think it was murder?" he asked.

The ball was in my court. But I didn't mind explaining. I watched his eyes as I outlined my reasons for rejecting suicide or accident. I saw a few faint flickers of interest, but nothing more. No surprises. I would have bet that he had been over this ground already. "And that leaves murder," I concluded, volleying back to him.

"That may be," he conceded. I leaned forward eagerly, ready for an intelligent discussion. "But we're still in the process of gathering information," he finished.

"Do you get that out of a book or what?" I asked in angry disappointment. "Every time I try to talk to you, you say you're 'in the process of gathering information.'"

"I'll tell you one thing," he replied, his eyes almost friendly.

"Yeah?" I prodded. Was he finally going to share information?

"You shouldn't dig into this," he rapped out. He shook his pencil at me. "Let us do the job."

I sank back into my swinging chair. Another vote of no confidence. That made it unanimous.

"Now, do you think you could answer some of *my* questions for a change?" Feiffer asked, his pencil poised. "For instance, who do you know who has visited Ms. Quinn's house and maybe played with her computer? I have a list here: you, your husband—"

"My ex-husband," I interrupted.

"Yeah, so I understand. I hear you're not getting along with your boyfriend either," he added breezily. His eyes smiled at me.

I squinted back at him. Why was he suddenly smiling?

The smile spread to his mouth. Then I recognized the expression. It was a leer. A subtle leer, but a leer none the less. Could he be interested in me as well as the pinball machines? It didn't seem likely. I was no femme fatale. Maybe this was a new interrogation technique. If it was, it was effective, I decided. I was completely rattled. I realized my mouth was gaping open and clamped it shut.

"Okay," Sergeant Feiffer said, his voice stern again. He glanced down at his notebook. "You, your ex-husband, the housekeeper Vivian Parrell, the gardener Jerry Gold, Peter Stromberg, Linda Zatara and Tony Olberti." He looked back up at me. His leering smile was gone. Had I imagined it? "Do you know of anyone else who's been to Sarah Quinn's house?"

I didn't answer. I was still trying to figure out the meaning of his smile. True, Feiffer had flirted with me the first time I met him. The second time too, for that matter. But I had assumed he was just playing.

"Ms. Jasper?" he prompted gently. "Anyone else?"

"How about the neighbors?" I offered, pulling myself back to the reality of Sarah's death. "She might have invited them in."

"We're checking that possibility out," he assured me.

"And her sister and her boyfriend?" I pressed.

"Yeah, we're checking them out too."

"I suppose you're also 'checking out' her ex-business partner, attorney and accountant," I concluded.

"You got it," he answered. He smiled again. I dropped my eyes quickly.

"And I suppose it doesn't look like anyone broke in or anything," I mumbled.

"They wouldn't have had to break in," Feiffer said, shaking his head slowly in disgust. "From what I understand, the woman didn't lock her doors."

"That's right, she didn't," I conceded. But I felt defensive on Sarah's account. "You've got to understand," I told him, "Sarah really believed in the benevolence of the universe. And that's usually what she got too." I sighed. "Until this, anyway."

"Well, I hope you lock your doors, Ms. Jasper," he said. "We wouldn't want anything to happen to you." His voice was affectionate. Too affectionate.

"No problem," I said in an effort at nonchalance. My effort came out sounding gruff.

Sergeant Feiffer seemed to catch my mood. His manner was all business when he asked me if I knew anyone with a motive to murder Sarah.

I shook my head. Sarah might have rubbed a lot of people the wrong way. But enough for murder?

"You know these people," Feiffer said. "Are any of them mentally unstable?"

I shook my head again. But I wondered. Someone had to be unstable, didn't they, to commit murder?

"How about drugs?" Feiffer went on.

"Drugs?" I repeated stupidly.

"Yeah, drugs," he said, smiling again. "You know what we say in the Sheriff's Department—if you find someone who looks dead on a Marin street, put a mirror under their nose. If they inhale, they're still alive." He pantomimed sniffing coke.

"No, Sarah didn't need drugs," I told him, laughing in spite of myself. "She was strange enough without them."

That comment started him on another round of intense interrogation. Just how was Sarah strange? Were her friends strange, too? Just what went on in our study group, anyway? Did we really meet in a hot tub? What did I know that I wasn't saying? And on. And on. By the time he had finished pummeling me with more questions, I wasn't sure which was harder to deal with, an affectionate sergeant or a serious one. An affectionate one was likely to become an angry one if spurned, I thought suddenly. My neck muscles tightened. I interrupted him before his next question to begin my own interrogation.

"Do you know who did it?" I asked, watching his eyes.

His eyes narrowed. "I'm asking the questions, not you," he reminded me. Did he know? I wished I had Barbara's psychic powers.

Feiffer stood up abruptly to leave before I could ask anything else.

"Those are some nice machines," he said, looking at the pinballs wistfully. "Maybe I can come over for a game when this investigation is all over."

"Sure," I said, without thinking.

He gave me a big smile and left. I let out a long, trembling sigh. If only Wayne had given me that smile, I thought sadly.

I shook my head violently. I wasn't going to worry about men anymore. I reached for the phone book.

Sarah's attorney, Janice Jackson, was listed as having an office in San Rafael. I began to dial her telephone number but put down the receiver before I completed the call. She might refuse to see me if I called first. But what if I just presented myself at her office? I jotted down her address, turned on the answering machine, put on my glasses, and left the house before my mind could stop me with rational objections.

The "Professional Building" that housed Janice Jackson's office was neither modern nor attractively Victorian. It was a fifties-vintage, long, low two-story building. Its age and lack of style were inadequately disguised by new redwood shingling. I entered the lobby and found Jackson's name on the directory among those of other attorneys, accountants and consultants. "Donald Simpson, Accountant," was also listed. I took the accessibility of both Sarah's attorney and accountant in one building as a good omen.

The sign on Ms. Jackson's door said, PLEASE COME IN, so I did. An attractive young black woman with warm, friendly eyes and cropped hair was perched on the receptionist's desk. I asked her if I could speak to the attorney.

"I *am* the attorney," she replied. Strike one for Kate. She saw my look and laughed.

"People often think I'm the receptionist. And, yes, I am awfully young, but I'm good, too! What can I do for you?"

"I wanted to ask you some questions about Sarah Quinn."

Her eyes narrowed, becoming less friendly, but she didn't kick me out. She invited me into her inner office. She had made the best of the low-ceilinged room. The cream-colored walls were decorated with Japanese silk hangings that complemented the simple teak furniture.

"Now, just who are you, and what do you want to know about Sarah?" she asked in a cool voice once I was seated.

"I'm Kate Jasper," I replied. "I'm a friend of Sarah's." There was no reaction from the attorney. "From her study group," I added.

"And . . . ?" she prompted.

"There were a couple of things . . ." I faltered. "You do know she's dead, don't you?" I asked anxiously.

"Yes, I know," she replied. Her eyes narrowed further.

"I'm looking into her death, kind of," I squeaked. I made an effort to lower my voice. "I wanted to confirm the contents of her will," I finished.

"Do you think you're in her will?" she demanded, a look of disgusted comprehension crossing her face. Strike two.

"No, no!" I assured her. "I just wanted to know what was in it."

"Ahead of everyone else, I suppose." She clicked her tongue. "Have you ever heard of confidentiality?" she asked, enunciating each syllable of the last word separately. I squirmed in my seat. Strike three.

"Confidentiality, oh sure," I said. I looked into her glaring eyes. "Maybe we can start this conversation over again," I suggested hopefully. "I'm just trying to find out what happened to Sarah, sort of investigating, you know." Her eyes softened a bit as I babbled. "I guess there's not a lot I can ask you that won't run into the confidentiality problem?"

"Probably not. Sorry about that," she said. She was smiling politely, but I knew I was definitely out.

"I won't take up any more of your time, then." I got up and walked to the door. At the door I turned to ask one more question. "Have you ever visited Sarah's house?"

"No, I haven't! Come and see me if you ever want to hire an attorney." She ostentatiously broke eye contact and bent her head over the papers on her desk.

I dragged my feet up the carpeted stairs to the next floor, wondering if I really had what it took to sleuth. Donald Simpson's door was standing wide open. Unlike Ms. Jackson, he had not made the most of his single-room office. There was paper strewn over every available surface. Computer printouts, ledger sheets and long curls of adding machine tape covered desk, couch, shelves and most of the floor.

As far as I could see there was no human form visible. I sighed and turned to leave. Then I heard a grunt from behind the desk.

– Seven –

My perception shifted instantly when I heard that grunt. Where I had only seen disorder before, I now saw the signs of a ransacked office. My adrenaline began to flow. Was that the grunt of a man returning to consciousness after a brutal beating? I stepped quickly toward the desk and cautiously peered over.

Lying prone in a great nest of paper was a short, middle-aged man. As I looked at him, he opened his eyes. They were small, dark eyes set closely together over a disproportionately large nose and dark luxurious mustache. He blinked and sprang up, extending his chubby body to its full five feet.

"A little cat nap, great thing for the mind. Donald Simpson," he introduced himself, sticking out his hand abruptly.

After an involuntary jump backwards onto slippery computer printouts, I remembered my manners and shook his hand. He energetically denuded a chair of its pile of papers and motioned me to sit down. He likewise sat, in his own chair, but without bothering to remove the paper which cushioned it. He kept his eyes fastened on mine as he began a lecture on the value of napping as opposed to sleeping. Midstream he asked, "Did I have an appointment with you?"

"No, I . . . I'm a friend of Sarah Quinn's," I said, startled by the sudden question. I could feel my eyes rapidly blinking under his intense stare. Then I remembered Vivian telling me this guy believed you could spot aliens because they didn't blink. I hoped I had proven myself a human life form to his satisfaction.

"Ah, Sarah," he sighed. "Terrible thing about Sarah." He shook his head sadly. "Good mind, that woman had. The best! Kept all her records and documents on her computer. She'd bring me her floppies at the end of the month. Really understood the value of the computer as a tool—"

"Did you ever get to see Sarah's computer?" I asked, cutting into his discourse.

"Never had the pleasure," he replied, then rattled on blithely. "A robot of hers delivered some floppies here once. Knew it was Sarah's doing 'cause I could hear her giggling out in the hall. Great little robot, but you never know about robots." He paused and frowned, his eyes leaving mine momentarily. "But, still, Sarah was straight. Sure going to miss that woman." His eyes returned to mine. He had a questioning look on his face. Did he realize I had never told him the purpose of my visit?

"Well, I've certainly enjoyed talking to you," I said, getting up out of my chair. I leaned forward and shook his hand briskly. He smiled automatically and escorted me to the door. I could hear him tapping on his computer keyboard as I walked back down the hall.

Once I had descended the stairway, I asked myself what I had gained by my last two interviews. Neither Sarah's attorney nor her accountant had admitted to having visited her house. Then again, why should they tell the truth? I could see why Sarah had chosen these two professionals for backup, though. Simpson must have matched her own untidy love affair with computers, and Jackson's "I'm good, too," would have touched her positive-thinking spirit.

A glance at my watch told me it was two o'clock, time to go shopping for Nick Taos. Guiltily, I realized I hadn't called in to the Jest Gifts warehouse yet that day. I found a public telephone in the lobby and remedied the oversight.

My warehousewoman, Judy, assured me everything was "cool." There were no problems with the manufacturers, no problems with the mail orders, and the inventory remained stable. This was not always the case. Not only did whole boxes of stock occasionally disappear, but sometimes they were even transformed. One hundred Freudian Shrink-Proof T-shirts had once turned overnight into fifty attorney's Faw-law-law Christmas mugs. Go figure. That day, however, everything was disconcertingly right at the warehouse.

I didn't have to go far to find the nearest Safeway. There was one right across the street from the office building. If my entree to Nick Taos involved the purchase of mass quantities of forbidden foods, I was ready. I loaded Mallomars, double-chocolate ice cream, Pop Tarts, candy bars, frozen cheesecake, Hostess pies and Coca-Cola into my cart. As I reached for the root beer, I considered the possibility that Nick was both a guilty murderer and a diabetic, and was arranging his own execution.

I chuckled the thought away and went to the meat department for hamburger and bacon. I've been told bacon is the consummate toxin, combining meat, fat, sugar, salt and nitrites. I grabbed three packages anyway, and six pounds of hamburger, before continuing my rounds. I zipped through the rest of Nick's list, picking up mayonnaise, potato chips and Wonder Bread. I laid one vegetable, iceberg lettuce, on the top of the pile and made my way to the checkout counter. I couldn't look the checker in the eye.

He picked up on my embarrassment immediately. "Planning a little binge, are we?" he smirked.

"It's for a friend," I replied with dignity.

"Uh-huh," he drawled. "I've heard that one before. Enjoy yourself."

I slunk out of Safeway, fat and glucose in hand, and drove to Nick's house.

The yard in front of his house was grown over with lush vegetation. Ivy and berry vines covered the fence and the trunks of the trees. Dandelions, buttercups and forget-me-nots poked their petals through the overgrowth. The path through the leaves, stickers and vines was barely discernible. Obviously, Sarah had never loaned him her gardener. It did make sense, if the man never left the house. I was curious what the neighbors thought of the place. I made a mental note to visit them on some pretext.

My Reeboks crunched the vegetation as I carried my two bags of offerings down the jungle path to Nick's door.

Once there, I dropped the bags and pushed the doorbell. I didn't hear it ring, though. I waited in the silence for a little while. Then I banged on the door with my fist. I wasn't in the mood for subtlety. The groceries were heavy, not to mention expensive. A curtain was pulled back from a window. Then the door opened.

The man who looked out the doorway left me gaping. This guy was breathtakingly handsome! He was about six and a half feet tall, exquisitely proportioned, with muscular arms peeking out of his shirt that made me want to see other parts peeking out. And on top of his body was a strong well-formed head with clear, blue-grey eyes. He reminded me of a picture I'd seen of Tom Selleck on the cover of *People* magazine. Most people this handsome were in the movies. When he spoke, I remembered why he wasn't.

"Are you Kate?" he bawled. "What'd you bring me?"

"Groceries," I answered briefly. The combination of that voice with that body was a cruel cosmic joke.

"Let me bring in this stuff for you," I suggested. I didn't intend to end up just passing groceries over the threshold. I wanted to get inside the house for a little chat.

"I guess so," he mumbled uncertainly. At least his volume was somewhat modulated.

He stepped back from the doorway and shifted his weight onto one leg, pulling the other leg up and tucking his foot behind his knee. There he stood, looking like a muscular stork. I picked up the bags and pushed past him. He didn't object. Nor did he offer to help. Or to pay me for the groceries for that matter. He just watched from his stork pose as I hauled the bags down the hall into the kitchen.

"How would you like a root beer?" I asked him once I had disposed of the bags. I used the voice I had developed working in a mental hospital. It's the voice most people use with children.

"Okay!" he bellowed. I tried not to wince. He brought his foot down from behind his knee and bounded toward me. Suddenly I remembered something else from my mental hospital days. Big and stupid can be dangerous. My neck prickled. Nick was sure big. Was he stupid? Worse yet, was he crazy?

"I'll have some tea myself," I squeaked as he came to a stop two feet in front of me. "I've brought some herbal." I took a deep breath and sat down at the kitchen table.

"I have some herbal tea, too!" Nick announced loudly and eagerly. "Here on the shelf, it's Sarah's." He grabbed a box of tea in his oversized paw and waved it triumphantly in front of me. "Mellow Mint," he read carefully from the label.

"Great," I said.

"I'll boil the water," he offered. A tearful look passed over his face as he banged the kettle onto the stove. My fear dissolved. It was a good bet he was thinking of Sarah. Poor guy.

"May I call you Nick?" I asked gently.

"Sure, if you want!" he bellowed back. I jumped in my seat. How the hell had Sarah stood his loud enthusiasm? He lowered his voice to the level of a Marine drill sergeant and went on. "Nick Taos is the name Sarah gave me. She said it was a spiritual name and was more descriptive of my 'artistic essence.' She said it might sell my sculptures better. I kinda like it now."

"What's your old name?" I asked.

"Herb Smith!" His answer shook the room. He smiled broadly

as he sat down across from me. "I was named after my uncle. He got real rich in the linoleum business. I liked him a lot. He died a couple of years ago." The smile disappeared. "It seems like everyone I really love dies."

"You know *Sarah* wouldn't just 'die,' " I said, feeling a need to reassure him. "Look at it this way, she's been . . . well . . . transformed."

His eyes were tearing over. Time for a story, I decided, my mental hospital skills coming in handy once more. I thought fast.

"A long time ago there were these two caterpillars who were very, very good friends," I began in my best once-upon-a-time voice. Nick cocked his head to listen.

"One was a girl caterpillar, and one was a boy caterpillar. They played during the day and slept soundly at night." A smile touched Nick's face. I had him. I cut to the bad news. "Then the girl caterpillar went into her cocoon. The boy caterpillar thought she had died and was very sad. He cried and cried. But then, after a little while, a miracle happened. His friend came fluttering out of the cocoon as a butterfly." Nick's eyes widened. "The boy caterpillar was filled with joy at the transformation. He waved happily as she flew away, knowing one day he would follow. And in the meantime he played during the day and slept at night as happy as—"

Nick let out a wail like an air raid siren. Then he put his gorgeous head in his huge hands and wept loud and long. So much for cheering him up. But as I watched him weep, I found myself wishing that I could cry as cleanly as he did. Maybe it was for the best.

"You tell stories like Sarah!" he bawled out finally. He gulped loudly a few times and went on. "I know Sarah is probably okay, but I'm so lonely. I don't know what to do."

"What do you need?" I asked him. He didn't answer me right away. "You'll probably be all right financially—" I began. Another wail interrupted me. But this time it wasn't Nick. It was the teakettle.

Nick got up and turned it off. "Ellen said that the two of us inherit!" he shouted over his shoulder. "And I still have Uncle Herb's money." He sat back down. "But I just don't know how to do regular stuff, like drive and shop and stuff like that." He looked at me like a forlorn child. A very large, handsome, forlorn child.

"I could teach you some of those things," I found myself offering. Damn. Just what I needed, a six-foot-six baby. "I mean, all of us," I amended quickly. "Sarah's friends: me and Peter and Tony." I could always twist their arms into helping later.

Nick grinned and clapped his big hands. "I feel like I know you all already!" he cried. "Grumpy Peter, sweet Tony, gossipy Vivian, quiet Linda. And your old husband, Craig. Sarah told me all about you guys!"

My ears perked up. At last, a willing informant.

"Did she say anyone was mad at her?" I asked nonchalantly.

"All the time!" Nick leaned back and laughed heartily. Pots and pans shook on their shelves. "Peter was always mad at her. And Vivian—and you—and her partner Myra—and her sister Ellen got mad at her. Craig used to get mad at her. Even Tony was mad at her sometimes."

"So she knew she drove us nuts," I said, somehow pleased. "Thanks, Nick. I was never really sure before."

He smiled, obviously gratified by the thanks. Suddenly I realized he had left someone out.

"What about Linda?" I asked quickly.

He wrinkled his handsome forehead with concentration. "Sarah never said Linda was mad at her, I guess," he said finally. "I'm sorry," he mumbled. He hung his head.

"That's all right," I assured him. Poor guy. He was really trying to help. But before I tried to cheer him up again, I had another question. "What did you think of Sarah's house?" I asked slyly.

"Oh, I've never been there!" he replied, shaking the room again. "She said it had lots of neat stuff. She said this house was 'sterile.'" He hung his head once more.

I looked around. It was certainly bare. There were no pictures on the beige walls, no mementos cluttering the utilitarian wooden shelves, only a scattering of cooking implements and foodstuffs.

"You're a big help, Nick," I told him. He lifted his head and sat up straight in his chair. "Did Sarah ever mention a computer program to you that had to do with the stock market?" I asked. "One that was going to make her a fortune?"

"Uh-huh!" His reply came without hesitation. "She was working on it forever! She said it would model everything a stock broker did, but on a program. She said it would 'revolutionize investing.' I think she was about to sell it. She was real hot on it."

Nick was watching me expectantly. I was pretty sure he would answer anything I asked him. But I just couldn't think of any more relevant questions. And we never had gotten around to the tea and root beer.

"So you're a sculptor," I prompted.

He nodded his head violently.

"I'd like to see your work," I told him.

"Really?" he bellowed.

"Really," I answered. A smile tugged at my mouth. I could almost see why Sarah loved him. Almost. "Have you ever had a show?" I asked.

"Uh-huh! Sarah made me two showings. We sold some, but not too many." He waved his hands in the air. "It doesn't matter. I have money. I did the sculptures for Sarah. An *homage*." He pronounced the word carefully. "She loved them. Maybe you'll like them too." He looked at me shyly. I stood up.

Nick led me across the hall into the living room. There were no sculptures there. The room was sparsely furnished with exercise equipment, a tanning lamp, a television set complete with VCR, and two cushions on the floor. For a moment I wondered if he just imagined he was a sculptor. But then he pointed to a door at the back of the living room.

He opened that door onto a barn of a workroom which overflowed with sculpted works. Shelves and shelves of sculptures in various sizes, colors and media lined the walls. All of them were the same shape, a vaguely floral one that looked somehow familiar. But I couldn't place exactly where I had seen it before.

We walked in. On one wall there were glistening bronzes, terracotta potteries and wood carvings. On another wall there were sculptures of papier-mâché and plaster. There were even cloth ones, painted and embroidered in a rainbow of colors. Against the third wall was a massive marble piece. Next to the door was a table with an ivory miniature on it. Nick patted each piece lovingly as he led me past. The display was overwhelming.

"How do you like them?" he asked, his eyes shyly lowered. For once he didn't shout.

His restraint deserved a positive answer. And the work *was* impressive. I tried to think like a friendly art critic. "There's a real harmony to the group as a whole," I told him honestly. "I especially like the wood carvings. You did those with such attention to the grain. Nice, very nice." His eyes came up, smiling. "Did you do them all?" I asked.

"Yes, every single one," he said. "Now that Sarah's gone, maybe I'll do something different. She loved these, but I was running out of stuff to do them in. Maybe we could arrange a showing, you know, for Sarah." He watched my face.

"An 'homage' to Sarah?" I asked.

He nodded eagerly.

I patted his elbow. I couldn't reach his shoulder without getting too close. "Could be," I said.

I contemplated Nick's creations for a while, focusing on individual pieces and then stepping back to look at the total exhibition. But I still couldn't figure out what the sculptures were meant to represent. I sighed and stole a look at my watch.

I turned to Nick. "I need to go now," I said gently. His face fell. "But I'll leave you my phone number," I added quickly. "And I'll be back. Don't worry."

"Thank you," he said. It was then that I realized he wasn't bellowing. His voice was still loud, but it had never regained its formerly painful volume the whole time we had been in this room. His sculptures were a good influence. I looked at him and wondered what kind of influence Sarah had been.

On the way home in the car, I mulled over Nick Taos. What a peculiar blend he was, with that gorgeous body and that trombone of a voice. And what about his mind? He couldn't, or didn't, do "regular stuff." But he could do what it took to create intricate sculptures. Was his intelligence really limited? Was he crazy, or something else altogether? And how could someone who ate all that junk food look so damn healthy, anyway? I turned into my driveway. Nick was certainly a paradox, but was he a murderer?

I walked into my house still wondering. Then I turned on my answering machine.

First I heard the distinct sound of someone spitting. Then the machine snarled, "Get off the case or you're dead!"

- Eight -

THE ROOM THAT had seemed so familiar suddenly looked grey and alien to my eyes. I stopped breathing for a moment and heard the sound of my own pulse pounding. Then I ran back across the room and locked the front door. In the years that I'd lived in a San Francisco apartment, I had been very careful to bolt my doors. But here in mellow Marin I had gotten out of the habit of locking myself in.

I sat down and focused on remaining calm. A death threat. Damn. I was shaking all over.

I took a big breath and told myself to think tranquil thoughts. *But it has to be the murderer,* a shrill voice inside my head insisted. No, I admonished, tranquil thoughts only. Think about flowers. Think about gardening on a sunny day. I imagined the colors in the garden and the buzz of sounds on a summer day. I concentrated on feeling the warmth of the sun on my hands. I took another big breath. My pulse was slowing back to normal.

I forced myself to sit a little longer. My mind was almost clear. Then a new thought jerked me out of my seat. *What if the murderer is already here?* I ran through the house, frantically checking rooms.

But I was the only one home. Besides C.C. She was cuddled up in my laundry basket, snoozing obliviously. I gave her head a reassuring pat, reassuring to me at least, and returned to the answering machine.

I replayed the message, listening carefully to the voice.

"Get off the case or you're dead," it said once more.

The speaker didn't sound like anyone I knew, even disguised.

Actually, it sounded like a Hollywood-style gangster. And the spitting! As far as I knew, none of my acquaintances was in the habit of spitting before speaking.

The second rendition was enough. I called the Sheriff's Department and asked for Sergeant Feiffer. I wasn't going to keep the message to myself. The police had all kinds of gadgets. A voiceprint, that's what I needed. Right? Didn't they have voiceprint kits or something? My phone call was promptly routed to the sergeant. I said the magic words "threatening message" and he told me he'd be right out.

I played the message over and over as I waited for him, hoping that the sound of the voice would call up a corresponding face. It didn't. The wait wasn't long. A Sheriff's car came sirening up to my door less than five minutes later. Sergeant Feiffer and a goofy-looking deputy hopped out. The deputy was a long, lean man with a classic hound dog face. They trotted up my front stairs in tandem.

"You don't need your guns," I joked weakly, opening the door and leading them inside. "The machine will talk without coercion." Gallows humor.

But Feiffer was not smiling. "This is serious, Ms. Jasper," he rumbled. "Let's hear the message."

I decided to believe his new gruffness was out of personal concern. The uncharitable thought did enter my mind, however, that it wouldn't do his career a whole lot of good if I ended up murdered along with Sarah. The three of us stood around the machine as I played the tape once more.

"Dead" was still echoing in the room when the dog-faced deputy piped up. "I know who that is," he said.

"You do?" the sergeant and I exclaimed simultaneously. We turned to him expectantly.

"Sure," he said. His sorrowful eyes crinkled in a smile. "It's this bad guy on *Philadelphia Beat*."

"What?"

"You know, the old TV show," he explained impatiently. He sketched the shape of a TV set with his hands, then continued. "See, there's this bad guy. And Red Cullen is closing in on him. So the guy calls Cullen, spits real nasty-like, and then says 'get off the case or you're dead,' but Cullen doesn't listen. So then the bad guy blows up his car, boom!" The deputy threw his arms outward. What a performer. "But Cullen isn't in it 'cause he knew that was going to happen. And then—"

"When was this show on?" asked Sergeant Feiffer. His voice was deep and ominous.

"Uh," the deputy answered, suddenly looking nervous. Had it just occurred to him that this was serious? He wrinkled his forehead in thought. "Musta been last week." He nodded fervently. "A rerun, you know. Yeah, last week," he confirmed.

"But how did the murderer know last week that they were going to need a threatening message this week?" I asked. I hadn't actually meant to speak out loud, but there it was.

"Maybe he—or she—didn't," answered Sergeant Feiffer thoughtfully. "Maybe they just videotaped it for themselves and then decided they could use it on you later." I noticed that he didn't correct me on the word "murderer." My pulse began to race again. He was as worried as I was. I tried to think clearly.

"It's someone with a VCR," I said after a moment. Suddenly it seemed easy. I straightened my shoulders. "So all we have to do is find out who's involved that has a VCR."

"Probably *everyone* in this case has a VCR," Feiffer said, sighing. So much for easy.

"Well, I don't have one," I insisted loudly, unwilling to give up the comfort of an easy answer.

"Everyone but you, then," he growled.

I looked him in the eye. Was he giving up already?

"Oh, we'll check into it," he assured me. But he didn't look excited about it.

"How about tracing it?" I asked. "Can't you find out where the call was made from?"

"Maybe," he said glumly. "But if it's a local call we're out of luck. And even if it wasn't, I doubt that the person who called was stupid enough to do it from their own telephone." He paused. "What time did the call come in?"

I thought for a moment. "Sometime this afternoon," I said slowly. "I was out for a couple of hours after you left the first time."

He gave me an accusing look. Did he know I was out sleuthing? Then he sighed. "We'll do what we can," he said apathetically.

His lack of enthusiasm was catching. I hung my head and hoped the death threat wasn't really serious. Fat chance! About as good as the chances of being only a little pregnant.

"I have a question for you," barked Sergeant Feiffer, jarring me out of my reverie. "Are you mixed up in anything else besides this

Sarah Quinn business? Some other 'case' that someone is warning you off of?"

"I don't think so," I mumbled. Then I considered the question more thoroughly. There was no one I could think of in my personal life. Except . . . Wayne. Wayne wanted me off the case. No, not Wayne, I told myself firmly. A business matter? I was late on some orders. But people don't threaten gag-gift peddlers with death, do they?

"No," I told him firmly.

"Well, that's a relief!" Feiffer snapped. He lowered his head so he could glare directly into my eyes. "Now we just have to worry about one person murdering you. A person who has already killed once. Are you listening to me?"

The hairs went up on the back of my neck. My childhood had taught me that a question like that always precedes something unpleasant. But I nodded, mesmerized.

"I want you to stop interfering with this investigation," he enunciated carefully, as if for a deaf person. "We will take care of it. Don't ask any more questions. Don't discuss it with anyone. Do you understand?"

I nodded my head again, vigorously this time. I had understood his words. I would decide later if I was going to abide by them.

"Now, if at any time you feel that you are in a dangerous situation, phone us immediately," he continued. Then he changed direction. "Do you have anyone you can stay with?" he asked.

"Not really," I mumbled automatically. I thought of Wayne, then dismissed the thought. "I do my business from my house, so I can't just go stay somewhere else," I said in a stronger voice.

"I would consider taking a little vacation from your business," he said, enunciating carefully again.

I blinked. He was serious.

"Yeah, I can see by your face that you won't," he rumbled. "But at least stay close to a phone. And open your door to no one, I mean no one."

He went on in this vein for a full fifteen minutes before he left. Even Howard Hughes would have rebelled at the restrictions on human contact that he suggested. Nevertheless, I thought about Feiffer's suggestions. I sat in my comfy chair and thought about them long and hard. But in the final analysis, one thing was quite clear to me. I was never going to feel fully safe until I found out who had killed Sarah.

I looked at my watch. It was almost four, time to leave for my appointment with Sarah's ex-business partner, Myra Klein of Word Inc. I paused for two final seconds to consider Sergeant Feiffer's advice, then got in my Toyota and drove.

All it took was one step into the corporate suite of offices that housed Word Inc. to realize that the company was thriving. A well-manicured receptionist at the desk offered me a seat on a mauve couch and buzzed an office somewhere down the luxuriously carpeted hall. Sinking into the couch, I looked up at soft-edged paintings of orchids. A tasteful sign on the receptionist's desk assured customers of the willingness of Word Inc. to do the best job possible. There was no clickety clack of typewriter keys, only the soft hum of computers and piped music. Was this the same music that Peter had on his telephone system, or were there varieties of canned music?

Before I could answer my own question, a petite blonde in a teal suit and high heels arrived to usher me into Myra Klein's office.

Myra was a tall, slender woman, dressed for success in a well-tailored navy blue suit with obligatory red scarf. But despite the stylish business suit, there was something about her that was just plain mousy. If they had been casting for the part of a schoolmarm, she would have won it. High cheekbones, a long thin nose and circles under her pale eyes defined her stiff face. She stood and offered a cold damp hand to me. I shook it gingerly.

"I understand you were a friend of Sarah's," Myra said. Her voice was as pale as her eyes. "Won't you have a seat?"

There was an awkward silence as I tried to think of what my next line was supposed to be. I couldn't say, "Sarah has told me so much about you," because she hadn't. And I didn't want to say anything glib about a "loss," because I wasn't sure Sarah's death was a loss to Myra.

"It looks like Word Inc. is doing well," I offered.

I must have said the right thing because Myra's face relaxed. She allowed herself a small smile as she resumed her own seat.

"Yes, we are," she agreed in a breathy rush. "We are doing quite well, even *without* Sarah Quinn." I detected more than a little hostility in the way she pronounced Sarah's name. I kept quiet. Myra tapped her fingers on her desk as she went on. "Sarah may have kept a ten per cent interest in Word Inc., but she hasn't bothered to grace us with her presence for a very long time."

"Oh," I said, leaning forward in my chair. "I suppose Sarah . . ." I trailed off invitingly.

Myra just stared back at me, her face stiff again.

"I thought maybe you could give me a little background on Sarah," I muddled on. "I've only known her for a few years. And she rarely talks about her past . . . or *talked* about her past," I corrected myself.

Myra sighed. "Sarah and I go way back," she murmured. She leaned back in her padded leather chair and looked up at the ceiling. "It must be twenty-five, maybe thirty years now. We shared a dorm room in college, you know, University of Pennsylvania." She brought her eyes down from the ceiling and met my gaze.

"It's hard to imagine Sarah in college," I prompted. Myra gave me a vague smile. I plodded on. "I mean she always acted like she just spontaneously appeared on this earth in full bloom. She did have parents, didn't she? Family?"

"Oh, yes," Myra answered. She leaned back to look up at the ceiling again. "I met her mother quite a few times. Mrs. Quinn was a very sweet woman. She seemed totally impervious to Sarah's shenanigans." Myra smiled softly again, lost in some memory. "Sarah would try to shock her mother by telling her about sex, drugs, religion—whatever she was into—and her mother would just nod and say 'Isn't that nice' or 'Isn't that interesting.' It just drove Sarah crazy."

I chuckled. Myra leaned forward and flashed an unexpected grin in my direction. Her face looked alive with that grin. She went on with more enthusiasm.

"I remember once, Mrs. Quinn was visiting and Sarah said to her, 'Mom, I've got some heroin. Would you like to shoot up with me?' and Mrs. Quinn says, 'No thank you, dear, but you go right ahead.'" Myra giggled in a little-girl way that clashed with her navy blue suit. "You should have seen the look on Sarah's face. She was incensed. And, of course, she didn't really have any heroin, so she ended up looking ridiculous."

I laughed aloud. I could just see it. "So that's where Sarah learned how to drive people up the wall," I said. "From her mother."

Myra shrugged and leaned back again. "Mr. Quinn never visited," she continued. "I think he and Sarah argued, and he got the worst of it, so he stayed away. She was really wild then."

Myra moved her head back and forth slowly, remembering. "Sarah changed her major every semester, breezed through her classes, and spent the rest of her time 'Living' with a capital L. I was her best friend, as much as you could be a best friend to someone like Sarah. And I was allowed to live through her vicariously.

She did all the things that I was afraid to do and shared them with me. I lived through her drug experiments and cosmic insights and her endless string of lovers." Myra's tone deepened. "I even got her throwaways. My first husband came to me on the rebound from Sarah." She frowned.

"Was Sarah ever married?" I asked quickly.

"Ah, yes," Myra said, meeting my eyes once more. "In our third year of college she up and left for India to find 'spiritual insight.' She sent me a postcard saying she had finally found a man she could learn from, and that she had married him. He had some Indian name, but I think he was really an American. She sent one long letter to me about the joys of being married to a 'spiritual master.' She was calling herself Serena." Myra snorted derisively. "As if Sarah could ever be serene! Then I didn't hear from her for a while. A few years later I got a postcard from New Mexico. She didn't mention the husband." She shook her head as she smiled softly.

"Do you think she's still married to this guy?" I asked.

"No," Myra answered briskly. "Sarah was quite practical about legal details. However, I think he actually managed to . . . to dominate her somehow. She probably never forgave him. She certainly never mentioned him again. And she went back to calling herself Sarah."

Myra tapped a finger on the armrest of her chair and smiled politely at me. Was she getting ready to throw me out?

"Have you met Nick Taos?" I asked. Keep that ball rolling.

"Oh, you mean Herb," she answered. She didn't just giggle this time, she laughed heartily. "Is he still doing *those* sculptures?" she asked, rolling her eyes upwards.

I nodded, politely joining with her in laughter, although I wasn't sure exactly what we were laughing at.

"You know, Herb wasn't always so strange," Myra said earnestly. "He really is, or was, a good artist. He was just overwhelmed by Sarah."

I nodded.

She continued. "Herb moved into that house and let Sarah take more and more responsibility for him until . . . until . . ." Myra threw up her hands, searching for the right words. "Until he lost the knack of taking care of himself," she finished. Bitterness had crept into her breathy voice. Was she just talking about Nick? Or was she talking about herself? "Sarah tended to overwhelm people like that. Her death is probably the best thing that could happen to him, the poor man."

A button on her telephone lit up. "Excuse me," she said and picked it up. She murmured soothingly and efficiently to whoever was on the other end. She was a good businesswoman. It was hard to remember that when she talked about Sarah. After she hung up the telephone, she rose from her desk, ready to usher me out.

I stayed glued to my chair. "Have you seen Nick lately?" I asked.

Myra shook her head. I pretended I was a cop and gave her a long, searching look. It worked! She let out a small sigh and lowered herself into her chair again.

"I haven't seen Herb, Nick, for a long time," she said. "Not since Sarah and I parted company. In fact, he had become pretty reclusive before that." She stared at the ceiling with all of the light gone from her face. Was she thinking about Nick or about the split-up with Sarah? I couldn't tell.

"How'd you and Sarah end up in business together?" I asked.

Myra brought her eyes down to mine. "I hadn't heard from Sarah, except for a few postcards over the years," she said, rushing through her words. "And in the meantime, I'd moved to sunny California with my second husband. Then my second husband walked out on me like the first, only he left me with two kids. So there I was, the mother of two children with a useless degree in anthropology and an equally useless minor in art history."

She stretched her face into an unnatural grimace. I nodded sympathetically. How many women have lived some variation of this story?

"So I started freelancing as a typist. And one of my customers had me trained on a word processor. Word processors were a new technology then. Most people were still using typewriters. Anyway, I got a lot of word-processing work and I was doing fairly well. Then Sarah showed up." Myra looked up again. Was this it? Was she going to throw me out?

"How'd she find you?" I asked quickly.

"I really don't know," Myra answered. She began pacing. I relaxed. She wasn't going to throw me out. "She just had that knack, you know, of showing up and acting like she had just gone around the corner for cigarettes or something instead of having been out of your life for ten or fifteen years."

I nodded. I could imagine.

Myra was pacing faster now. And talking faster. "So Sarah

showed up and asked what I was doing. I told her. Then she started asking if I had more business than I could handle, and why didn't I have any employees. Blah, blah, blah!" Her angry syllables echoed off the walls. "The next thing I knew we were Word Inc. and raking in business. And we were best friends again. I really loved her, like I did during our school years. I began relying on her emotionally again." Her voice deepened. "That was my mistake."

Myra stopped pacing and turned to me. I squirmed in my chair. I could feel her anger, even smell its acrid scent. "I want to use the full potential of the computer, and of my mind!" she pronounced.

I jerked in my chair involuntarily. She had done a perfect imitation of Sarah's voice. I shivered. Myra was staring at me now. No, she was staring *through* me. And her pale eyes were full of hatred.

– Nine –

MYRA BEGAN PACING at full speed again. Her voice paced with her. "Sarah told me she wanted to use her 'full potential,' and then she was gone," Myra rapped out. "Not from Marin, but from my life. She sold me most of her company shares. Then she left me for newer and better things. I couldn't believe I'd been taken again!" As she paced, Myra aimed a glance in my general direction, but her pale, angry eyes never connected with mine. I suppressed the urge to wave my hand in front of her face. She probably wouldn't have seen it anyway.

She was too busy railing. "By the time I realized how angry I was, Sarah was gone, and I couldn't tell her," she ranted on. "We talked a few times after that, but she deflected me any time I wanted to talk about my feelings. All she wanted was her checks in the mail! I was left with a successful business and a load of bitterness."

Myra came to a halt in back of her chair. She rested her hands on its leather and looked at me, seeing me this time.

Her voice softened. "Sarah gave me a tremendous boost financially. I couldn't have done it without her. But she ran my feelings over in the process. I haven't seen her in over five years, and we both still live in Marin." She circled back around her chair and flopped down into it like a spent boxer.

"Sarah did that kind of thing, all right," I whispered. I didn't know what else to say. Myra had been badly hurt by Sarah's betrayal.

I tried to think of a tactful way to ask Myra what had happened to Sarah's ten per cent upon her death. But she was talking again, in a soft murmur now.

"So after years of therapy, I had finally decided I'd talk to her, have it out with her," she sighed. She looked at the surface of her desk as if for answers. "It wasn't just her. It was the pattern in my life." She raised her empty hands in the air. "I never was able to tell my father what I felt because he died before I made up my mind. And I don't even know where my ex-husbands are. So I was going to talk to Sarah. And now she's dead." Myra shook her head slowly and sadly.

I shook my head with her. I was all out of words. My stomach was churning with her turmoil. And a nasty thought kept intruding into my mind. How therapeutic might it have been for Myra to murder Sarah?

Myra stood up abruptly. Had she realized the content of my thoughts? Guiltily, I jumped out of my own chair. She offered me her hand. It was even colder and wetter than before. I murmured my thanks for her help, all the while restraining myself from bolting from her office. I wanted out! We exchanged a few more polite words and I left with carefully measured steps.

When I got to my Toyota, I sat in the front seat trying to shake off the interview. I felt grimy, splattered with her feelings. Her anger was frightening. And her pain and sense of betrayal had been all too palpable. Had she been the one to leave the message on my answering machine? Suddenly cold, I rubbed my hands together for warmth. I wanted a long, hot shower. I looked at my watch. I didn't have the time.

I had ten minutes to get to my tai chi class. And I needed that class, especially the stillness of mind it could bring. The martial arts aspect seemed pretty appealing too. And if I died any time soon, at least my spine would be straight and my thighs relatively trim.

I drove to the class with a chattering mind. Was Myra's the character of a murderer that I had been seeking? The requisite hatred was certainly there. I could even smell it in the acrid odor of her sweat when she spoke of Sarah. She had seemed sincere about wanting to have it out with Sarah. On the other hand, I had only her word that she hadn't already had it out . . . by murdering Sarah. But if that were true, why would she have agreed to speak to me and reveal her motivation?

I parked my car around the corner from the tai chi classroom as my mind continued to spiral outward. As owner of Word Inc.,

Myra must have had some understanding of computers in general. But did she have access to *Sarah's* computer? To Sarah's house and robot? I shook my head. How could she?

I found myself wanting Myra to be the one, wanting anyone who wasn't my friend to be the one. But she just didn't fit. It was like seeing the perfect sweater in the ideal color, style and price range, but in a size too small. I wanted to squeeze Myra into the role of murderer. But I just couldn't.

As I walked into the classroom filled with women and men wearing baggy pants and peaceful expressions, I could only think of Myra. And Sarah. What about Sarah's ten per cent interest? Would Sarah's heirs sell that interest to Myra now? I put on my Chinese slippers quickly. Was that what Myra wanted? Control? But again, why had she told me about Sarah's share in the business if that was her motive?

With an abrupt return to the here and now, I realized that the whole tai chi class was waiting for me. Everyone was positioned to start the form, except for a few students who were turned and staring at me. Their expressions were no longer peaceful. They were aggravated. I nodded apologetically and hurried to take a place in the back row, trying to file Myra and murder in a back drawer of my mind.

The room was silent as fourteen bodies began the tai chi form. I let Myra and the murder go. Sinking the weight down through my torso, through my legs, and into the ground, I began the slow dance, enjoying the sensation of shared purpose as we all took the first steps in synchronization. Then the shift, turn, press and release. I was lulled into inner quiet.

But when I brought my knee up for the first kick, my mind blasted me.

My visit to Nick. His room of sculptures. Suddenly it was clear. I knew.

"Kate!" hissed someone behind me.

My knee was still in the air. Everyone else had finished their kicks and turned toward the opposite wall. Damn. I turned to catch up with the others, but my overflowing mind turned with me.

I knew what Nick's sculptures were. How could I have missed it?

As I bent down for the low punch I couldn't suppress a snort of laughter. I could hear it reverberate in the silence like blasphemy in church. I kept my eyes low, avoiding the instructor's. But I knew.

Nick's sculptures were representations of female genitalia.

I drew my body up and followed the others in the turns and shifts and punches and kicks. But my mind stayed with Nick's sculptures. How Sarah must have loved Nick's labial "homage." And it had taken me all afternoon to figure it out. At least I had solved one mystery.

I apologized to the tai chi instructor after class. I told her I had been struck by a flash of insight during the form. She nodded gravely. I didn't tell her what the insight was. I just left.

Once I got home I checked my answering machine for death threats. There weren't any. Then I called Barbara. I needed a sanity check. But as I sat down in my comfy chair, C.C. burst into the room yowling. She jumped into my lap and stared unblinkingly into my eyes with an expression of feline concern. I gave her a reassuring pat, wondering if she knew something I didn't. She settled down into my lap. I dialed Barbara's number as C.C. began clawing. I stuck a notebook between her claws and my thighs. C.C. shot off my lap with an outraged yowl, cheated once more of a good dig.

I told Barbara about my conversations with Vivian, Janice Jackson, Donald Simpson and Myra. I didn't tell her about the death threat. I didn't want to talk about it. I didn't even want to think about it. Then I topped off the recap by telling her about Nick's sculptures.

"What a kick!" she shrieked. Her laughter came pouring out of the telephone receiver.

I was glad to hear it. I hadn't been able to decide if there was something creepy, even threatening about Nick's sculptural obsession, or if it was just funny. I let my tense muscles relax. But not for long.

"You know, kiddo," Barbara began, her voice serious. "If this is actually murder, the killer isn't going to be amused by your snooping." She paused. My neck muscles tightened. This isn't something you want to hear from a psychic. She went on. "I'm surprised this guy hasn't attacked you, or at least threatened you," she said.

Damn.

By the time I hung up on Barbara I had less than an hour left to work before meeting Peter for dinner. The eternal pile of Jest Gifts paperwork on my desk radiated an uncharacteristic appeal that day. I dove into it gratefully, trying to forget Barbara's warning. Trying to forget that someone had threatened my life. But I had only worked a few minutes when the doorbell rang.

As I stood up I felt a pang of fear and suddenly wished I had a chain lock for the door. I peered out my office window and saw a tall figure lurking on my doorstep.

It was Wayne. I rushed to the door to let him in. But he made no move to enter when I opened it. I reached out and grabbed his hand. It was stiff and unresponsive. If it hadn't been warm, I would have sworn it was plastic. I dropped his hand and looked up under his eyebrows. There was nothing in his eyes. They were blank, chilling, a bodyguard's eyes.

"Are you still investigating?" he asked. His words were exact, his deep voice curt.

I shrugged.

"Are you all right?" he inquired. There was still no feeling in his eyes or his voice.

I nodded.

"Wayne—" I began.

He turned his back on me and walked down the stairs carefully, slowly. No conversation. No hug. Nothing.

Then there was a flash of black and white at the door. C.C. shot down the stairs, running after him.

I closed the door slowly and went back to my desk. I picked up my pen and continued work on a payroll tax deposit form. But something was wrong with it. The writing wavered. I looked again. My tears had blotched the ink.

The doorbell rang once more. This time I didn't even bother to look out the window. I just didn't care anymore.

"Who is it?" I shouted from my desk.

"Felix!" came the reply. I didn't think my heart could sink any further, but it did. Felix Byrne was at my door.

Felix was Barbara's boyfriend and, worse, a reporter. Where murder was involved, he was a pit bull of an interrogator. Once he had you by the throat he never let go. I wasn't up to being questioned by Felix. I put my head down on my desk and covered it with my hands, hoping that if I was very quiet he would go away.

"Kate!" he shouted and pounded on the door. He wasn't going away.

I left the sanctuary of my paperwork and opened the door cautiously. Felix was an attractive man, small and slender with a luxurious mustache reminiscent of Mark Twain's. His dark, soulful eyes were what usually hooked the women. But they didn't look soulful right now. They were narrowed with anger.

"Why didn't you call me?!" he bellowed. What a lot of voice for such a small man.

"Hello to you, too," I said.

He ignored my greeting. "You find another body, and I read about it in that . . . that scuzzbag trade rag! Not my paper, nooooo!" He drew out the word so long I thought he'd run out of air. No such luck. He clamored on. "I'm your friend, and you treat me like a piece of slime! I'm a reporter—"

"Sarah was my friend too, Felix!" I cut him off with my own shout. It felt good. I was almost glad to have someone to yell at. His eyes widened. "How do you think I feel?" I finished in a softer tone.

He was silent for a moment. Then he put his hand on my shoulder comfortingly. He smiled gently. "How *do* you feel?" he asked.

I could almost see the tape recorder switch on in his brain. This was the interview. I didn't answer his question. I stuck my tongue out at him instead. It seemed to be the safest strategy. With my tongue out of my mouth, I couldn't use it to speak.

"Come on, Kate," he cooed.

It was useless to try to avoid him. I knew he'd alternate cooing and bellowing and anything else he could think of until I talked. I retracted my tongue.

"All right," I said gracelessly. "I'll give you half an hour. Then you've got to go. Agreed?"

"Agreed," he said, pushing past me into the kitchen.

I told Felix about Sarah, her life, her friends and her death, over the tea that he made. Felix was a great one for making tea. And when he wasn't ranting, he was a good listener. He had a way of fixing his round eyes on me that made me feel he was intent on my every word. His nods of assent punctuated the unfolding of my murder theory in all the right places.

"If she was murdered, it'll be a nut-buster of a story," he said finally, pushing away his empty teacup. "Not only the method but her. What a wacko! I wish I could have met her."

I shook my head. "Don't be so sure you'd have liked her," I told him. "Sarah could be pretty cruel. And she didn't even know she was being cruel half the time. She was just insensitive and selfish and—" I broke off. Was this any way to talk about a dead friend? To a reporter? "Sarah had her good qualities," I corrected myself. Then I tried to think of some of those good qualities. "She was great for personal transformation and prosperity consciousness and all of that . . ." I faltered.

"Prosperity consciousness," snorted Felix. "What bull-pucky! Do you really believe that prosperity consciousness had anything to do with her success?" He shook his head pityingly at me.

"I don't know whether it actually works," I said defensively. "But I figure a little creative visualization can't hurt anything. And sometimes I . . ." Felix's amused stare stopped me before I admitted any other New Age practices.

"What do you do?" he smirked. "Imagine lawyers thinking, 'Gee, I'd sure like a case of shark ties—' "

"All right, all right." I gave in. "Maybe it's all silly. But Sarah believed it! She used to drive people crazy with this stuff. If anyone complained about their life she'd just tell them 'you create your own reality.' Or she'd say, 'There is abundance in the universe available to you.' " I sighed. "She never bothered to explain how to get a piece of that abundance, of course."

"Jeez, I hate those kind of bliss-ninnies," Felix said. "I live in mellow, friggin' Marin. I hear it all the time." He bent forward and hissed. "Even Barbara does it to me! I work my nuts off, and I sure don't 'have it all.' Marin may be mellow, but it's expensive. All I can afford is my rat-cage of an apartment and my old Chevy." I nodded. I'd seen them both. "But if I complain, Barbara says, 'Just open your mind to receive, Felix.' I could kill her. It's all a crock if you ask me."

I chuckled. Felix was so upset he had forgotten to interrogate me. He sat there glaring at his empty teacup.

"Prosperity consciousness just means that when you're rich you get to gloat," he finished in a sullen tone. But then he jerked up his head and smiled. "I wonder if that's what got Sarah killed?" he said slowly. He looked into my eyes. "What do you think?"

"I don't know," I answered. But my brain was rapidly cataloguing the people she'd driven crazy with her ideas. Peter, Vivian, Myra . . . me. I shook my head. "No, I don't buy it," I told him. "I can see someone being driven to strangle Sarah in a momentary fit of rage, but to carefully plan a murder like this? It doesn't make sense, Felix. There has to be another motive."

"Money?" he asked.

I hesitated. Should I tell Felix everything I knew?

"Come on, Kate," he prodded.

What the hell. "The sister and the boyfriend inherit," I told him. "Have you met Nick Taos yet?"

"No. I've knocked on his door, but he doesn't answer. His

friggin' yard's a disaster area." Felix directed a big smile at me. "I hear he's a real weirdo," he offered enticingly.

"You can say that again—" I began, but stopped myself. The subject of Nick's sculptures wasn't for discussion in mixed company. Let Barbara tell him. Felix opened his mouth, but I cut him off before he got a word of protest out.

"Then there's this computer program that Sarah was working on," I said softly. "It'd be worth stealing if it was for real."

That got his attention. "What program?" he demanded.

"Oh, something to do with the stock market. Craig says it's probably worthless."

"Seeing old Craig again?" Felix asked snidely.

Why did I put up with Felix? Then I remembered. He was a *source* of information, too. Knowing Felix, he'd probably interviewed every female member of the Marin County Sheriff's Department by now.

"So what have you gotten from the police?" I asked.

"Doo-doo," he said with a frown. "They're locked up tighter than George Bush's jockstrap."

"George Bush's . . . ?" I began. No, I didn't want to know what Felix meant by that. "Come on, Felix," I said. "They must have told you something."

"Zilch!" he exploded. "It's like they've all been ordered to avoid me." His eyes went to the ceiling thoughtfully. "Maybe they really have been told to avoid me." He brought his eyes back down. "But something's going on, Kate. Like maybe they know who did it, but they don't have doodly-squat to prove it." He shook his head in disgust. "Everyone's doing their jobs, but no one will talk to me. It's like a friggin' monastery there."

I could imagine it. A Sheriff's Department filled with Linda Zatara clones, moving but not speaking. "Linda Zatara—" I began.

"Linda Zatara?" demanded Felix, suddenly sitting up straight. "What's Linda Zatara got to do with this?"

"She was in our study group," I said. "Didn't I tell you that?"

"No, you didn't 'tell me that,' " he said acidly. "You just said Linda." His eyes narrowed.

"What about Linda?" I demanded. Was she a notorious murderer? What was he so excited about?

Felix changed the subject. "How's Wayne doing?" he asked innocently.

"What about Linda Zatara?" I changed the subject back.

He looked at his watch. "It's been half an hour to the friggin' minute," he said. He got up from the table. "Nice talking to you. Gotta go."

I jumped out of my chair and stood in front of him. "Felix," I whispered in a tone of menace.

He wasn't impressed. He stepped around me and headed for the door. I raced after him and blocked him at the threshold.

"Tell me," I demanded.

"Will you share *everything* you know?" he asked.

I hesitated.

He pushed past me onto the porch.

"All right, everything!" I shouted. "Now tell me about Linda."

"Dinner tonight," he offered, turning back to look at me.

"Sure—" I began. Then I remembered Peter. "I've got a date," I said. "How about tomorrow?"

"You're on. Dinner tomorrow night. You tell me everything and I tell you about Linda Zatara." He paused. "No deal if you hold back," he threatened in a low whisper. "*Capeesh?*"

I nodded.

"Bring your credit card!" he shouted happily and clattered down the front stairs.

I stood in the doorway fuming. Then I remembered. Felix had his sources. But I had mine. I ran to the telephone to call Vivian. Maybe she knew Linda's secret. She knew everyone else's.

I didn't waste any time when Vivian picked up the phone. "What do you know about Linda Zatara?" I demanded.

"Who?" she asked.

"Sarah's friend," I told her. "Brown skin. Grey hair. Grey eyes."

"Oh, her," Vivian mumbled. I could barely hear her voice. "Yeah, she visited Sarah once when I was cleaning."

"And . . ." I prodded eagerly.

"And nothing!" Vivian shouted. I could hear her clearly enough now. "Kate, cut it out! Stop nosing around. It's dangerous!"

Then the phone went dead.

I was punching out Vivian's phone number again when the doorbell rang.

"I'm coming, I'm coming!" I shouted impatiently. I banged the phone down and ran to the door.

I yanked it open and found myself looking into a pair of cold grey eyes. Linda Zatara's cold grey eyes.

"Did Peter do drugs in college?" she asked.

- Ten -

"PETER DO DRUGS?" I repeated stupidly, unable to pull my eyes away from Linda's. What went on behind those cold grey eyes? Did Felix really know?

Abruptly, Linda let my eyes go and stepped past me. She walked quickly into the living room and parked herself on my couch. I came out of my trance and followed her. But I didn't sit down. I stood in front of her, hoping that my relative height would give me an advantage.

"Well?" she pressed, staring up at me, unintimidated. There was no eagerness in her voice or her face, but I could feel it emanating from her.

"I'm sure Peter didn't do any more drugs in college than anyone else," I snapped defensively, realizing as the words left my mouth that I should have just said I didn't know.

I turned away from her, away from her eyes. Peter and drugs? What kind of question was that? Peter! I looked at my watch. I was late for dinner with Peter! Unless I rushed.

"I've got a date," I said, turning back to Linda.

She didn't blink an eye. Maybe Donald Simpson was right. Maybe people who didn't blink were aliens. You couldn't disprove it by Linda, who continued to sit on the couch gazing at me with the impassivity of a Vulcan.

"You've got to go now," I told her firmly. I was all out of politeness. And I didn't want Linda in my home anymore.

She shrugged her shoulders in a pointed show of indifference and walked with exaggerated slowness back outside. I grabbed my purse and followed her, pausing only to lock up the house. She was opening her car door as I raced down the stairs.

"Linda!" I shouted.

She turned back to face me.

"Do you know how to program a computer?" I demanded.

She smiled enigmatically. "Why?" she shot back.

I didn't answer. I gave her an enigmatic smile of my own. At least I hoped it looked that way. I'd never practiced enigmatic in the mirror. Then I got into my Toyota to watch her leave. Once she was gone, I raced the car out of the driveway, popping gravel.

I flew into the Safari Café parking lot at seven twenty-nine with a sigh of relief. Peter Stromberg was very picky about punctuality. I could see him through the glass front as I jogged up to the café entrance a precise minute later. He stood ramrod straight in his grey pinstripe suit, hands clasped behind his back, his foot tapping impatiently. The clatter of plates and aroma of expensive coffees greeted me when I opened the door. Peter merely nodded.

Once we were seated, I stared at Peter and wondered whether I was looking at the face of a murderer. And what about drugs in college? Peter squinted back at me intently. With his high cheekbones and sensual mouth, he was actually almost handsome. In a gaunt kind of way. I wondered why I had never noticed before.

"So, what's up?" I asked, breaking the eye-to-eye standoff. Peter jumped a little in his seat and then impatiently motioned for menus, without answering.

I turned and saw the waitress bearing down on us. She was wearing the Safari uniform: hiking boots, khaki shorts and khaki top tied just under large breasts. Her slim legs and midriff were very brown. (The Safari Café also sported an in-house tanning salon.) Her body was perfect. Her face wasn't as impressive, snub-nosed and small-eyed. But I guessed from the direction of Peter's furtive glances that her face wasn't at issue.

The decor was definitely safari. Our table was a mock elephant leg. Fake animal heads looked down at us through lush potted plants. At least I hoped the heads were fake.

The waitress handed us menus that proclaimed "natural safari cuisine" at the top. I looked at the first choice and blanched.

"Got any questions?" she demanded.

"Are the zebra burgers made from real zebra meat?" I asked weakly.

"Naah," she assured me. That was a relief. "Just plain old hamburger." She paused for a beat. "Natural of course, real natural."

"Do you have any vegetarian dishes?" I inquired hopefully.

"Oh, yeah, vegetarian." She took her pencil and scratched her ear lob thoughtfully. "Uh, let me ask," she said finally and turned away from us.

"Hey, Johnny!" she shouted across the room. "What's vegetarian?"

"Do you come here often?" I whispered to Peter.

"It's conveniently located," he snapped, his face reddening.

"I didn't mean—"

"Native's fare," interrupted the waitress, turning back again. She pointed her pencil halfway down my menu. "Rice, beans and papayas, no meat." I looked closer. "Native's fare" was priced at ten dollars! *Don't be cheap,* I scolded myself. The ingredients probably cost at least fifty cents, and I would have bet the waitresses got free tanning sessions. That had to put a dent in the Safari's profits.

"I'll take it," I said.

"The zebra burger for me," Peter requested.

I avoided his eyes. I didn't care if he ate hamburger. I was a vegetarian upon doctor's advice. I dreamt about roast beef at least once a month. I wasn't about to proselytize. But I knew that no matter what I said, he was going to get defensive. Somehow, a vegetarian at the table has that effect.

"Kate, you really need to be more flexible in your eating," he told me. "We eat macrobiotic at home, of course. But when I'm in a restaurant I can allow myself to enjoy meat." His voice went a shade higher. "There's just no reason for your obsessive self-denial."

"You're absolutely right," I said. That stopped him cold.

He opened his mouth, then closed it again, foiled.

"Listen, Peter," I said, changing the subject quickly, "I'm going to arrange a seance with my friend Barbara. Probably Monday evening. To see if we can get in touch with Sarah. Would you come?"

"A seance?" His eyebrows went up. "Are you going crazy?"

"What is with you, Peter?" I shot back. "You practice all kinds of metaphysical hoo-ha. I don't believe in half the cosmic connections that you do. But I'm willing to try a seance if there's even an outside chance that we can communicate with Sarah. Why can't you?"

"I am not Shirley MacLaine," he protested. He jutted his head forward. "The mysticism I practice is more subtle, more pure." He waved his skinny white hand in the air in an effort to explain himself. I could see he was weakening. "Connecting to the higher self for spiritual progress is not the same thing as playing psychic games," he finished.

"But you'll do it?"

He looked down at the table and groaned.

"For Sarah?" I pressed.

"Perhaps," he said. "For Sarah." Then he surprised me by smiling one of his rare smiles. "This is just the sort of thing she'd want us to be doing, making total fools of ourselves. I guess we'd better not disappoint her." He leaned back in his chair again. "Is Tony going to come?" he asked.

"I'll invite him when I see him tomorrow," I answered. Peter frowned and opened his mouth. Time to move on.

"I hear you took Sarah's dog, Freedom," I remarked slyly. "I thought you hated dogs."

Peter let out another groan. "I do, but Freedom was Sarah's dog," he said, as if this explained everything. His voice rose in pitch as he continued. "Freedom irritates me almost as much as Sarah did. The first thing that damn dog did when I took him to our house was to run away back to hers." His face grew pinched in annoyance. "I had to retrieve him!"

I stifled a giggle. I could imagine Peter retrieving Freedom, mutt hair all over his pinstripe suit. "How's your wife like him?" I asked.

"God!" Peter exploded. "Nancy hates dogs! Especially ones who defecate in her garden." He looked at me. "You know what a sweet woman she is, spiritual and loving."

I nodded. She seemed that way. And even if I hadn't known from personal experience, I figured she had to be a saint to live with Peter. Peter continued.

"When she sees a dog in her garden, she loses all reason." He lowered his voice. "She karate-kicks them."

"You're kidding!"

He shook his head sadly.

"I've never seen Nancy act like that," I said wonderingly. "She's always so . . . so serene."

"If you were a dog, you wouldn't think she was serene. Just try making a mess in her garden. Even a human who bothered her garden might get karate-kicked."

Our waitress brought our dinners before he could expand on the theme. She handed me a plate of rice, beans and papayas. I sniffed it suspiciously. It smelled good. I dug in for a bite. Peter picked up his zebra burger and munched fastidiously.

"So, Kate," he said a moment later, wiping his chin with a khaki napkin. "I'm learning a new computer system. Maybe you could give me some assistance."

"I don't know anything about computers," I mumbled through a mouthful of beans. "Except how to use a word processor and spreadsheet." The rice and beans were surprisingly good and spicy. And the papaya was a good complement.

"What makes you think I could help you?" I asked after I swallowed. Then I remembered that Sarah's murderer must have known how to program a computer. I grabbed my opportunity. "You're pretty good with computers yourself, aren't you?" I prompted.

"Oh, I hack around a bit," he replied modestly. "But I don't really have the expertise that Craig does, for instance."

"Peter, do you have a VCR?" I asked abruptly.

"Yes," he confessed. "I own one." I watched his face go red. Was this a sign of guilt? I sucked in my breath. Had Peter been the one to leave the *Philadelphia Beat* message?

"We use it to tape educational programs," he explained shrilly. "And occasionally for quality films. I know you don't own a TV, but there really are some good shows on PBS. It's not all pablum for the masses, you know!" I let out my breath. He was probably just embarrassed to be caught enjoying the pablum of the masses.

"Why do you want to know?" he finally thought to ask.

"Oh," I mumbled, taking another bite. "I was just curious."

"Indeed?" Peter glared at me suspiciously for a moment before continuing. "I remember Craig really seemed to enjoy Sarah's computer setup. Did you two go over there often?" he said.

It finally hit me.

"Peter, are you interrogating me?" I asked loudly, clattering my fork down on the table.

He jerked his head around nervously to see if anyone had heard me.

"Yes, dammit!" he hissed.

"Welcome to the club," I said. "I'm interrogating you, too." I picked up my fork again, laughing.

"This is no laughing matter," Peter snapped. He thrust his head forward and glared intently. "I'm going to get to the bottom of this. Were you jealous of Sarah?"

"Well," I considered. "A little. But I wouldn't have wanted to be her." I looked back at him. "Why? Is that your idea of a motive?"

Peter shrugged. "I'll admit I couldn't think of a very good one for you. Or for Linda."

"Linda's been asking me about you," I told him.

Peter stiffened in his chair. "What's she been asking about?"

"Drugs in college," I answered softly, keeping my eyes on him. It was worth the effort. The blood drained from his face, leaving it a gaunt white mask. His hamburger slipped from his hand back onto his plate, splashing a thin spray of juice onto his white shirt cuff.

"Oh, no," he whispered, more to himself than to me. He rocked his head back and forth slowly. "I had hoped the past wouldn't haunt me. I'll never get a seat on the bench if . . ." His voice trailed off. I watched him as he visibly pulled himself together. He straightened his shoulders and dabbed at his shirt cuff with a napkin. Then he turned his glare on me in full force.

"Do you know where Sarah met Linda?" he demanded.

"No . . . I don't," I said slowly. "Do you?"

He shook his head in short jerking motions. "Do you know anything about her?" he pressed.

"No," I answered honestly. I didn't know anything yet. "All I know is that Sarah seemed to like her."

"But why?" Peter asked. He wrinkled his forehead as he began cutting his zebra burger into neat little pieces with his knife and fork. "What in the world did Sarah see in that woman?"

I thought about it. "Linda listened," I decided. "Sarah liked people who listened to her."

"Dammit!" Peter exploded. He dropped his knife and fork abruptly. "I never wanted that woman in our group."

"But Sarah wanted her, so she stayed," I reminded him. I watched Peter as I spoke, remembering how angry he had been over Sarah's intransigence. Peter met my eyes.

"I did not murder Sarah Quinn," he said firmly. I was glad to hear him say it. I just hoped he was speaking the truth.

"Well, for the record," I replied, "nor did I."

I saw his face relax. He was relieved too. I dropped my eyes to my plate, suddenly embarrassed by my suspicions. I ate for a while in silence, working my way through the rice and beans and papayas. When I looked up again Peter was making notations in a small leather notebook with his silver Cross pen. I smiled. He would take notes. He caught my look and shoved the notebook and pen into his breast pocket. Then he speared what was left of his zebra burger.

"About Craig," he said in a nonchalant voice. "Did he ever use Sarah's computer?"

I sighed, but answered. "He never really *used* it. He played with it a few times."

Peter nodded with satisfaction. He reached for his notebook again.

"Peter, that was over two years ago," I pointed out irritably. "While Craig was still in the study group. I doubt if he's even seen Sarah since."

"Are you sure of that?" Peter asked in an insinuating tone. He opened the notebook.

"No," I admitted. "But you're barking up the wrong tree. Craig can be a jerk at times, but he's not murderer material."

Peter smiled smugly and put his pen to paper. "Let me be the judge of that," he said.

"All right, all right," I told him. "You can be a judge if you want to." The smug expression left his face. His eyes narrowed.

"Are you making fun of me?" he asked.

"No, not me," I assured him in a voice of pure innocence. I bent forward. "But before you write anything else down, let me remind you that you're the one who was always threatening to strangle Sarah."

Peter laid his notebook on the table and sighed heavily. "I know," he admitted. "I don't feel very proud of that now. But, dammit, she was the last person I would have expected to actually die."

"Don't worry," I said, taking pity on him. "I think she really liked you threatening her. That's how she could tell that she really had you stirred up."

"Thank you, Kate," he said quietly. Now I wondered if *he* was teasing. Then I remembered. Peter didn't know how to tease.

"Did you ever go over to her house, besides the times we had the study group there?" I asked.

"A few times with Nancy," he answered. He didn't pause to think it over. "But not for a year at least." He opened his notebook again and riffled the pages. "The group only met at Sarah's fourteen times in three years." He looked up at me. "I counted the days on my calendar. I would doubt that any of us were in her house long enough to learn how to operate the computer. Or the robots."

"*Could* you have programmed her robot?" I pressed on.

"It's possible," he replied earnestly. "Given enough time to familiarize myself with her system." I looked into his clear eyes. Was his honesty just a ploy to convince me what a guileless person he really was? I had to keep reminding myself that this man was a skilled trial attorney. I observed his face closely as I asked my next question.

"How much do you want to be a judge?" Peter popped up in his seat, his eyebrows raised.

"Dammit, that could be a motive, couldn't it?" he barked. He shook his head ruefully. "Blackmail. I hadn't even considered it." He reached for his notebook again.

"Peter, you don't have to write down your own motives, for God's sake!" I let out a hoot of laughter without thinking.

Peter's face reddened once more. I smiled at him, inviting him to smile back. He didn't. He didn't even accuse me of making fun of him. He shot me a hurt look, bent his head over his plate, and ate the remains of his burger in silence. I finished off my "native's fare" quickly. I had run out of questions for Peter.

I was deep in thought when I got home. Was Peter a superb and evil actor? Or merely a pompous innocent? I opened the door and stepped into the house. As I did, I heard a rasping sound and saw movement out of the corner of my eye.

Instinctively, I stepped back. The movement I had seen resolved itself into the hurtling form of a potted plant, which crashed to the floor at my feet. I stood there, stunned for a moment, staring at shards of clay pot, fern fronds and scattered dirt on the wooden floor.

Then the residual buzz of adrenaline kicked in. My body began to shake as I looked up and saw the remains of the macrame network which had held the potted plant. One of the three suspension ropes was hanging down, revealing its frayed end. Time to breathe, I told myself. But as I sucked in a deep, trembling breath, uninvited questions began shouting for my attention.

Was this a murder attempt? Was someone really trying to kill me? I looked at the pot. It was only four inches in diameter. I doubted that it would have even knocked me out, let alone killed me. Was I dealing with a stupid murderer or perhaps just a naively hopeful one? A picture of Nick formed in my mind. Or was someone just trying to scare me? I could see the end of the rope from where I stood. It didn't look cut. It looked worn through.

I dragged a ladder to the scene and climbed up to examine the other end of the rope. It too looked frayed and worn. The individual threads which had made it up ended at slightly different lengths and were spread outward. If they had been cut with a knife, wouldn't they have been more even? And how could it have been arranged to finally break at the exact moment that I walked in? I briefly considered calling Sergeant Feiffer as I climbed down from the ladder. Very briefly.

Lighten up, I told myself. It had been twenty years since I had bought the macrame hanger. Who decorated with macrame any longer? In Sarah's terms, the universe was probably telling me it was time to hire an interior designer. With that in mind, I cleaned up the mess, listened to my answering machine's messages and returned to the business of my business. But my fear had blossomed like a spring daffodil.

I worked until midnight. Avoidance of fear is a great incentive for boring work. At midnight I put on my purple-striped dropseat pajamas with the feet in them and rolled into bed exhausted. C.C. materialized in front of me and climbed onto my chest. I put my arms around her gratefully and fell asleep.

It was nearly two o'clock in the morning when I woke with a start. C.C. was gone. And someone was calling my name.

– Eleven –

HAD SOMEONE REALLY called me? Or had I dreamt it? I lay there under the covers, straining to hear. There was a rustling sound, then the muffled voice again.

"Kate," the voice called.

Who the hell was it? I sat up groggily and waited for the voice to call once more. Maybe then I could recognize the person it belonged to. But all I heard was a loud bang on the door that led from my bedroom to my back deck. At least the sound was loud enough to convince me I wasn't dreaming. Reluctantly, I pulled myself from my warm bed. Why was someone banging on my back door in the middle of the night? Why weren't they knocking on my front door?

There was another loud bang on the door.

"All right, all right!" I shouted, stepping around the bed toward the door.

But I paused when I reached it.

"Who's there?" I called out nervously.

There was no answer. But the rustling sound was getting louder. Was that the wind?

Raccoons, I thought suddenly. It was just some raccoons playing on the deck. I had forgotten what a racket they could make. I reached for the doorknob with a sleepy sigh of relief. By the time it occurred to me to wonder how raccoons could call out my name, I had already turned the knob and pulled back the door.

An explosion of sound and light and heat blasted me back a step. In the instant of that backward step my sleep-sodden mind took in what was in front of me.

Fire!

In the yard, a few feet away from the deck my neatly stacked log pile was on fire. It was now a four by ten foot log itself, alive with orange flames writhing and pirouetting into the sky like Halloween spirits. And the roar! The crackling blotted out everything else. How had I heard my name and the banging over that sound? For yet another instant I wondered if I was indeed dreaming. A fire three feet from my back deck? Three feet from burning down my redwood-shingled house? It didn't seem possible in the waking world. But another instant of heat and sound was all it took to convince me that it was real.

Move! my mind shouted. I slammed the door shut and ran through the house to the telephone, barely noticing as I caromed off a wall in the hall. I dialed 911, muttering "please, oh please," under my breath to a god I didn't really know. They put me on hold.

I screamed "Fire!" into the silent phone.

It must have been less than a minute before they came back to me, but it was an eternity too long. "Fire!" I screamed again and babbled out my address as the man on the other end of the line told me to calm down.

Calm down? I carried the telephone receiver into the kitchen, causing the rest of the phone to clatter to the floor. I looked out the glass of the kitchen's back door and saw orange flames writhing higher and closer. The man repeated my address and cross street. I hung up and moved. I ran out my front door and down the stairs. The hose I had used to fill my hot tub was now hooked up to a faucet in the front yard for watering the garden. I tripped on the bottom stair, falling onto my knees in the tan bark, then picked myself up and sprinted the last few steps to the faucet under the stairs.

I grabbed the working end of the hose that was connected there and turned the water on. I held the end tight and tore around the corner of the house. The unwinding hose caught under the edge of the front porch, jerking me to the ground.

I scrambled to my feet, ran back to the front and untangled the mess. Would the hose reach the back of the house? I frantically tried to remember how many feet I had. Should I unscrew the hose from the front faucet and attach it to the back one? It would take too long, I decided instantly. The hose would just have to reach. I grabbed a spray nozzle and screwed it on as I went tearing around the side of the house again.

The logs were blazing fifteen feet into the sky now. And the fence they were stacked against was burning too. I ran toward the fire. Yards away from the flames, I could already feel the scorching waves of heat flapping back and forth in the wind. I couldn't get much closer without burning my face. I needed that spray nozzle. It would give me at least a yard more reach. Bright cinders were raining down everywhere like kamikaze sparklers.

I moved as close as I could to the heat and squeezed the trigger on the nozzle, spraying a jet of water onto the center of the log pile. The fire hissed where the water hit and retreated ever so slightly, then roared back as I moved the jet of water to the next section. Damn.

Forget the logs, I told myself. If the fence went, the house wouldn't be far behind. I turned the nozzle on the nearest section of burning fence and sprayed. The flames faltered and then died where the water hit, sizzling and popping their death rattle. Thank you, God, I thought as I sprayed the next section of fence.

Once the fence was out I turned my hose back on the logs. The flames bent back like ballerinas, but didn't die. I kept spraying.

I heard a thin voice shouting nearby. Was that the fire department already? I squinted over the side fence at a shadowy figure who was almost invisible beyond the flames. It was my neighbor Grace, an unsociable old woman I had spoken to maybe ten times in six years.

"Your deck!" she screamed.

I turned and saw the flames digesting the corner of the deck. Oh God! Would the flames stop before they reached my new hot tub?

"I'll get it!" she cried. She swung her own hose over the fence and turned it onto the deck, splattering me with cold drops as she did. I blessed Grace as I turned back to my log pile. A cinder hit my cheek. I felt its brief burning sting and a surge of new fear. What if my hair caught fire? What if it was already on fire? Could I even feel it in all this heat? I raised the nozzle of my hose over the top of my head and squeezed the trigger. A shock of ice water drenched me from my hair to my pajamaed feet. I became a snowball in hell, freezing in the inferno.

"Have you called the fire department?" came a new voice shouting over my back fence. Another neighbor, Steve.

"Yes!" I screamed back.

"I'll get your roof!" he promised.

Neighbors! My neighbors. I turned my hose back on my log pile, alternately shivering from cold and reeling from the blasts of heat when the wind shifted the flames in my direction. I concentrated the water on the edge of the log pile where the fence had gone up. Out of the corner of my eye I saw Steve climbing up a ladder with a streaming hose. He directed the stream onto my roof.

Then I heard the fire sirens.

"Thank you, God. Thank you, neighbors. Thank you, fire department," I whispered.

By the time the fire truck arrived, I had vanquished the flames in one corner of the woodpile, Grace had taken care of the deck, and Steve had made a good start wetting down the roof. My hands were glued to the hose as I moved to the next flaming section of wood.

"Ma'am!" came a call from behind me.

I turned my head for a moment and saw the yellow-slickered figures pulling their giant hose toward me. I nodded acknowledgment and returned my attention to the burning log pile.

"Ma'am!" came the call again.

I jerked my head impatiently toward the firefighters. Couldn't they see I was busy?

"Get out of the way!" someone shouted.

My mind couldn't take in the words. I had to keep spraying the fire. I had to save my house.

"We've got more water power than you!" yelled another voice, a firewoman this time.

Slowly, her words sank in. I stepped back from the log pile in a daze. The firefighters pushed past me with their great-granddaddy of hoses and let loose.

Within minutes there were no more flames anywhere, only a pile of steaming charred firewood.

I sat down hard on the deck, feeling the cold wet wood on my bare skin. Bare skin? The dropseat pajamas! I had been standing outside in front of my neighbors, the fire department and God, with my fanny hanging out of my purple-striped dropseat pajamas. I had to be dreaming.

But I wasn't.

"Are you okay?" a fireman asked me. I could just make out his concerned face in the shadows.

"Fine," I said. At least he couldn't see the worst if I remained sitting.

"Do you know how this started?" he inquired gently.

Damn. How *did* it start? I began to shiver violently.

"Bring her a blanket," the fireman ordered. I heard footsteps as some kind soul obeyed.

"I think someone set it on f-fire," I stuttered through chattering teeth.

I felt a blanket being draped around my shoulders. But before I could turn to thank the person responsible, the fireman in front of me had another question. The sixty-four-thousand-dollar question.

"Do you know who did it?" he asked.

I shook my head. Who? This was no worn-out macrame. This was arson. I might have . . . I could hardly complete the thought. I might have burned alive. My shivering escalated into uncontrolled shaking. And with the shaking came the bile of fear in my throat.

"You'd better get inside, ma'am, where it's warm," counseled the fireman.

Warm, I thought. Warm would be good. But not hot. As I stood up I wondered if I'd ever make a fire in my woodstove again. I was leading the way back around the house when I remembered my neighbors.

"Thank you, Grace!" I shouted. "Thank you, Steve!"

"Anytime," came Grace's thin voice. I thought I heard a quiver in it.

Steve's voice wasn't quivering, but it was an octave higher than usual. "Right on!" he squealed enthusiastically.

I smiled. At least someone had enjoyed the fire. I would think of wonderful gifts for both of them. I let my mind drift. What would please them? I knew Grace knitted. A gift certificate from that incredibly expensive yarn shop downtown might please her. And for Steve—

"May I come in, ma'am?" asked the fireman at my side, startling me back to the present. Back to the fear.

"Sure," I answered wearily. I had to face what had happened. I might as well talk to the fire department. We walked up the stairs into my house and the questioning began.

It was four in the morning by the time all the firefighters had left. The fireman who interviewed me had been polite, but insistent. I told him about Sarah, about the threat, about everything. He told me he would inform the police and left me alone in my house. My house. I looked at the walls lovingly. My house was intact!

I knew I should go back to sleep, but it seemed out of the question. I walked to the kitchen to make a pot of herbal tea. C.C. was curled up on her favorite kitchen chair, snoring softly. I looked down at her fondly. I wondered if she had slept through the whole thing.

I set the kettle on the stove and turned on the burner. The flame!

I gulped down fear as the flame came alive. I quickly turned the burner off. Forget the tea for now. Think. Whoever had set the fire had banged on my door. They had called my name. Why? To make sure I caught the fire before it did any real damage?

The arsonist hadn't intended to kill me. Suddenly I was sure of it. Whoever it was had only meant to warn me, to frighten me. But if the arsonist was the same person who killed Sarah, that person had no compunction about murder. So why had the arsonist saved me by banging on my door? Because it was someone who knew me. Someone who liked me. A friend?

I began shivering again.

I had to find out who did this! I couldn't wait for the next attack.

I strode toward my desk. It was time to begin a suspect list. But as I walked past my answering machine, I saw its light blinking.

Probably a concerned neighbor, I thought. I rewound the tape, then hit PLAY.

"That's our last warning," a gangster's voice rasped. "Next time it'll be you."

– Twelve –

I TOPPLED INTO my comfy chair like a felled tree. Another death threat. Damn. I had already figured out that the fire was a warning. At least intellectually. But the rasp of the gangster's voice brought the reality home to my body. I pulled my trembling knees up to my chest and hid my face on top of them. I didn't need to replay the tape. The message, especially the "next time it'll be you" part, was repeating itself in my mind all too clearly.

Oh God, I was scared. If arsonists could set my log pile on fire, they could set my house on fire. Set me on fire! What a horrible way to die. Suddenly I stopped breathing, the leftover smell of smoke smothering me.

I dropped my knees, pulled my head up and inhaled. If I hadn't asphyxiated while I was fighting the fire, I wasn't going to now. I concentrated on breathing for a couple of minutes, then yanked the threatening message tape out of the machine and replaced it with a blank one. That was my last blank tape. There had better not be any more phone threats.

I called Sergeant Feiffer, but he wasn't in. Then I remembered, it was four thirty in the morning, time for all reasonable human beings to be asleep.

I shuffled down the hall and into the bathroom where I gulped down two NatuRest tablets. Then I climbed into my cold bed, hoping for some rest. But the moment I closed my eyes I saw orange flames writhing against the darkness. My eyes flew open again. I focused on the soft glow of the stars through the skylight above my bed until my lids gradually descended with me into sleep.

When I woke again it was nearly eleven on Saturday morning.

I jumped out of bed and yanked open the door leading to my charred deck. No, I hadn't dreamt the fire. The heavy scent of smoke was still in the air. And I could see the black heap of charcoal on the ground where my woodpile had been. Grey ash covered my charred porch. Then I noticed the fireman. He was kneeling in front of the charcoal, picking out small pieces and depositing them into a plastic bag. He turned and waved.

"Ms. Jasper—" he began.

I lowered my eyes. I didn't want to talk to another fireman. Not while I was in my pajamas. As I lowered my eyes I saw two softball-sized chunks of concrete on my door step. Concrete? Was that what had banged on my door the night before? I shivered.

"About last night's fire," the fireman was saying. "Could you—"

"Give me a couple minutes," I shouted and closed the door.

I showered and dressed in less than five minutes. Then I opened my back door again. But the fireman was gone. It was just as well, I thought as I walked down the hall to my answering machine. The light was blinking. I rewound the tape and pushed the playback button gingerly. I sighed thankfully as I listened to one voice asking me if I was interested in an investment in strategic metals and another selling a class which explored the connection between metaphysics and eroticism. No death threats so far.

The last message announced that the funeral service for Sarah Quinn would be held Sunday at the Jasmine Mortuary Chapel in San Rafael. My stomach knotted. I was alive, but Sarah was still dead.

C.C. tore into the room yowling. Breakfast was late!

I dialed my friend Barbara's number and carried the phone into the kitchen while I searched for KalKan. C.C. urged me along, batting at my leg impatiently. I was a criminally slow slave.

"Hi, Kate," said Barbara when she answered on the fourth ring. C.C. did figure-eights around my legs.

"How did you know it was me?" I asked as I scooped out cat food.

Barbara just chuckled. Psychics!

"Never mind," I told her, throwing out the can. "Will you go to Sarah's funeral with me tomorrow?"

"I wouldn't miss it for a rerun of *Dallas*," she assured me cheerfully.

"What do you mean by—" I stopped myself. Obviously she

meant yes. "Listen, Barbara," I continued. "Probably a lot of the, uh, people who knew Sarah will be there."

"You mean the *suspects*, don't you?" Barbara corrected me blithely.

I nodded. One good thing about psychics. They know when you're nodding over the phone.

"That's cool," she assured me. "I'll check them out for eee-vil vibrations."

"Do you think you can spot the murderer?" I asked her.

Her voice turned serious. "I don't really know," she said softly. "But I'll do my best."

"Thanks, Barbara," I said. "Talk to you later."

But she stopped me before I could hang up. "Kate," she said slowly. "I'm getting something weird on you. I don't know what it means but I see—"

"Fire," I finished for her.

"Yes," she said. "What happened?"

"Someone set my log pile on fire."

"Oh, I see," she remarked.

I was glad someone saw. I opened my mouth to tell her about my night, when the doorbell rang.

"I'll let you get the door," she said and hung up.

I wished she hadn't when I saw who was at the door. It was Sergeant Feiffer. And he wasn't smiling as he walked in.

"Jesus, what did you do!" he shouted. Then he slammed the door behind him.

C.C. came loping in to check out the action.

Sic 'im, I ordered her silently.

Feiffer took another step forward and brought his head down so that he was glaring directly into my eyes. "What do you know?" he snarled.

C.C. skidded to a stop, turned and walked nonchalantly back to the kitchen. Her mama didn't raise any foolish kittens.

"I . . ." I faltered.

"You what?" he asked, his eyes glued to mine.

'I don't know what I know," I answered weakly.

"Well, someone thinks you do," he told me. He straightened his shoulders and spoke in a nearly normal tone. "The fire marshal says it's arson."

Then he just stared at me. What did he want from me?

"Do you want to hear the message?" I asked finally.

His eyebrows went up.

"What message?" he asked. Then I saw his eyes narrow. "Did you get a new one?" he demanded.

I led him to the answering machine and stuck in the tape. Then I hit the play button.

"That's our last warning," the tape rasped. "Next time it'll be you."

Feiffer dropped into my comfy chair and shook his head back and forth. I resisted putting a consoling arm around him. I didn't want to be misunderstood. But he sure looked like he could use some consolation. He wasn't the only one.

"What did you find out about the first message?" I asked softly.

"Nothing," he said, shaking his head harder. "It must have been a local call. There's no record of it." He looked up at me. "We've sent it to another lab. They'll try to filter out the TV show and get some background noise, but . . ." He threw his hands up despairingly.

"Could you assign someone to guard my house?" I asked in a small trembling voice I didn't even recognize.

Feiffer rose from the chair and shrugged his shoulders. "I can put in a request, but I can't promise much."

He must have sensed my heart sinking. "I'm sorry," he said. "We just don't have the people to go around. Maybe we can get someone to drive by every once in a while but—"

"That's all right," I told him. No use in his feeling bad.

Suddenly he glared at me. I could see the lecture forming in his eyes. "Ms. Jasper, take my advice. Get out of town for a while—"

The doorbell rang again. Sergeant Feiffer and I both jumped.

It was Felix. He came stomping into the hallway, his eyes full of hurt, his mouth moving furiously under his mustache. "What's the deal here?" he demanded. "How come you didn't call—"

Then he saw Sergeant Feiffer. Feiffer glared at Felix. Felix glared back at Feiffer. Reporter versus cop. I didn't bother to introduce them. It was obvious that they had met each other before.

"You ought to take better care of your friend," Feiffer snapped at Felix. Felix's eyes widened. Feiffer glared at both of us for a moment, then strode out the door and down the stairs.

The moment I closed the door Felix started in. "I thought you were my buddy, my *compadre*," he whined. Then he escalated to shouting. "But noooo! Every time something big happens you forget all about me! You tell Barbara but not me! A story like this and all you can think of is—"

The doorbell rang again. Oh boy. Someone else to yell at me?

I opened the door and saw Vivian. Was this her day to clean? I couldn't even remember what day it was.

Vivian tilted her head toward Felix. "Who's he?" she demanded brusquely.

"Felix Byrne," I answered. "Ignore him."

Felix's face reddened.

"What's up?" I asked Vivian. I remembered now. It wasn't her day.

"I was doing a house down the street," she explained. "They told me about the fire." She put her hand on my shoulder. "Are you okay?" she asked.

Finally. Someone cared if I was okay. "I'm all right," I lied. "Thank you for asking." I shot a pointed look at Felix. He had the grace to look down at his shoes. That was probably as close to an apology as he would consider making.

"What happened?" Vivian asked.

"Arson," I answered. The word was out of my mouth before I could stop myself.

"Why?" Vivian pressed. She stared at me unblinkingly.

I wiggled impatiently. Was she going to tell me I brought it on myself? "To stop me from asking questions about Sarah's death," I admitted.

"*Are* you going to stop?" Vivian asked in an even voice.

"No, goddammit!" I exploded. Why was everyone on my case?

Vivian stepped back, hurt on her face. I was immediately sorry for shouting.

"I just—" I began.

"That's fine," she muttered angrily. "You don't have to explain anything to me. I'm just the hired help."

Felix smirked as she turned and left.

"Out!" I shouted at him.

The smirk left his face. "But—" he began.

"I've got a lunch date," I insisted. "I'll see you later."

"Kate—"

I centered myself, put my hands on his chest and gave him a light tai chi shove. He stumbled backwards a step. All right! I hadn't been sure it would actually work.

"Cool, I'm cool," he assured me, putting up a restraining hand. "But remember, dinner's on you tonight. Catch you at six."

As he walked down the stairs I felt a pang of guilt. He was Barbara's sweetie after all.

"Felix!" I yelled after him. "I'll tell you everything tonight. I promise."

He turned back to me, a gleam in his eye. His mouth opened.

"Tonight," I repeated and closed the door quickly.

I trotted into the bathroom to fix my hair and brush my teeth. I was meeting Tony at his restaurant at twelve-thirty. I smiled at the mirror. Tony might be a murderer, but at least he wouldn't yell at me.

The Elegant Vegetable greeted me tastefully, as always. As I walked into the restaurant, the aroma of herbs and garlic wafted toward me. That was a big improvement on smoke. I breathed in happily and realized I was really hungry. I never had eaten breakfast. Vivaldi played softly in the background. Large watercolors of flowers were hung on the walls, and real ferns, philodendrons and palms grew in abundance. Tony walked up to greet me and gave me a long, warm hug. I sank into the comfort gratefully.

"I've made some very special dishes in honor of your visit today," Tony told me once we came out of the clinch. He held me at arm's length and looked into my eyes. "In addition to the regular menu we have gingered eggplant salad, cauliflower mousse and tofu bourguignonne. And today's soup is miso watercress." He gave me a second, brief hug.

"I'm salivating," I assured him enthusiastically. But my genuine gustatory anticipation couldn't stop me from staring at Tony's face. Why were there dark circles under his round blue eyes? Was he mourning for Sarah? Maybe he just had a late date last night, I told myself. Or did he stay up past his usual bedtime to light my log pile on fire? I lowered my own eyes guiltily.

Tony didn't seem to notice. He led me to a corner table and whispered to our waitress that he wished to be considered a patron rather than host for the next hour or so. She was dressed in an olive-green sweatshirt over black tights, one of the more conservative outfits in the place. She nodded, bobbing her hot-pink and black-streaked hair, and then slunk off.

"How come you hire these punkers to wait tables?" I asked in a whisper. For the moment I wanted to talk about anything besides murder. Or arson.

"At first I took them on because the poor kids can't get work anyplace else," Tony explained gently. "They're just expressing their feelings, but you wouldn't believe the discrimination they run into." He shook his head sadly.

"I can't imagine why," I remarked insincerely as I watched the busboy filling my glass. His face was chalk-white. I hoped it was makeup and not natural. He wore a rhinestone nose ring, leather pants and a shirt that had torn shoulders and came down to just above his navel. The strip of hair that divided his skull down the middle was fanned into gold-tipped spikes. Tony didn't seem to notice the insincerity of my words.

"But then I found they were a drawing card," he want on placidly. He leaned forward and spoke in a hushed tone. "People who aren't vegetarians come here just for the enjoyment of watching the kids serve. Isn't that amazing?"

I smiled. "It sure is," I agreed honestly.

"But enough business," Tony said, sitting back in his chair. "What'll you have to eat? Tofu bourguignonne? Cauliflower mousse?"

"I'm overwhelmed," I told him. "How about if you order? I'll have whatever you suggest." Tony flashed me a sweet smile, then motioned the waitress over and ordered a series of dishes and a bottle of Navarro pinot noir grape juice.

"God, it must be heaven to eat here all the time," I purred.

"It is sometimes," Tony agreed seriously. "Though most of the time I'm too busy cooking, or smoothing someone's feathers, or doing all the——" He broke off with an embarrassed smile. "Enough complaining. Today is special. I'm going to get comfortable and appreciate the food and the company." Then his face went serious again. "Since Sarah has gone, I've come to cherish my remaining friendships more than ever." He looked so sincere as he spoke. But was he?

"It doesn't seem possible somehow that Sarah is really gone," I prompted.

"No," said Tony, his sorrowful eyes staring out past me. "I'm thirty-four years old and I go to funerals every month. I study the obituary column like an old man. So many of my friends have died. I should be used to it."

AIDS, I thought. He's talking about AIDS. My stomach spasmed. I knew he did hospice work, but he rarely talked about it. I reached out to touch his hand. He was such a good man.

"*You're* all right, aren't you?" I asked, suddenly worried by his mood.

He brought his eyes back to mine and smiled weakly. I could tell it was an effort. "So far, so good," he said, squeezing my outstretched hand. Then he leaned forward. "What I don't understand is Sarah dying," he whispered. "She wasn't sick. And she was . . . she was . . ."

"Immortal," I finished for him.

"Yes . . ." he agreed slowly. "I suppose I actually believed that." He shook his head. "I just don't understand how it could have happened." He stared at me intently. What answers did he want from me?

"You mean how she was murdered?" I asked, retrieving my hand.

"Murdered!" Tony yelped. "She wasn't murdered, was she?" His face paled. Was it possible that he hadn't realized? He certainly looked shocked and horrified.

"I'm sorry, Tony," I said hurriedly. "I really don't know if she was murdered. I just—"

Our waitress arrived with our salads before I could say anything else foolish. I studied Tony's face as she served us. He stared down at the table with unseeing eyes as she set his salad in front of him. He certainly looked like he was a man in shock.

I decided to concentrate on my gingered eggplant. I dug in and brought a bite to my lips.

"Murder?" Tony repeated in a faraway voice. "I read the paper, but I never really believed . . ."

Damn. I laid my fork back down and reached for Tony's hand again. I shouldn't have done this to him. "Tony," I scolded gently, "you're right about enjoying ourselves. Now eat. Or I'll feel bad." He continued to stare at his plate in a daze until his natural graciousness reasserted itself.

"Of course," he murmured. I let go of his hand and he speared a piece of eggplant. I didn't know if he meant "of course we should eat," or "of course she was murdered." I let it go.

We ate in uneasy silence. I couldn't think of anything to say, except to ask him where he was at two o'clock this morning. So I praised the eggplant salad. Tony brightened a little. I turned up the heat as the rest of the dishes came. I sighed over the cauliflower mousse made with soy milk instead of cream, and moaned unashamedly over the tofu bourguignonne and clove-spiced pilau. Very few men can resist loudly orgasmic recognition of their skills. Tony was no exception. By the end of the meal he was smiling again, albeit wanly.

I planned my interrogation as we drank our herbal tea. But before I could begin, our waitress brought over one of the customers who just *had* to speak to Tony personally.

"I hate to interrupt you," the woman whispered urgently. "But you have ants crawling on the floor."

"Yes, I know," Tony replied quietly. "But we wouldn't want to kill them, would we? So we'll just have to share our space with them for the time being."

"Uh, well, I guess so," she mumbled and toddled off in confusion.

"Everyone's after me to kill those ants," he told me, shaking his head unhappily. "But I'd have to use pesticide. I just couldn't." This was the man I was suspecting of murder? I reminded myself that ants were not people and plunged in.

"Tony, remember the last study group when Sarah said she knew your secret. What was she talking about?"

He was silent for a moment, his brows lowered in confusion. Then recognition filled his eyes and he blushed.

"She was just trying to get my goat, Kate," he muttered. "And she did. But I'm not going to talk about it."

I just sat and stared at him, hoping to wear down his resistance.

"I could make up something," he said after a few minutes of this torture. "Then you would think you had it. But I'd rather be honest. Okay?" His round blue eyes looked beseechingly out of his open face.

"Okay," I sighed, giving in. "But I really do have a reason for asking." He just continued to look forlorn. I pressed on. "Do you have a VCR?"

"Yeah," he answered slowly, confusion evident in his face once more.

"Peter has a VCR too," I said hurriedly. "But he's uptight about his."

"Peter is really okay, Kate," Tony lectured me gently. "He's trying so hard to be perfect that he gets a little critical. He's actually a harsher judge of himself than he is of other people."

I thought for a moment. "You're probably right," I finally agreed. I had never looked at Peter that way. "But he can sure be annoying." I changed the subject. "Listen, are you going to the funeral tomorrow?"

"Of course," Tony murmured. "Do you want an escort?"

"No, no," I said. "I have a friend coming with me." I leaned forward and whispered. "What I really wanted to ask was whether you'd come to my house on Monday evening for this seance I'm arranging."

"What do you mean by seance?" Tony asked, tilting his head to the side.

"Well," I began. I took a big breath. I felt so silly talking about it. "I have this friend who's into psychic stuff," I rattled off. "The idea is that she'll try to get in touch with Sarah's spirit and ask some questions. If there's any way Sarah can answer, I'll bet she will."

"Yeah, she would," said Tony, smiling reminiscently. "It's worth a try. Sarah would love it." Then his smile faded. "Oh, Kate," he breathed. "Do you really think she was murdered?"

– Thirteen –

"I DON'T KNOW for certain that Sarah was murdered," I answered carefully, adding silently that I wouldn't take any bets against it.

Should I tell Tony about last night's fire? It would be a relief to talk to someone who wouldn't yell at me. I could trust him, couldn't I?

"Tony, I . . . last night . . ." I faltered. I looked into his stricken eyes. I just couldn't. He didn't need any more shocks. "I don't know," I repeated.

Tony dropped his eyes, graciously allowing my withdrawal. We sipped our tea silently, both lost in our own anxieties. Once we were finished, we shared another long hug, and I thanked him for the meal. He told me to "take care," and I left, ninety-nine per cent certain that Tony was incapable of murder. Then I went shopping. I had neighbors to thank.

By the time I reached home, I had deposited a magnum of champagne on the front seat of my neighbor Steve's pickup truck, and a gigantic woven basket filled with balls of mohair-and-silk yarn on Grace's doorstep, Easter bunny-style. I had also changed my mind about Tony. My confidence in his innocence had dropped to ninety-two per cent. When no one seems a likely candidate for murderer, the nearly impossible suspect becomes merely improbable.

The first thing I saw when I opened my front door was the blinking light on my answering machine. I approached the machine and pushed the buttons cautiously. But all the tinny speaker produced was an invitation from Craig to accompany me to Sarah's funeral. I slumped into my comfy chair. Why hadn't *Wayne* called?

I didn't have the time for a major moan-and-whine break. I had bookkeeping to do. Even murder and arson don't count as excuses to forgo work when you're your own boss. I left a brief message on Craig's machine telling him I already had an escort, then sat down at my desk and began punching the keys of my adding machine.

The doorbell rang a little before six. I switched off my adding machine and switched on my memory. It must be Felix. I wondered where he was going to take me to dinner. Since I was paying, I assumed it would be expensive.

I flung open the door with sarcasm on my lips. But Felix wasn't on my doorstep. Wayne was. I didn't stop to think. I just leapt toward him and caught him around the waist with the grasp of a drowning woman. He didn't struggle. He just held me like a good lifeguard. I pressed my face against his sweatered chest, filling my lungs with his scent. Then C.C. got in the act, purring and squeezing herself in the space left between our ankles.

"Heard about the fire," Wayne growled.

"Mrph," I answered into his chest.

"Barbara called," he went on.

I loosened my grip on Wayne slightly, feeling a sudden surge of guilt that encompassed Sarah's murder, the fire and the man with his arms around me. I hung my head.

"You're coming to my house," he ordered quietly.

I didn't answer. My brain was issuing a cacophony of conflicting instructions.

"Stick with you night and day," he promised. "No one will get to you."

"No, I need to be here to work," I heard myself say.

He withdrew the comfort of his arms abruptly. I looked up and saw the hurt in his face.

"It's not just work," I said quickly. "I need to find out who murdered Sarah. Who set my logs on fire."

I watched his face harden into an expressionless mask.

"Would you be able to watch me talking to possible murderers without interfering?" I asked desperately. He said nothing. "Well, would you?" I demanded.

His eyes flickered ever so slightly. "Probably not," he stated in a low, impassive voice.

He stared down at me for a few moments. "You're too close to this," he said finally.

I grabbed his hand. "Whoever set the logs on fire didn't want to kill me," I argued. "If they had, they would have torched the house." I didn't tell him about the warning on my answering machine.

"Kate—" he began, life and frustration back in his voice. Then he sighed. "Right," he rumbled.

I grabbed him again. He returned my embrace tentatively. I squeezed him tighter, trying to squeeze his doubt away.

I heard footsteps coming up the stairs. Wayne pushed away from me gently.

"Call me when you want my help," he whispered and turned to leave.

As Wayne passed Felix on the stairs, C.C. gave out a long, low-pitched yowl of distress. I looked at her wonderingly. Was she finally exhibiting the fabled feline sensitivity I had heard cat lovers twitter about? She batted my leg impatiently. No, I decided. She was just hungry.

Felix pumped me as I served the evening's KalKan. I answered all of his questions and more. I wanted what he knew about Linda Zatara in exchange. I told him all about the fire. I told him about the telephone message. I even gave him a quick tour of my charred back deck.

"Far friggin' out," he murmured blissfully, gazing at the remains of my log pile.

"Felix!" I protested.

"Jeez-Louise, Kate!" he shot back. "Don't pop your tonsils."

I closed my mouth. Should I tell him my tonsils were popped years ago? Felix took my moment of silence as an opportunity to further harangue me.

"What's the deal here?" he demanded. "Every time I try to talk to you, you're pricklier than a pit bull with hemorrhoids."

"The deal," I said slowly and carefully, "is my life."

"Holymoly, Kate," he muttered. His eyes widened in a show of hurt and innocence. "I didn't torch your friggin' wood—"

"Forget it, Felix," I cut him off quickly. It was no use trying. You can lead a reporter to sensitivity but you can't make him drink. "Let's go to dinner."

"I hope you feel better," he murmured solicitously as we climbed into his car, a turquoise vintage '57 Chevy. "Watch the paint job," he added as I slammed the door.

"I'm fine," I lied.

Felix pulled out of the driveway and onto the street carefully. I had forgotten how much he pampered his old Chevy. The sound of a car starting up behind us drew my eyes up past the pink foam dice to the rearview mirror they hung from. I leaned closer to Felix to get a good perspective. A bottle-green Jaguar was following us. Now I really *was* fine. Despite the understaffing of the Marin Sheriff's Department, I had my guard. My own personal bodyguard, Wayne Caruso.

"So, who'd you have lunch with?" Felix asked. His tone was still solicitous. Such restraint deserved a reward.

"Tony Olberti, from the study group," I answered. I might as well tell all. "And Peter Stromberg last night for dinner," I added.

"Give," he ordered, his voice thick with anticipation.

So I gave. I told him everything I could remember about the lunch and dinner conversations. Well, almost everything. I wasn't about to hand him Tony's mysterious secret. Or Peter's worry about his college drug days. Anyway, I had my own question.

"So what's the big deal about Linda Zatara?" I demanded.

"Later," said Felix. "We're here."

"Here" was a few blocks from the University of Marin campus. A carved wooden sign announced "The Crêpes of Wrath." A restaurant, I hoped. Felix motioned me ahead. I pushed the door open and saw mismatched, scarred wooden tables and folding chairs. The specials were scrawled on a black chalkboard. And no one waiting tables looked over twenty-five. I took a relieved breath. A student hangout. It had to be cheap.

Felix turned to me as if he had read my thoughts. Taking lessons from Barbara, no doubt. "Hey, I'm your buddy," he assured me. "I wouldn't burn you for a megabucks meal."

I was impressed. He really was on his best behavior.

"So," he whispered. "What do you think Tony's secret is?"

I jumped. Hadn't I left Tony's secret out of my debriefing? "I don't know—" I began. Then it dawned on me. I wasn't the informant. "Who told you about Tony?" I demanded.

Felix shrugged his shoulders and smirked.

He was saved from a demonstration of the tai chi low punch by the arrival of a young man whose name tag read "Chad, Your Host."

Chad was browned to perfection, with long blond bangs that fell into his face. He jerked his head to flip the bangs out of his eyes and asked "How many?" in a world-weary voice.

Felix held up two fingers.

"Two," I announced, afraid Chad couldn't see Felix's fingers through the bangs that had slipped back into his eyes.

Chad led us to a rickety wooden table and handed us some gloppy menus.

"Soups are minestrone and clam chowder," he informed us drearily, then slouched away.

"Local surfer?" I guessed in a whisper.

Felix laughed. "Chad's a concert pianist. He was a child prodigy. I did a story on him last spring."

"Who told you about Tony?" I asked quickly, hoping to catch Felix in his informative phase.

"Not you," Felix snapped.

"Felix," I protested. "You don't know Tony. No secret of his would be enough to murder over." Felix lifted an eyebrow. "I tell you Tony is out of the running," I insisted. Felix lifted both eyebrows. "Anyway, he wouldn't tell me what his secret was," I admitted.

Felix chuckled his forgiveness and looked down at his menu. I followed suit.

Crêpes and more crêpes. Tuna crêpes, ham and cheese crêpes, spinach crêpes, Spanish crêpes and Roman crêpes. I wasn't sure where the wrath came in. I found salads on the back of the menu. Avocado and sunflower-seed salad. Perfect. I was still full from my lunch with Tony. But I figured I was nervous enough to stuff myself anyway. Might as well stuff myself with salad.

I looked up. Felix was eyeing me speculatively. "Anything else you haven't told me?" he asked.

I shook my head.

"It's your turn, Felix—" I began. A blast of "Jumpin' Jack Flash" drowned out the end of my sentence. Our table began to dance, shaking the silverware into new arrangements.

Felix tilted his head back, closed his eyes and smiled happily. So, this is why he chose the place. If there was anything he loved more than his fifties car, it was the high decibels of sixties rock 'n' roll.

A tall young woman with long blond hair shuffled over to our table. She was dressed in a black miniskirt and tank top. She wore it well. Her legs were long, tanned and perfect. I let loose a sigh into the music, thinking of my own white legs that hadn't been on intimate terms with the sun for over a decade.

"So, whadya want?" she shouted over the music. Ouch! Her shout was shrill and whining. Maybe she and Nick should get together.

Someone turned the music down a few notches. Our table stopped shaking just as a fork shimmied up to the brink of suicide.

"I'll start with the minestrone and spinach salad," Felix announced, his eyes traveling down the menu rapidly. "Then two crêpes, the cajun shrimp and the three-cheese—"

"That just for you?" demanded the waitress. Her voice hadn't improved. But it was a good question. Felix wasn't much bigger than me. Where was he going to put it all? Not going to burn me for the meal, indeed!

"All for me, you gorgeous thing," Felix drawled. "I'll take a decaf espresso too. I need a lot of coal for this train," he added, rubbing his flat stomach and winking extravagantly. Ugh.

The waitress smiled back at him.

"I'll take the avocado and sunflower salad," I cut in.

"Sun-avo," the waitress confirmed shrilly and sashayed away with an over-the-shoulder glance at Felix.

I thought of Barbara. "Felix—" I began.

"So, do you want the poop on Sarah Quinn's nearest and dearest?" he asked briskly.

"Sure," I answered. Barbara could take care of herself.

Felix leaned forward across the table. His eyes were alive with information.

"First, there's Sarah's sister, Ellen," he told me. "She's a hot-shit insurance saleswoman from Jersey. She brings in the bucks and doesn't spread them around. And the police are buying her alibi." He paused. "She seems to be out of the running."

"Seems?"

"Nobody knows but Oz, man. She might have a double, or maybe she snagged a computer hit man, or something equally bizarre. That filly's still in the race as far as I'm concerned." He looked at me for confirmation. I nodded. He went on. "Second, two of the players have been busted for sticky fingers—"

"Sticky fingers?" I asked.

"Shoplifting," he clarified. Then he lifted an eyebrow at me. "Guess who," he ordered.

I thought it over. "I don't know," I said finally. "Ellen, Vivian, Myra, maybe Nick? Tell me."

"Two out of four ain't bad," he congratulated me. "Myra and Vivian. A long time ago for both of them and it probably doesn't mean diddly."

"Any arrests for arson?" I asked hopefully.

He shook his head impatiently and started back down his mental

list again. "Your gardener, Jerry, he used to be a lawyer." Felix pronounced it "liar," but I got the point. I nodded. "Do you know why
he quit law?" he challenged me.

I shrugged my shoulders. "Something about mellowing out, I
think."

"Huh!" Felix grunted triumphantly. "The man *had* to cool his
jets. He was deep in ethical doo-doo." Felix watched my face and
added, "without a pooper-scooper." Then he leaned back in his
chair.

"Go on," I ordered impatiently. Felix loved the big buildup. I
hated it.

Felix complied. "Under the code of ethics," he intoned, "attorneys aren't supposed to be playing hide-the-salami with their
clients—"

"Hide the salami?"

"You know," he insisted. He was blushing. That should have
been a clue. "Bouncy-bouncy," he explained. "Four-legged frolic,
blanket drill—"

"I got it," I cut him off hastily. Why couldn't he just speak
English?

"Well, anyway," he pressed on, eyes lowered. He was embarrassed! Maybe that explained the exotic euphemisms. "Your gardener Jerry wasn't just diddling his own client. He took it a step
further." He brought his eyes up. "Guess," he said.

"Felix!" I exploded. I lowered my voice. "Just tell me, all
right?"

He shrugged his shoulders. "Jerry's representing this poor
sucker in a divorce." He lowered his voice. I could tell the punch
line was coming. "And he was having it off with his client's soon
to be ex-wife."

"Wow," I said, trying to look suitably impressed. I still couldn't
see how this tied in with Sarah's murder.

"Yeah," said Felix smugly. "Fraternizing with the enemy, so to
speak. And," he went on, "he appeared in court a few times totally
baked on some pretty potent chemicals. The State Bar was taking a
good look-see at old Jerry, so he just sleaze-balled it out the back
door into a gardening business."

I made myself a mental note to talk to Jerry soon, while Felix
continued down his list.

"Your friend Peter, however, is squeaky clean," he told me.
"There's a lot of buzz about a judicial appointment for him. The
only naughty whiff in his past is his dalliance with left-wing poli-

tics. He might have had S.D.S. links. But nothing that can be proven."

Good. Even Felix hadn't been able to uncover the drug angle. Maybe Peter had a chance.

"Same clean slate for your friend Tony," Felix grumbled. "Aside from his being gay as gathering nuts in May, which he's completely up front about, there's nothing I could dig up."

"How about Linda—"

"Sun-avo for you, poppy seed dressing," came a shrill voice at my side. Damn. Was Felix paying this woman to distract me? "And salad, soup, two crêpes and espresso for you," our waitress purred at Felix. "I brought them all at once. I thought you'd be too hungry to wait."

"You've got it, sweet thing," Felix purred back, beaming up at her.

Should I tell her *I* was going to be the one in charge of her tip? She walked away before I had a chance.

Felix began slurping soup noisily. I looked down at my salad without interest.

"Come on, Felix," I cajoled. "Tell me about Linda Zatara."

Felix grinned at me. "You mean you really don't know who she is?" he asked.

I shook my head. He went back to his soup.

"Felix," I snarled.

He finished his soup, unperturbed, spoonful by slurping spoonful. Finally, he looked up at me.

"Have you told me everything you know?" he demanded.

"Yes, I have told you everything," I lied through clenched teeth.

He blotted his mustache with his napkin and settled back in his chair. "Linda Zatara," he announced, "is an investigative reporter."

"Oh no," I groaned. One was bad enough.

"Oh yes," he assured me. "She used to work for the *San Francisco Chronicle*. Now she writes best sellers," he said in an awed voice. He pulled his salad in front of him.

"I've never heard of her," I objected.

He took a bite and crunched, then smiled. "Have you ever heard of Z. L. Harvard?" he asked.

"Linda is Z. L. Harvard?" I yelped.

He nodded. I took a bite of my own salad. I needed time to assimilate this information. Z. L. Harvard. She infiltrated various groups, then wrote pseudo-documentaries about the gnat-brains that were in them. Of course the names were always changed to protect the innocent, but still . . . I chewed without tasting. I had read her book on the members of the prostitutes' union. She had exposed them down to the roots of their dyed hair. Their sad self-delusions, their abysmal mothering attempts, their foolish prattling, their sordid childhoods. Those poor women must have felt skinned alive. The pen can be crueler as well as mightier than the sword.

I looked up at Felix. He had finished his salad and was going for the crêpes. I put down my fork.

"Did you read the one about A.A.?" he asked cheerfully through a mouthful of cajun shrimp.

I shook my head. Though I could imagine her pitiless review of recovering alcoholics.

"How about the one on funeral homes?" he went on eagerly after he swallowed. "Holy socks! No wonder she writes under a pseudonym. That woman's lucky she isn't laid out under lilies herself. And the one about women who marry prisoners sure must have pissed off some of San Quentin's finest. She's lucky they didn't chew through the bars to get her." There was a glazed expression in his eyes as he took another bite.

"Felix, do you actually admire her?" I asked.

"Holymoly, Kate, of course I do," he said. "That woman's so big she's in a different time zone. Do you know the bucks she gets for just one book—"

"Do you know what she's writing about now?" I asked, cutting him off. I couldn't wait. I had a nauseating suspicion it might be human potential support groups.

He shook his head. He must have seen the look on my face. "Hey, Kate, I don't know everything," he apologized.

I finished my salad slowly as Felix gobbled up his crêpes and washed them down with espresso.

"Do you know Linda's address?" I asked as he took his last bite.

"You mean this?" he said, pulling a slip of paper from his pocket. He leaned forward with a grin. "That woman thinks nobody knows her address, but I do." He put the slip back in his pocket.

"May I have the address, please?" I asked as calmly as possible.

"Buy me dessert and it's yours," he bargained.

My mouth dropped open. How could he stuff any more into that short, skinny body? Never mind. I told myself and looked for the waitress.

Felix ordered the chocolate mousse crêpe and another round of decaffeinated espresso. The waitress was clearly impressed with his appetite. She was giggling as she sauntered back to the kitchen.

Felix handed me the slip of paper with Linda's address. I glanced at it and dropped it in my purse. Then Felix bent forward across the table. "I've got more, you know," he whispered enticingly.

"Give," I ordered.

"Guess who's spent time in the loony bin," he said.

I sighed, but played the game. "Myra maybe," I hazarded. "No," I corrected myself, "Nick."

"Bingo," Felix caroled. "A few years ago he wigged out totally. Wouldn't talk. Wouldn't eat. Sarah hauled his keister down to the local mental health facility. He wasn't there long. Being forced to spend time with other people was enough to get him functioning again."

I laughed appreciatively. "I'll bet that's exactly why Sarah did it," I told him.

A picture of Sarah chuckling flashed into my mind. I smiled, then shook my head to rid myself of the specter. She was dead. I'd go for nostalgia after I found out who killed her.

I watched Felix eat his dessert crêpe and paid the bill. Funny how expensive a student place can be when your guest is eating for three.

By the time Felix drove his Chevy carefully into my driveway we were all out of conversation. We had pumped each other's brains dry as the drought.

Felix didn't even bother to turn off the engine of his car. He pulled up to the house, bent across me and opened the car door.

"Thanks, Felix," I said sleepily.

As I got out I heard another car turn off its engine. I looked over my shoulder. Wayne's Jaguar was parked across the street.

I walked into my house and headed for the bedroom. It might have been only eight o'clock on Saturday night, but I was tired. I picked up my pajamas. They smelled of smoke. I dropped them into the laundry basket and went back out into the night. I crossed the street and knocked on Wayne's car window. He looked up, startled. Some bodyguard. Then he rolled his window down.

"Don't you think you could protect me more efficiently if you were in the same room with me?" I asked conversationally. "The bedroom, for example?"

– Fourteen –

WAYNE'S BROWS DROPPED like a curtain over his eyes. Was he angry at my flippant proposition?

He opened the door and got out of his Jaguar slowly, then straightened up to his full height and stared down at me without speaking.

Damn. I felt myself wither under his towering gaze. "Sorry," I muttered.

Then he smiled.

He hoisted me up in his arms and hauled me back to the house. He wasn't playing coy maiden anymore.

I woke up late Sunday morning in a state of sleepy optimism. I turned to look at Wayne sleeping by my side. His long, muscular body was curled into a fetal ball. His rough face was softened by sleep. He didn't look like a bodyguard anymore. He looked like a child. I kissed him softly on the forehead. He smiled sweetly from his dreams.

I decided to let him sleep. He needed some rest. We had made love ravenously the night before, gluttons after three months of famine. And once the initial hunger had been sated, we had savored the touch and taste and scents of old territories more slowly, assuring ourselves nothing important had changed.

I curled my body next to Wayne's, at peace with the world. I could hear birds calling and the sounds of my more industrious neighbors mowing, hammering and shouting. The light from the twin skylights made glowing, square imprints on the wall across from me. Warm and comfortable, it felt like a birthday morning or maybe Christmas. Then I remembered it was the day of Sarah's funeral.

Suddenly I was nauseated. Mourning sickness, I diagnosed quickly. I remembered the last funeral I had attended. Almost everyone had wept, the protocol being mass indulgence in a public outpouring of sorrow. It was like being in the movie audience when Bambi's mother died. I don't like to cry in public. Or in private for that matter.

I groaned. Wayne opened his eyes and looked at me, his face full of the same innocent optimism that I had been feeling moments before.

"Sunday morning, breakfast in bed," he mumbled and reached for me.

I took his hand from my body and kissed it softly. "I've got a funeral to go to," I whispered.

The optimism left his face abruptly. His brows lowered. He got out of bed slowly.

"I'll go with you," he growled.

I looked up at him, wondering if I would learn anything pertinent at Sarah's funeral with my bodyguard in tow.

"You're going to ask questions there?" he asked. I nodded my head.

His brows dropped further.

"It's dangerous, Kate," he said quietly.

"I know that," I told him, keeping my tone even with an effort. I swung my legs out of bed and stood up quickly. Too quickly. I swayed dizzily as I tried to remain standing.

Wayne stepped toward me and laid a hand on my shoulder to steady me. I put my arms around him.

"I love you, you know," I whispered into the hair on his chest.

He didn't respond. Maybe he didn't even hear me.

I broke away and pulled open the door to the back deck. I pointed at the charred woodpile. "I have to know who did this," I told him. "I have to know who killed Sarah."

But—" he began. Then he stopped.

He shrugged his shoulders. "I'll go," he said quietly.

He began dressing. I closed the door, suddenly aware of my own nudity. I hoped none of the neighbors were peeking. Dropseat pajamas were bad enough.

His face was stone when he turned to say goodbye.

"Call when you're ready," he said.

I didn't have a chance to ask him, "ready" for what. He left too quickly.

I threw myself into the shower and tried to think of other things. Funerals, for instance. I knew they were important rituals, though I couldn't remember exactly why. As I soaped, I switched my thoughts to Jerry, my unobtrusive gardener. I had never really talked to him in the same way I talked to Vivian. He was no friend, just the man who came and did things in my garden. I paid his bills by mail. Felix's revelations about Jerry had surprised me into considering him seriously as a suspect. Could he have set my logs on fire? I assured myself that it wasn't too late to investigate and dried off.

It took me ten minutes of searching through my jumble of business cards to find Jerry's phone number. And when I called the number, all I got was his answering machine. I hung up without leaving a message. Then I went to the garden and picked some orange chrysanthemums for Sarah.

Barbara picked me up at twenty after ten in her souped-up Volkswagen bug. She had insisted on driving. Funeral services were set for eleven at the Jasmine Mortuary Chapel. I didn't want to be late. I didn't want Barbara to have to speed to get there.

Barbara's driving was, at best, flamboyant. She liked to keep eye contact with her passengers while she was talking. And her car tended to swerve in time with her emphatic head movements. This was actually quite an effective form of communication. I have never forgotten some of the things she has said in her car, but only because her words were burned into my memory by fear. After an intense session of mobile conversation with Barbara, my right leg usually ached from trying to put on the brakes for her. And it got worse when she was in a hurry.

She had never actually hit anyone. I always reminded myself of that while riding with her. And I kept closing my eyes. But even with my eyes closed, I could still feel the swerves, accented by the anxious honks and beeps of other drivers.

On the way to the mortuary I tried to keep conversation at a minimum. It was no use. While drifting into the right lane, Barbara asked about the people that she was likely to meet at Sarah's funeral. She talked about doing her psychic best to discover the murderer among them. Then, while switching lanes for the highway turnoff, she discussed her plans for Monday's seance. Finally, she turned her attention to my relationship with Wayne. I gave her an edited version of the night before and the disastrous morning.

"Kate, you love that man," she insisted as she cut off a Safeway truck. She didn't seem to notice the blare of its horn. I winced and gripped my seat.

"Why do you always push him away?" she continued.

"It was him that—" I began. Then I stopped. It was both of us. I changed tack. "Where are we supposed to live if we get married?" I demanded instead. "Where would I do business? Actually, between the bedroom suites, cathedral living room, library, game room and indoor spa, I'm sure I could find a spot," I admitted. "But where would I feel *comfortable* doing my business? Where could I pile up my messy stacks—"

"How about your house?" she suggested.

"My house, huh!" I snorted. "My house would fit into one of Wayne's bedroom suites. It just doesn't have enough room—"

"You're just afraid Wayne will leave you like Craig did," she diagnosed.

I didn't answer her. I crossed my arms and stared resolutely forward. What a low blow.

She turned her steady gaze on my face.

We veered into the next lane.

"All right, all right!" I screeched, matching the sound of the car behind us. "Maybe I am a little paranoid about marriage."

"A little," she snorted, meandering back into her own lane. She turned down the road that led to the mortuary.

"What kind of service do you think they'll have for Sarah?" I asked. "She wasn't a member of any church, she was just . . . just New Age."

"We'll find out soon enough," Barbara answered, skidding into a parking space marked "For Mourners Only."

The main lobby had a tasteful bulletin board directing us to the Serenity Room for Sarah's funeral. The Serenity Room seemed preferable to the other choices, which included the Quietude Room and the Eternity Room. My stomach tightened with dread.

"This stuff is so spooky," I whispered to Barbara and clutched her arm. "It really gets to me."

"Just pretend we're on another planet visiting aliens," she replied. As we passed the ladies room she said, "Hey look, the Eternal Rest Room!" We softly giggled the rest of the way down the long corridor.

Peter was at the door to the Serenity Room. He looked like the stereotypical funeral director in his impeccable black suit.

"Hello, Peter," I said, injecting seriousness back into my tone. "This is my friend Barbara."

He looked at Barbara, an expression of disapproval tightening his lean face. I assumed the disapproval was directed at her low-cut jumpsuit. Or maybe that was just the expression he felt was appropriate at a funeral.

He forced a "Hello, Barbara" out of his stiff mouth, then turned his face to me. "It appears I'm the unofficial usher here," he complained. "This operation isn't very well-organized."

"What exactly is the operation here?" I asked nervously.

"Do you see that woman over there in the orange and purple robes?" he said. My eyes followed his and saw a tiny dark-haired woman dressed in Sarah's favorite colors. "Her name is Teala. She's from the Trancenjoy Foundation," he said.

"The what?" I asked.

Peter's tense face tightened further. A tic had developed at his temple. "It's some kooky organization that Sarah was involved in," he explained in a censorious tone. "Sarah's sister Ellen brought this woman in to do the service today. She wants to talk to all of us who knew Sarah, including you, Kate. We are going to be assigned parts in this . . . this ceremony." His nostrils flared in evident disgust.

My stomach spasmed. I might need the "Eternal Rest Room" after all. A funeral was bad enough. Public speaking didn't even bear thinking about.

"Peter, it's twenty to eleven," I whispered urgently. "How can we be assigned parts now?"

"I said this operation lacked organization," he snapped. Then he remembered his role as unofficial host. "Shall I introduce you around while we wait for Tony?" he offered.

"Sure," I said and turned to look at the rest of the mourners. I saw my ex-husband, Craig, first. He was in animated conversation with a man who was a stranger to me, a lean man with handsome Japanese features.

"Who's that talking to Craig?" I asked Peter.

"His name is Dave Yakamura," Peter whispered. "He worked with Sarah." He gave me a meaningful look.

"I thought she worked alone—" I began.

"Wayne's here," Barbara whispered in my ear. I forgot all about Craig and Dave Yakamura.

I turned slowly to look at Wayne. There he was, all alone at the back of the room, his face exhibiting all the animation of concrete.

Barbara and I strolled his way nonchalantly, leaving Peter at the door.

"Hiya, big boy," I greeted Wayne in a whisper.

He didn't return my greeting. He didn't even blink. My back stiffened. I told myself he just wanted to remain incognito. It wouldn't be easy with his mashed face. On the other hand, no one was hanging around trying to make social chitchat with him. Maybe isolation was what he craved.

Barbara and I wandered back across the room. I heard a familiar voice behind us.

"Howdy, hi, Kate," said Felix. Then he planted a big kiss on Barbara's nose. "Yum, yum," he murmured, peeking down the top of her jumpsuit.

I watched them sadly. As obnoxious as Felix was, at least he was being nice to his sweetie. Why wasn't Wayne kissing me on the nose? I took a look back at him. Wayne wasn't alone anymore. Linda Zatara had joined him. I smiled a malicious smile, thinking of the frustration she would endure if she tried to get any information from him. He could do the silent treatment every bit as well as she could. A rock talking to a hard place, I mused.

"Wanna meet the main folks?" Felix asked.

"I suppose you already know everyone in the room," Barbara teased him.

"Just doing my job, babe," he said with a big grin.

Felix introduced us to Sarah's neighbors, the Baums, a kindly old couple who said "she was such a nice girl," some of the people who Sarah had worked with on the Nuclear Free Marin campaign, and a few people from the local dramatic society who had used Sarah's robots in various roles for their plays. The conversations seemed like party chatter, except that the tones were hushed and the subject was usually Sarah.

As soon as I could do so politely, I disengaged myself and strolled up to Craig and Dave Yakamura. But my mind wasn't strolling. It was racing. I hadn't realized before that Sarah worked with anyone. I had assumed she was an independent. If Dave Yakamura worked with her he might have a motive, as well as the requisite knowledge of computers.

"Craig," I said, touching his shoulder. I glanced back at Wayne quickly, hoping the touch hadn't bothered him. Nothing showed on his face. He and Linda were standing side by side like a mismatched pair of gargoyles.

Craig, however, was delighted by the touch. "Kate," he said in a low purr. He stared at me for a moment with obvious longing in his eyes. Too obvious, I concluded. I didn't want to be manipulated by Craig anymore.

"Introduce me to your friend," I ordered briskly.

"Kate, this is Dave Yakamura," Craig said obediently. "Dave, this is my ex-wife, Kate."

If Dave found anything strange in this introduction he was too polite to mention it. He just smiled and shook my hand vigorously.

"So, Dave, I understand you worked with Sarah," I plunged in.

"I didn't actually work with her," he explained in a soft, pleasant voice. He was certainly quick with his denial, I thought suspiciously. "It's been years since I saw her personally. But she wrote software for us. She uploaded it to us in San Rafael by modem." He shook his head sadly. "She sure loved computers. And robots," he added as an afterthought.

I stiffened for a moment, thinking of the robot that had killed her. I told myself to calm down and ask questions.

"What does your company do?" I prodded.

"Robots," he answered. My pulse jumped. Dave fished into his pocket, pulled out a business card and handed it to me.

I looked down at the silver-on-black logo. It read "2020 Robots, Dave Yakamura, President."

"Are these the robots—" I began slowly.

But Dave was looking over my shoulder.

"Linda!" he shouted and waved. "Excuse me," he apologized, "I see an old friend."

Linda Zatara was his old friend? Was this the connection I had been looking for? I watched him walk over to her. He seemed to be limping. I wondered if his limp was permanent. Or did he hurt himself in some extraordinary physical activity like, for instance, setting a log pile on fire? I told myself to forget it. The man just limped. He reached Linda, and the two of them walked off together leaving Wayne in stony isolation.

"How are you, Kate?" Craig asked softly.

I jumped. I had forgotten all about him.

"Fine," I lied. I looked over his shoulder and spotted Janice Jackson talking with Donald Simpson. What an opportunity.

"Craig, I see someone—" I began.

"So introduce me," a loud voice with an East Coast accent demanded from somewhere behind me.

I turned and saw a large blond woman with a big grin on her face. She stepped forward and slapped Craig on the back. Craig hastily identified me as Kate Jasper and the blond woman as Ellen Quinn. Then he smiled weakly, murmured his apologies and disappeared.

I turned back to Ellen. Even if I hadn't been told her name, I would have guessed she was Sarah's sister. Although she was taller than Sarah, probably close to six feet, heavier and older-looking, that Howdy Doody smile was so close to Sarah's it was spooky. She wore a navy blue suit and a red blouse which strained over her massive bosom. Her upper torso tilted forward as she looked at me with Sarah's direct stare.

"Oh boy! Are we gonna have some fun today," she boomed out.

"Fun?" I mumbled nervously. "What exactly are we going to do?"

She leaned her head back and laughed. It was a good laugh, full and resonant. "You and your friend Peter are sure uptight about the details," she told me. "I thought you Californians were supposed to be mellow."

"I—" I began.

"Hey, Teala!" Ellen shouted, cutting me off. "Over here!" Now we had everyone's attention. Peter was glaring ferociously. Other mourners were staring at us with expressions ranging from shocked and appalled to amused.

Myra and Tony came in the door just as Teala and three other women dressed in brightly colored robes walked toward us with serious expressions on their faces.

"I am Teala of the Trancenjoy Foundation," the leader announced in deep rhythmic tones. "And these are my assistants, Sonia, Neva and Tasha. We will release Sarah with joy today." She paused. Her assistants murmured approval. "The purpose of the Trancenjoy Foundation is to promote joy in all transition, transformation and transcendence," she continued. "Today we will release Sarah with chantings of love and thanks."

Peter, Tony, Myra and Craig had joined us during Teala's speech. Linda Zatara chose to stand a few feet away with her back to us. I guessed she wasn't interested in participating in Teala's program. I wasn't sure I was either.

"What, specifically, are we supposed to do in this ceremony?" asked Peter, his voice tight with impatience.

"All of those assembled here today will be asked to join in the chanting," she declared. "You who knew Sarah so well will each stand when I call your name and tell the group what you have received from Sarah. Then you will affirm that you release her from this earthly plane."

"Oh, I couldn't possibly do that," protested Myra.

"Only say what sincerely comes to your mind," Teala advised her. "I can leave you out if that's what you really want," she continued, her tone stuffed full of disgust over Myra's cowardice.

"Yes, please. Leave me out," Myra begged.

I didn't have the audacity to stand up to Teala's glare, so I began desperately searching my brain for something sincere and profound to say. Sarah had been inspiring, funny and irritating. But none of that sounded good enough to say in public. I decided to simply wait and say whatever came up when I was called on. Not that this approach had ever worked very well in school.

Peter had been eyeing his watch nervously throughout Teala's instructions. It was after eleven o'clock. Teala announced that it was time to begin and Peter led us to our chairs. Those of us involved in the ceremony were given front-row seating. I was seated between Ellen and Craig, with a view of the closed coffin. I turned my head away from its black presence. It wasn't time for that yet.

After a brief introduction, Teala began the chanting. "Sarah, we love you. Sarah, we thank you. Sarah, we release you." Soon her assistants joined her. "Sarah, we love you. Sarah, we thank you. Sarah, we release you." Teala nodded toward the front row and we chanted the words with them. Then she spread her arms wide in a gesture that included the whole audience and everyone began to chant the three phrases. My mind shifted into an altered state of consciousness as the chanting increased in volume and tempo. It was frightening and exhilarating at the same time. Sobbing broke out from somewhere behind me. Then Teala brought her arms down in a gesture to stop.

"Peter, what do you thank Sarah for?" she asked.

"I thank you, Sarah, for your constant challenge to the rigidity of my thinking," Peter said. "I release you from this earthly plane." Peter spoke in an unusually gentle tone. His eyes were glistening.

Teala raised her arms and we chanted again. Then she asked Tony what he thanked Sarah for.

"I thank you, Sarah, for showing me the positive and divine purpose in any and all situations," he announced clearly and released her.

The pattern continued. Craig thanked Sarah for telling him that success is a state of mind. I thanked Sarah for showing me that I always had choices, and Ellen thanked Sarah for the ability to laugh in any circumstance, and then proceeded to laugh maniacally. A sprinkling of nervous laughter from the mourners echoed through the room. Then we chanted for a seemingly infinite amount of time the same words of love, thanks and release over and over again. Toward the end, Teala increased the pace of the chanting until we sounded like a room full of crazed auctioneers. I was dizzy by the time she brought her arms down again.

Then one of Teala's assistants opened the lid of the coffin. Teala stepped up to Ellen and led her by the hand toward the now open coffin. Peter acted as a sheepdog and herded the rest of us in a line behind them. Ellen and Teala looked down at Sarah. Teala said, "I release you." Ellen repeated her words.

It was my turn. As I moved forward I felt a reassuring hand on my shoulder. Wayne's hand. I whispered a thank you and looked down at Sarah. Her skin had an orangish cast which I attributed to the makeup, although it might have been the lighting or even the aura of all those years of orange. The bones of her face were more prominent than ever. She was sunk into the coffin in her favorite orange and purple jumpsuit. Nestled in her hands was one of Nick's sculptures, the little ivory one. I stared down and finally knew that she was really dead. As I felt my tears sneaking out and down my cheeks, I remembered what the ritual was for. I said, "I release you" and moved on and back to my seat. Soon we were all chanting words of love, thanks and release for the last time.

Outside, the air felt crisp as those of us who were going to the cemetery climbed into the cars Peter had assigned us. I was in Craig's car. Barbara and Felix sat up front with him. I sat in the back between Ellen and Wayne. I speculated upon the malicious intent that might be behind Peter's assignment of cars as we slowly drove in a procession to the cemetery.

"Hey, are you guys all dinks?" Ellen asked, her raucous voice breaking into the somber mood.

"What's a dink?" asked Craig.

"Double Income, No Kids," she replied.

"We're all single," I said pointedly.

"But at least you're yuppies, right?" she steamrollered on. "I mean, this *is* California. I read in *Newsweek* where you guys had a government task force to promote self-esteem!"

"Did we?" chuckled Barbara. "Far out. You know more about California than I do. Where are you from?"

"New Jersey"

"What exit?" wisecracked Craig. Ellen broke into a roar of

laughter. I leaned against Wayne without looking at him. But I could feel his body heat, even smell it. I put my hand on his knee, then felt his hand cover mine.

"Where'd you dig up old Teala and the Trancenjoys?" Felix asked Ellen. A bad choice of words when driving to a cemetery, I thought. But no one else seemed to notice.

"I looked through Sarah's address book," Ellen explained. "It was the only entry resembling a religious organization, right? Anyway, Nick said she went there a few times and liked them, so I called them up."

"Why isn't Nick here?" I asked.

"He couldn't handle it," Ellen said, her voice a little softer. "Cute kid, but he doesn't go out much."

"How about Vivian and Jerry?" I asked. "I hope they were invited."

"Oh, they were," Ellen boomed. "Vivian's Information Central, right, the mouthy cleaning lady? She said the 'hired help' don't go to funerals. And Jerry the gardener, right? He said he was working."

"How long are you going to be out here, Ellen?" Barbara asked.

"Oh, a coupla weeks," she replied. "I'm calling this a paid vacation." Was she talking about her inheritance?

"Would you like to come over for dinner tonight?" I offered. I had interrogation in mind.

"What'll you feed me, tofu burgers?" she rasped. She laughed loudly for a while at her own wit. "No offense. Sure, I'll come over," she said finally.

We pulled slowly into the cemetery and parked. Once the rest of the procession had arrived, Peter led us to the gravesite, which was set off from the rest of the neatly trimmed graves by a brightly striped canopy of orange and white. The attendants had already lowered the coffin into the grave. A neat pile of dirt was on a tarpaulin by its side. We still had most of the crowd from the funeral chapel, with the exception of Teala and her assistants, who had mysteriously vanished. Apparently, they were only hired to play the Serenity Room and their contract did not extend to the graveyard. We all stood around expectantly, waiting for the ceremony to begin. Ellen stepped forward.

"Ashes to ashes, dust to dust, laughter is healing, so laugh we must," she proclaimed. Then she began telling a joke about a donkey as she threw some dirt onto the coffin.

The gathering around the grave was temporarily immobilized.

Mouths gaped as we all stared at Ellen. She finished that joke and began another.

"What do you get when you pour boiling water down a rabbit hole?" she asked. There were no takers.

"Hot cross bunnies," she answered herself. There were a few scattered snickers.

I dropped my now wilted and crushed chrysanthemums onto the coffin as she asked, "What do you call a row of rabbits walking backwards?" A few more people stepped forward to drop dirt or flowers on the coffin.

"A receding hareline!" Some people were laughing aloud now. The attendants were smirking. But Peter was not amused.

"The time has come to take leave of Sarah," he announced, his voice bursting with reproach.

"May the divine spirit continue to guide her," Tony offered more gently.

"Amen," I said. Not that I meant to use the word in its religious sense. I just wanted to end the event. A few more "amens" were spoken and Peter shepherded everyone back to the cars.

"Hey, Sarah, remember where you're parked," Ellen shouted as we left.

I turned to see Wayne's reaction. But he had disappeared.

When we got back to the mortuary I snagged Linda and invited her to the seance. Her eyebrow lifted infinitesimally. For her, I guessed that this was the equivalent of a gasp. I wondered what it might mean. She recovered herself quickly and agreed to come.

Felix stood close by, drooling for an invitation. But Barbara headed him off easily, kissing him every time he opened his mouth until it was finally time to leave.

The minute Barbara and I were alone in her Volkswagen, I asked her what she thought.

"I think Wayne is hurting," she replied seriously.

"Not Wayne, goddammit!" I cried impatiently. "Who's the murderer? Did you get anything?"

"Not really," she said, swerving the car a little as she pondered. "I got all sorts of mixtures of anger, sorrow, fear. Nothing that I could exactly say was murderous energy. But a person can consciously or unconsciously shield themselves . . ." Her voice trailed off.

"Who was angry?" I asked hopefully.

"Peter was the angriest," she said. "But you can tell that by looking at him. Anyway, his anger is really more impatience than anything else."

Suddenly I felt tired. I had wanted something conclusive, and I had a feeling I wasn't going to get it. I leaned back in my seat and closed my eyes.

"Myra is some confused woman," Barbara went on. "And Linda is as blank as she looks."

I sat up straight. "Do you think she's shielding on purpose?" I asked.

Barbara shrugged her shoulders. The car sidled gently into the next lane, then floated back.

"I guess I don't know how to calibrate a murderer," she admitted. "Sorry, kiddo."

"Thanks for trying," I said. I kept my voice cheerful. I didn't want Barbara to know how disappointed I was. "Anyway, there's still the seance."

We rode along in uncharacteristic silence. Poor Barbara. I knew she felt guilty for having failed me.

"I do miss Wayne," I offered softly.

"I know," she said. Then she turned the full force of her smile on me as she swerved in front of a gasoline truck.

- Fifteen -

BARBARA REGAINED HER proper lane amid blaring horns and screaming brakes.

"Isn't one funeral enough?" I demanded.

"You know I never hit anyone," she replied calmly. And then, without any transition, she asked, "Why don't you marry Wayne?"

I groaned.

"Well?" she prodded.

"You're the psychic," I snapped. "You tell me."

"I just might," she said, grinning my way. The car began sidling up to the next lane.

"I'll tell you what," I bargained quickly. "If you stay in your lane all the way home, I'll explain why I don't want to get married."

"Done," she agreed and looked straight ahead.

I took a breath and began. "Here's the worst-case scenario," I told her. "I marry Wayne. I become dependent on him. I get used to having money. I don't put in my sixty hours a week on Jest Gifts. Jest Gifts withers from neglect. And then the marriage goes bad—"

"But Kate," Barbara protested. The car moved crabwise toward oncoming traffic as she turned to me. "You don't have to be so negative."

"Eyes on the road!" I ordered. "I'm explaining."

She looked ahead obediently and brought the Volkswagen back to center.

"I've been married," I reminded her. "To a perfectly good human being. And it didn't work out."

"That was Craig," she objected. "Wayne is different."

"I was just as in love with Craig then as I am with Wayne now," I shot back. That wasn't quite true. There was a qualitative difference between the ways I cared for the two men. But I didn't want to get into it.

"I was headed for law school when I met Craig," I went on, remembering. "I fell for him and forgot all about my career. Craig seemed more important. Craig and his business. I put over a decade of my life into *his* business!" I was surprised by the anger in my own voice. It was like hearing someone else speak. Was I that angry?

"So marry Wayne and don't depend on him financially," Barbara suggested breezily.

"It's not that simple," I argued.

"Of course it's not," Barbara said. "I'll tell you what really scares you. You cared for Craig and he left you. Now you're afraid of any emotional commitment—"

"That's enough," I interrupted. I was tired of the subject.

Barbara turned to me with a searching look. The car wandered into the left lane.

"All right, all right!" I shouted. "I'll think about it."

Barbara didn't press me. She began talking about Felix instead. Strangely enough, she adored the man. I allowed the happiness in her voice to flow over me and warm me as we oscillated home. She walked me to the door and gave me a quick hug. Then she veered off into the afternoon sun.

The light wasn't blinking on my answering machine when I walked into my house. I took a deep breath in relief, then dialed Jerry's phone number. But all I got was his answering machine again. I hung up and sat down to the stack of paperwork on my desk. Sarah's smiling face popped into my mind.

"Do you want me to keep trying?" I whispered aloud.

The face in my mind nodded and disappeared. Damn. Now I was speaking to the dead. I rubbed the sudden crop of goose flesh on my arms vigorously and reminded myself that Sarah was only in my mind, subject to my control. But when I tried to get her face back, the image wouldn't come. I grabbed a bunch of invoices angrily. I had been through enough spookiness for the day, thank you. I blocked out the world and wrote checks.

C.C. came wandering in a few hours later. She jumped up on my desk and batted my pencil. It slid across my neat ledger columns leaving a thin graphite trail. She let out a heartbreaking cry of starvation before I had a chance to yell at her. It was dinnertime.

I remembered my invitation to Ellen Quinn as I was scooping out KalKan.

I pawed through my cupboards frantically, looking for the ingredients of a meal. I pulled out a couple of cans of chili and a sack of cornmeal. There were some onions, garlic, peppers and a few vegetables in my refrigerator. I added them to the pile. It began to look like a tamale pie. I dug deeper and unearthed a package of tortillas and some salad greens. Fifteen minutes later, the tamale pie was in the oven.

The doorbell rang. I put the teakettle on the stove and sprinted for the front door as C.C. slunk off unsociably. I pulled the door open. Ellen Quinn stood in front of me with an unusually serious expression on her face. She wore the same navy blue suit she had worn at the funeral, but now carried a briefcase. She stared at me intently.

"Have you ever really considered your own death?" she asked quietly, unlocking her briefcase.

My body went rigid with fear. Then I remembered my tai chi training. I centered myself and lifted a defensive hand up in front of my chest. I was ready. But how helpful was my hand going to be if she had a gun in that briefcase? Now she was shouting at me. Slowly, I tuned into her words.

"Insurance, insurance!" she was screaming, her face thrust into mine. "I'm selling insurance, not trying to murder you!"

I stared at her until my mind finally processed the meaning of her words. Her face broke into the trademark Quinn Howdy Doody grin. She leaned back and laughed lustily. I managed a weak smile. At least she wasn't angry. My body wasn't rigid anymore. It was weak and trembling.

"God, I don't believe it," Ellen guffawed. "You thought I was going to kill you, right? You shoulda seen your face!"

"Shall I frisk you before I let you in?" I joked feebly.

"It'll be a long wait if you take the time to frisk me," she answered in a Mae West drawl. She wiggled her extensive bottom. "I'm a mighty big woman."

"Come on in, then," I invited, remembering my role as hostess. "Would you like some herbal tea?"

"Sure, what the hell," she said, stepping into the hall. "I'm game."

"What kind of game are you, venison?" I sallied as I led the way into the living room. It was one of Craig's old lines.

She laughed raucously as she followed me.

"You're okay," she pronounced approvingly. "Better than your friend Peter. Sometimes I think that Sarah was the only one of you guys who had a sense of humor." She lowered herself into one of the swinging chairs without missing a beat. "Though I'm never quite sure when people are joking out here. On the way over I saw this car with a bumper sticker that said 'Inner Peace Now' like it was a demand."

"There's nothing worse than a militant introspective," I deadpanned as I sat down across from her. I studied her face. God, she looked like Sarah.

"Ain't that the truth," she boomed. She pushed off with her feet, setting the chair to swinging. "Take that Teala broad of the Trancenjoys. Man, I wouldn't want to argue with her. Is she intense!"

"What's the foundation about, anyway?" I asked. I had wondered all afternoon.

"Oh God, they're about everything," Ellen groaned. She shook her head, then laughed. "Anything you do can be turned into a spiritual experience, according to them. For thirty-five an hour one of the devotees will introduce you to shopping as a transformational experience! I kid you not. Or if you don't wanna take novocaine when you go to the dentist, they'll hypnotize you so you won't need it. I told them they should call it Transcen*Dental* Meditation but no one got the joke." She shook her head again, then pinched her brows together in a look of confusion. "They told me I was very fifth and second chakra, whatever that means."

"I think the fifth is at the throat," I said slowly, trying to remember the order like a musical scale. "It means you're a good communicator."

"How about the second?" she demanded.

"Sex," I said brusquely, hoping I didn't have to explain its location.

"Hey, let's hear it for the second chakra!" she cheered. She sounded like Sarah, too, I realized with a pang.

Ellen tilted her head wistfully as the chair swung back and forth. She spoke more softly. "I haven't had any of that for a while. I want a nice sweet honey who will be there when I want him and won't pull any bullshit on me when I travel around. Someone who'll keep the house clean, have dinner waiting and keep the bed warm." She winked heavily. "Not necessarily in that order, either."

"You want a housewife who's male," I concluded.

"That's right, honey," she agreed, nodding her head emphatically. "But I don't think they exist."

The teakettle screamed from the kitchen.

"I don't know about the rest of it, but I'll be glad to cook you dinner," I said. I stood up. "Come on in the kitchen. I still need to do the salad and steam the tortillas. We'll have some tea while I cook."

She followed me to the kitchen and started up with the jokes. As I turned the teakettle off, she asked me if a dog wore more clothes in the summer or winter.

"Winter," I guessed. I poured boiling water over Red Zinger tea bags. It seemed to be the right brand for Ellen.

"No, summer," she shot back triumphantly. "In the winter he wears a coat, but in the summer he wears a coat and pants."

"That's terrible," I said, grimacing. I looked closely at her. "Did you ever think of becoming a comedian?" I asked.

She took a seat at the kitchen table. "I didn't only think of it, I was one for a while," she told me. "I never made it big-time, though." She sighed, then brightened. "I gotta tell you the one about the minister," she began. "You'll love it—"

"So why did you end up in insurance?" I asked quickly, averting her story. I put the tortillas in the steamer.

"When you're selling life insurance you gotta have a sense of humor," she explained. She took a sip of tea. "Everyone either makes fun of you, or gets mad at you, 'cause life insurance makes them so nervous about death. So you laugh or drink or do drugs." She grinned, reminding me of Sarah again. "I drink a little and laugh a lot. I'd probably do drugs too, if someone offered me some."

Ellen stopped for a breath and stared up at me with wide-open eyes. Was she waiting for an offer? I didn't make one. She sighed and continued. "I thought everyone in California smoked grass, but so far nobody's so much as invited me to share a joint."

"You're dating yourself," I told her. "We don't smoke dope anymore. We're health nut purists these days. Or else we snort coke."

"I'm not dating myself," she protested. "I never date older women." She paused for the audience reaction. I obliged her with a halfhearted smile.

"I know all about Marin residents and their coke habits," she informed me. "Did you hear there's going to be a new game show in Marin called *Where's My Line*?"

"Enough with the jokes," I groaned. "I can't stand it."

"I always say if you can't stand it, sit down," she finished with another expansive wink.

I took her advice. I brought the salad and tortillas to the table and sat down.

Over salad I tried to extract Ellen's feelings about Sarah. Ellen certainly had a compelling financial motive for murder, I thought as I watched her eat. Half of Sarah's estate had to amount to something. A big something. And if Ellen had really wanted to murder Sarah for her inheritance, I was sure she was capable of orchestrating her sister's death while providing herself with an unbreakable alibi. But subtle prods like "Sarah must have been an interesting sister," and "a shame about Sarah" got nowhere.

Finally, I just asked, "How did you feel about Sarah?" outright.

"Sarah could be a real pain in the ass as an older sister, but I loved her," Ellen said quietly, dipping a tortilla into the salad dressing.

"I thought she was your younger sister," I said, then realized I had jammed my foot firmly in my mouth.

"You and everyone else," Ellen replied lightly. It didn't seem to bother her. "After that 'youthing' business Sarah got so much younger-looking that people assumed she was younger than me, right?" She shook her head. "No, she was three years older." Ellen took a bite of tortilla, then continued seriously. "Sarah was always good at anything she took on. It didn't matter if it was calculus or getting under people's skins, she succeeded."

I waited for Ellen to go on. But she didn't. Her face was sad as she stared at her empty plate. I got up and brought the tamale pie to the table. I put a big scoop on Ellen's plate and mine, then sat back down.

Ellen started up again. "I was kinda a screw-up as a kid," she confessed. "Back then, I was so overwhelmed, watching Sarah take the world on, that I just took a seat in the audience. I couldn't compete. I didn't have much personality." She sighed. "I got married right out of high school and had two babies. They're okay kids, all grown up now." She took a bite of tamale pie.

"What do they do?" I asked, genuinely curious. Ellen was a character in her own right, almost as mind-boggling as Sarah had been.

"The girl's an auto mechanic," she mumbled through her mouthful. "The boy's in college, studying anthropology. Josie takes after her father. He was an auto mechanic before he turned into a full-time bum." Her face brightened. "Did you ever meet Sarah's ex-husband?" she asked.

I shook my head.

Ellen laughed. "You shoulda met the guy," she said. "His name was Swami something-or-other, but he was really just Lew Fields, this asthmatic kid from New York." She took another bite. "He's a gofer for a porno film company now," she mumbled. "I couldn't believe she fell for his line of bull. Though it was kinda nice to see *her* screw up for a change."

With that, Ellen stopped talking and ate in earnest. I gobbled up my own portion and wondered if she was as straightforward as she appeared to be. Ellen's fork scraped her plate. She asked for more tamale pie.

"Not bad for health food," was her grudging compliment.

"What were your parents like?" I asked as I put another scoop on her plate.

"My dad was kinda like me, I guess," she said. She tilted her head and thought for a moment. "He was a big guy, always making jokes. But basically he was pretty conservative. He sold insurance too." She took a bite and swallowed before going on. "Sarah drove him wild. She was real successful, but she always did crazy things, even as a kid."

"Like what?" I prompted.

"Oh, she would get all A's and then turn around and run away from home on summer vacation," Ellen told me, smiling at the memory. "Not because she was unhappy or anything, just because she wanted some excitement. Or she would pour Jell-O in someone's swimming pool, or let the air out of a police car's tires." She chuckled. But then her face grew serious again. "Her and my father were locked into a battle of wills till the day he died. In a way, I was even jealous of that. She got a lot of attention from him with all the stuff that she pulled." She leaned back in her chair and laughed abruptly, asking, "Did you know she married a sailor when she was fourteen?"

I shook my head. I had learned more about Sarah's past in the last few days than in all the time I had known her.

"Yeah, what a stunt! Sarah was halfway across the country with this guy on a train before she got bored and came home." Ellen shook her head, but kept smiling. "My parents had it annulled."

"What about your mother?" I asked. "What's she like?"

Ellen's smile faded. "Oh, Mom's okay," she mumbled. "She's in an old folks' home now. And Dad's gone. But Sarah! God, that shocks me." She slapped the table with her hand. "It's so hard to believe she's dead. I even remember the last time I talked to her on the phone. She told me this great joke. This guy goes to a psychiatrist—"

I derailed her quickly. "You remind me of Sarah," I told her.

"Yeah, it's funny about me and Sarah," she mused. "When we were growing up I thought we were so different, but now I see how much alike we really are. *Were,*" she corrected herself sadly. "And I'm successful now too. I sell a lot of life insurance."

"Do you make much money selling insurance?" I asked slyly.

"Enough," she assured me, shoveling tamale pie into her mouth. She swallowed and looked me in the eye. "And, yes, Sarah's money comes in real handy. But, no, I didn't kill her for it."

"Oh," I whispered. I guess I hadn't been as sly as I thought.

"I know that's why you invited me here tonight," Ellen informed me. She thrust her head forward and glared. "You have buttinsky amateur detective written all over you."

"I wanted to get to know you too," I protested weakly.

"Yeah, and you got to hear some great jokes." She waved a hand magnanimously and smiled again. "Look, it's okay. I want to know who killed her too, right? Much as we didn't get along all the time, she was my big sister. So, go ahead with your questions." She swallowed her last bite of pie and leaned back in her chair.

"Do you know how to program a computer?" I asked.

"I do a little programming," she answered easily. "I'm working on a spreadsheet package with a friend back home. She does the designing. I just do the coding."

As she was talking, a picture formed in my mind of how the murder could have been done. But I didn't have enough technical expertise to be sure it was possible. I made a mental note to call Craig.

"If you ask me, it was Peter," Ellen offered. "That guy is wound up tighter than a Mickey Mouse watch." She paused. "Or Linda. Jeez, that broad is weird."

"Weird, yes," I agreed. "But where's the motive?"

"You should know. These guys are all your friends."

Friends? Certainly not Linda. I even wondered about Peter and Tony. Did friends set fire to other friends' log piles? I shook off the thought.

"One more question, Ellen," I said nonchalantly. I watched her eyes. "Do you have a VCR in your motel room?"

"Yeah, I do," she answered unblinkingly. Then she rubbed her chin thoughtfully. "Why?" she asked.

"Oh, nothing. Just curious," I lied. Were VCR's in hotel rooms set up to record? Or did they just play movies?

"So don't tell me. Be that way," she muttered. She shrugged her shoulders. "I've got one for you. Are you hot for Nick?"

"Nick?" I asked. The name didn't connect with romance at first. Then I realized. "Oh, Nick Taos! Are you kidding? I've only met the guy once."

"I'm always kidding," she claimed. Then she tried to prove it with a complex story involving a lawyer, a crocodile and a one-eyed nun.

I protested in earnest, but to no avail. Ellen continued with the jokes while I cleared up, did dishes, and made her three more cups of tea. After that she halfheartedly tried to sell me some life insurance.

I was working myself up to show her the remains of my log pile as she explained the value of whole life coverage. I wanted to see her reaction. But she rose abruptly to leave in the middle of her own lecture. She was out the door before I had time to think. Shades of Sarah. I hurried out behind her just in time to see her drive away in her rental car.

As soon as I was sure Ellen was gone, I called Craig at his office. I knew I'd never get him at home. He picked up the phone on the fourth ring.

"Sunday evening and still working," I diagnosed.

"I'll bet you could persuade me to take fifteen minutes off to visit if you tried," he cajoled.

"No," I said crisply. "I just wanted to ask you some questions about modems."

"Come to dinner tomorrow night?" he invited. "I'll answer all of your questions then."

I hesitated. I didn't want to encourage any romantic expectations of reconciliation. On the other hand, Craig was the only computer expert I knew.

"I can tell you a lot about modems," he said.

"All right," I surrendered ungraciously. "But it's got to be late." I had a seance to host.

I agreed to meet him at his office at eight or nine and hung up.

I tried Jerry again and banged the receiver down in frustration at the sound of his tape. I didn't want to leave a message. I wanted to talk to him personally, before he had time to get his guard up.

Suddenly, I wondered if Sarah's neighbors had seen anything. The police must have talked to them. But still . . . I grabbed a phone book. What was the name of that nice old couple I had met? Baum, that was it. I found their number and dialed before I could chicken out.

"Hello, I'm Sarah's friend, Kate," I announced quickly when Mrs. Baum answered. "I met you at the funeral."

"Oh, yes. I remember you, dear," Mrs. Baum assured me.

I took a big breath and started lying. "I'm planning a memorial for Sarah," I said. "I'd like to get your input. And the input of some of Sarah's other neighbors too." I told myself that finding Sarah's murderer would be a sort of memorial to her. "Do you think it would be possible for me to talk to you and some of the others tomorrow?"

"Of course, dear," Mrs. Baum answered in a voice so kind that I blushed at my own deception. "Why, I'm sure everyone would just love to help. Now, tomorrow's Monday so a lot of people will be at work, but I can introduce you to Marianne Johnson and Cynthia Voss . . ."

"Thank you," I said a few minutes later. "I really appreciate it, Mrs. Baum."

"It's nothing really," she protested. "It's the least we can do for Sarah. She was such a sweet girl, never any noise, except for that nice music she used to play." She paused. "And the lovely inspirational books she used to bring over. I'm afraid I didn't understand them too well, but it was so sweet of her to bring them to us." What kind of books had Sarah given the Baums? "Can you tell me a little more about the memorial you were planning, dear?" she asked.

"Uh," I said, caught off guard. "A written memorial. Yes, a written memorial," I improvised. "Maybe it could be dramatized or something," I added, embellishing the lie.

"Oh my," Mrs. Baum trilled. "That sounds nice."

"Yes, nice," I parroted guiltily. "Would ten o'clock be okay for you tomorrow, Mrs. Baum?"

"Of course, dear," she assured me. I was sure she would have patted my hand if we'd been talking face to face. "Any time is fine. We're retired, you know. I'll call Marianne and some of the others to tell them you're coming. And please, call me Betty."

"I really do appreciate this, Betty," I told her. "I look forward to seeing you."

Once I had hung up the phone I realized I was alone. True, I was alone most evenings, but this evening the aloneness felt different. It felt heavy, clinging. I searched the house for C.C. She was gone. Or hiding.

Wayne, I thought, and headed out the front door into the cool darkness.

- Sixteen -

I SEARCHED THE length of my block, but I couldn't see Wayne's Jaguar anywhere. Maybe he was hiding with C.C. Maybe he was just gone, no longer interested in guarding my body. No longer interested in my body at all, I thought sadly.

I came back to my lonely house, put on a fresh pair of dropseat pajamas and slid in between the sheets. Alone.

But not for long. A few hours later, I awoke to a whiff of KalKan. C.C. was perched on top of my chest, breathing in my face. She was better than no one, I decided sleepily and fell back asleep as I stroked her silky fur.

The next morning, I drove to my Oakland warehouse before nine and left off some paperwork. I didn't catch so much as a glimpse of Wayne's Jaguar on the way there or the way back. But Vivian was behind me when I turned onto my street. It was Monday, her day to clean. Vivian and I drove our cars up the driveway in tandem and climbed the short stairway together.

"Where ya been?" she asked, cocking an eyebrow. The scent of J&B wafted my way along with her words.

"At the warehouse. Gag gifts wait for no woman," I answered gaily. Vivian didn't smile. I shelved the gaiety. "Yesterday was too busy, so I took my orders over this morning," I told her.

"Oh," she grunted. "How was the funeral?"

"Interesting, but strange," I said, opening the door. I turned to look at her. "Why didn't you come?" I asked.

"I wouldn't have fit in," she replied flatly.

"That's not true—" I began.

"So what was strange?" she demanded, moving past me into the house. I stood for a moment, just watching her. How well did I know Vivian? Could she be the murderer? The arsonist? I just hoped it wasn't her. Or Tony. Or Peter.

"Let's make some tea, and I'll tell you about it," I suggested.

"In a minute," she shouted over her shoulder, heading down the hall. "Your answering machine's blinking. You'd better check it. And I gotta get my stuff from the back room."

I put the kettle on and rewound the tape to play my messages. On the third message I could hear television laughter in the background, and some faint words closer to the telephone. Whoever had called was talking to someone else while my tape ran. I hate it when people do that. I caught a snatch of words ending in what sounded like "at the computer." Then the voice directed itself back to the receiver.

"This is Jerry Gold, your gardener," he rattled off. "It's about Sarah. Give me a call. You know my number."

Damn. Why did he have to phone while I was out? But at least I had an excuse to call him back now. I dialed his number eagerly, and heard the tape on his answering machine for the umpteenth time. There wasn't any reason to keep him off guard anymore. I told his machine to call my machine and then dragged Vivian out of the back room to talk.

"I only have five minutes left for tea," I told her, looking at my watch. If I wanted to visit Sarah's neighbors by ten, I needed to get on the road to Betty Baum's.

"Where ya going to?"

"To—" I started to say where, but immediately thought better of it. Telling Vivian about my investigative attempts would be like broadcasting on the radio. "A business appointment," I finished succinctly.

"Yeah?" questioned Vivian, her eyebrows raised.

"Someone to help with some of my paperwork," I lied. I must have been getting good at it. Vivian didn't even blink. She believed me.

"So who was at the funeral?" she asked.

I gave her a four-minute rundown and flew out the door.

I was almost to Sarah's house when I noticed Jerry Gold's green-and-gold van parked in front of one of the better-kept yards. I honked and waved as I passed. If he was still there when I came back, I'd talk to him then.

I drove past Sarah's house slowly, gazing sadly at the whimsical hedges. Would Jerry keep them trimmed into fish shapes now that she was gone? I resisted pulling into her driveway and turned instead into the Baums' driveway next door.

The Baums' house was small and neat, painted white with pale blue shutters and topped by a sloping grey shingled roof. There was a storybook look about it. This impression was heightened by the white picket fence, the manicured front lawn, and the brightly colored flower beds filled with foxgloves, alyssum, fairy primroses and violas. I could smell the newly mowed lawn as I walked up the brick pathway to the door. I pressed the doorbell and was rewarded with a tinkling music-box version of "Wouldn't It Be Loverly" and Betty Baum's pink and smiling face at the door.

"Oh, my dear, come right in and sit down," she trilled, clasping my hand and drawing me through the doorway. She sat me down on a plump, floral sofa and offered me a cup of coffee. I hesitated. I didn't want to hurt her feelings by refusing.

"Oh, I can just see by your face that you don't approve of coffee," she said. She patted her tight silver curls as she thought. Then she brightened. "I'll just make you some fresh tea the way I used to for Sarah. I have to get Jake anyway."

She disappeared toward the back of the house. I settled back into the sofa. I barely had time to take in the room's fluffy curtains and lovingly arranged knickknacks before she returned with her white-haired husband in tow. She was holding some sprigs of fresh rosemary in her hand.

"Now Jake, you keep Kate company while I go make her tea," she commanded and bustled into the kitchen.

"You certainly have a beautiful home, Mr. Baum," I said politely.

"Jake, just plain Jake will do," he replied gruffly. But his toothy smile eased the tone. "Built this house ourselves we did, way back, thirty-five years ago. Couldn't afford it now if we had to buy it, that's for sure. House around the block, no bigger than this one, sold for four hundred thousand dollars last week." He grunted disapprovingly.

"You sure did a great job building it," I offered. "And landscaping it, too."

"Yep, we do a little gardening," he said modestly. "Some of the folks around here don't keep up their yards." He grunted again.

"Here you go, dear," said Betty returning with a cup for me.

"This is fresh rosemary tea. Just a sprig of rosemary steeped." She watched my face eagerly.

I took a sip and gave her the verdict. "This is great," I told her. "Genuine herbal tea."

"Let me give you some rosemary cuttings when you go," Betty said as she sat down. "You can plant them and do the same thing yourself. Now, I know you really came here to talk about Sarah, so I won't chatter on. What did you want to know?" She gazed at me out of bright blue eyes.

"Oh, just your general impressions," I said. "Did you visit her often?"

A quick look passed between her and Jake. It occurred to me that they might know exactly why I was here asking questions.

"Actually, the last time we really visited Sarah at her house was a few years back," Betty answered carefully. "She invited us over to meet her robots." Betty lowered her eyes. "Her house was certainly—well—interesting."

"At least that gardener of hers kept up her yard," Jake put in.

"Did she have a lot of visitors?" I asked.

"Nope," answered Jake brusquely. "She didn't do a lot of entertaining, thank the Lord." Then he frowned. "The last people who lived there had parties all the time. Up till all hours of the night, music blaring, screaming and yelling."

"Drugs," said Betty knowingly. "But Sarah was a real nice, quiet girl. That music she used to play sounded just like a choir of angels. She came over here fairly often, to show us her new robot tricks or bring us books."

"What books did she bring you?" I asked.

"Oh . . . inspirational books, that's what she called them," answered Betty hesitantly. *"Autobiography of a Yogi* was one I remember."

"And *Truly Tasteless Jokes,"* added Jake, smiling. "I read that one. Had some pretty good ones. Nothing I could tell in mixed company, though. She had her robot bring it over. Quite a gal, Sarah."

"What about her dog, Freedom?"

Betty lowered her eyes again. She turned to Jake, who answered the question.

"Lucky we have a fence around our lot," he rapped out. "Dogs can't get in to leave their messes. Cats can, though. Little devils dig up my plants to do their business. That dog sure had people upset." He looked down at the floor uneasily. "But Sarah wasn't the only one with an unleashed dog. Cynthia Voss, now, she has six. Pretends to keep them in her yard and then lets them out real early in the morning, when no one's up. At least Sarah never pretended."

"No, she wouldn't," I agreed. "It wouldn't be her style."

"Yep, Sarah was quite a gal," he said again. "We got a real kick out of her." He sighed and went silent.

"We've kept you captive long enough, Kate," Betty said briskly. "Why don't I take you around to meet some of the others?" As I stood, Betty scooped up my empty teacup and handed it to Jake.

"I think we'll start with Rose Bertolli," she said. "Rose has been in this neighborhood for almost as long as we have." She counted on her fingers for a moment. "Must be close to twenty years ago she moved in with her husband, Frank. He's gone now. Died a couple of years ago. Rose just loved Sarah. Sarah helped her out a lot after Frank passed on."

We walked across the street toward Rose's house. As we walked, I asked Betty if she had noticed any visitors at Sarah's house right before her death.

"No, I didn't, dear," she answered with a sly look in my direction. "I do wish I had now. Those policemen asked the very same question. And that nice young man from the newspaper—"

"Felix Byrne?" I broke in, stopping short in the middle of the road. Betty stopped with me.

"Why, yes," Betty answered mildly and looked into my eyes.

"Sorry I interrupted," I mumbled. "Go on. Please."

We both continued toward the house on the other side of the road.

"The hedges around Sarah's house were so high," Betty explained. "Once a car was inside them, you couldn't really see it." She sighed. "I wish we had kept a better eye on her."

We walked up the short driveway to Rose's rambling white stucco house in silence. Betty was about to ring the bell when a wiry, grey-haired woman in an electric blue caftan shot through the doorway. I assumed this was Rose. She immediately grabbed my hand and started to pump it vigorously. She looked familiar to me.

"You must be Kate, Sarah's friend," she said, still gripping my hand. "I can't tell you how much Sarah meant to me. Her death—I mean transcendence—has been an incredible learning experience." She dropped my hand. Her voice gained volume. "I'd been going through a heavy growth period when Sarah turned me on to my own power. It changed my life. I now realize I am an unlimited human being. I can do anything, be anyone, have anything!"

Rose paused in her declaration and looked at me expectantly. I guessed that she wanted validation that she'd said the right things, the positive things that Sarah would have liked to hear.

"Sarah must have really inspired you," I offered.

"Oh, yes," she said earnestly. She clasped her hands together. "I'd love to help you on any book that you might write about Sarah. She taught me the truth about positive thinking, creative visualization, universal abundance. Oh, so many things! She was a great teacher."

"Did you visit Sarah often?" I asked, trying to remember where I had seen Rose before.

"No, she usually visited here," Rose answered quickly. "Sarah was a great healer, you know, a truly holy woman." She looked at me expectantly again.

I stood there, smiling foolishly. Rose's enthusiasm had derailed my planned questions. And even if I remembered my questions, they would probably be answered in positive-speak, which meant I'd have to translate simultaneously.

I had learned to translate Sarah's statements over the years. "I'm going through a growth period" stood for "I'm miserable." "My body is cleansing" meant "I'm sick as a dog." A "learning experience" was a "bummer" updated. I wondered how I could best ask this Sarah devotee about murder. Maybe I could ask if she had any idea who "guided Sarah in her transcendence." Betty rescued me from the awkward moment.

"Rose works in the local health food store, you know," she said conversationally.

"Oh, that's where I know you from!" I burst out. That was one mystery solved. "I thought you looked familiar. You're the organic vegetable lady."

"That's me," Rose said. She mugged a big smile. "I'm the afternoon carrot-juice queen. Would you believe I never worked outside of my home before I met Sarah?"

I shrugged. Rose went on.

"Sarah was the one who pushed me into going to an assertiveness class," she told me. "And now I have a part-time job!" Not enough to pay the mortgage on that house, I thought.

"And my house is paid off," she said as if in answer to my thought. She opened her arms wide in an all-encompassing gesture she must have learned from Sarah. "I have investments creating abundance and I am free to create whatever reality I choose."

"Did Sarah introduce you to her dog, Freedom?" I threw in casually.

"Yeah, Freedom. The super-pooper." Rose's shoulders slumped. "That was going to be my next project in assertiveness. I was going to tell Sarah to do something about that dog. It's hard to be assertive with someone as advanced as Sarah, though," she said in a softer, wistful tone.

"Amen," I agreed spontaneously.

"I would have, though," she added, brightening. "I can do anything I put my mind to."

I nodded my understanding and thought about leaving. I wasn't up for any more positive-speak.

"You've given me a wonderful view of Sarah," I told her. "Thank you." I reached out and shook Rose's hand once more.

Rose gave me the high sign, then turned and strode positively into her mortgage-free house.

Betty and I rambled down the street to the next home. Large pine trees surrounded this square redwood-shingled house. The chimney, porch and porch swing gave it a comfortable vacation feeling. I was sure Jake wouldn't approve of the overgrown yard, but Betty seemed adjusted to it. She led the way up the dirt path and lifted the brass knocker.

The door was answered by a solemn, blond little girl with large hazel eyes.

"My mama is in the bathroom peeing," she enunciated carefully.

"And what's your name?" I asked.

"My name is Tayu Amanda Johnson-Jekowsky," she answered carefully. "I am four years old."

I hoped Tayu's mother would arrive soon. I had a feeling the child was close to exhausting her conversational resources. At Betty's suggestion, we pulled up a couple of wooden folding chairs and sat on the porch, while Tayu stood guard at the door. A buxom, blond woman emerged from the house soon after we were seated. Her hair was cropped close to the scalp. She wore paint-speckled blue jeans and a woven top that looked Guatemalan.

Betty introduced her as Marianne Johnson, filled her in vaguely on the purpose of our call, and then sat back in her chair, smiling. The ball was clearly in my court.

"What can you tell me about Sarah?" I asked.

"Sarah was a far-out lady," Marianne said in a surprisingly deep voice. "We worked together on the Nuclear Free Marin campaign. She had a real sense of global responsibility, of the ecological consequences of our actions." She paused and glared at me. "Except where it came to her shitting dog."

"Damn shitting dog," interjected Tayu. Her mother smiled fondly. Tayu continued in a slow, clear, high-pitched voice. "People must learn to be responsible for their shitting dogs."

"Tayu is absolutely right," Marianne said. "It always amazed me that Sarah could be so clearly on the path and still be irresponsible about Freedom. I told her someday we'd barbecue that dog, but she just laughed." She tapped her foot angrily.

"We're going to barbecue some dog meat," announced Tayu.

Marianne's foot stopped tapping. She chuckled. Tayu continued to stare at us solemnly.

"But other than that, the woman was definitely enlightened," Marianne continued, her tone lighter now. "She even bought some of my weavings. Not very many people appreciate them." She sighed. "It's hard to believe Sarah's gone. Do you know if the police have made any progress?"

"No," I confessed. "If they have, they haven't bothered to tell me."

"They questioned all of us, you know," Marianne said. She nodded toward Sarah's house. "But it was hard to see what went on at Sarah's. Those hedges were too damn high. I hope the whole thing is cleared up soon. I don't like the idea of a murderer running around." She tapped her foot again. "My weaving is definitely off."

"So you assume that Sarah was murdered?" I prodded.

"It seems obvious to me," she replied brusquely. "And that reporter said it's what the police think." Felix again, I thought as Marianne continued. "You only had to meet Sarah once to know it couldn't be suicide or an accident."

"Exactly what I said to Jake," added Betty.

"Do either of you have any ideas about who did it?" I asked. There was no use pretending any longer that I was writing Sarah's memorial.

They both shook their heads glumly.

"Was anyone in the neighborhood upset enough about the dog to kill Sarah?" I pressed. The question sounded foolish the moment I asked it.

But Marianne treated it seriously. "No," she replied with a frown. "If dog shit were the cause, the murderer would have killed Cynthia, not Sarah. Her and her six dogs. It's ridiculous! But most people liked Sarah. Pretty much, anyway."

It was more than an hour of fruitless conversation later when Betty and I said our goodbyes to Marianne and Tayu. Betty looked as discouraged as I felt as we headed back across the street to the home of the infamous Cynthia Voss, owner of six dogs.

Cynthia was an athletically built young woman with large moist brown eyes. She invited us into her dog-scented house and told us all about her pets as soon as we were seated. I could hear the pets in question barking and whining as they banged against the closed kitchen door. I wondered how long it would take them to break the door down. I led the conversation back to Sarah as fast as I could.

After a few polite phrases about Sarah's death, Cynthia bent forward and whispered, "I've been worried about that man who came to Sarah's house."

My adrenaline started flowing. "What man?" I demanded.

"The one that took Freedom," she answered. "He said his name was Peter something-or-other—"

"Was he tall, thin?" I interrupted.

She nodded impatiently and continued. "I'm afraid he won't take good care of Freedom." Concern radiated from her brown eyes. "Dogs need lots of love, and he didn't look like a man who loves dogs to me. I could take on Freedom if I had to."

"Don't worry, Peter will take care of Freedom," I assured her as my excitement drained. Peter was responsible, if nothing else. And I would let him know about Cynthia's offer.

Cynthia looked unconvinced. She lectured on dogs and their needs for a full fifteen minutes. I was trying to figure out how to extricate myself when Betty looked at her watch and rose from her seat.

"It's been so nice visiting with you, Cynthia," she trilled and led the way out the door.

Betty spoke more quietly as she walked me back to my car.

"I really did love Sarah," she told me. "She livened things up so. And she had a wonderful spirit. I certainly hope your memorial investigations bear fruit." Her eyes scanned my face for a moment. "I just couldn't bear the thought that we'll never know what happened," she said finally.

We talked by my car a little longer, then parted with mutual promises not to be strangers. Once Betty had walked back through her gate, I looked over at Sarah's house. How could I get in? I wanted to see the inside of her house one more time, not only to investigate, but because it would be my last glimpse of the heart of

Sarah's home. I stood and stared at the fish-trimmed hedge. Then I heard a voice behind me.

"I really wouldn't do it, dear. The neighbors here are so nosy . . . and the police wouldn't be amused." I turned to look at Betty. "Here are those rosemary cuttings I promised you," she finished.

"You're a lot sharper than you pretend," I told her. "I can see why you and Sarah got along."

Betty's cheeks grew a little pinker with the compliment. She grasped my hand for a moment, then gave me the cuttings. I slid into my car, waved and drove away.

On my way home I saw Jerry's van still parked where I had seen it earlier. I braked and pulled over to the curb. I was tired of missing opportunities to talk to my gardener. If he had any information for me, I wanted it now.

I jumped out of my car and marched up to the van shouting, "Jerry!"

No one yelled back. Damn. I had yelled loud enough to reach the yard. Where was he?

I walked around the van and saw the answer to my question.

– Seventeen –

A BODY LAY face down in a bed of impatiens and alyssum. A litter of broken pink and white blossoms obscured the body's edges.

"Jerry?" I whispered, trying to persuade myself that I was seeing a man who was merely asleep.

But the body was too still, the limbs positioned too awkwardly for sleep. And the back of the head didn't look right. It was misshapen under the blood-matted hair, like dough that had risen improperly.

"Jerry!" I called out urgently. The body didn't move.

My brain was buzzing with adrenaline, my vision preternaturally clear. A voice in my head told me that I was looking at Jerry's body, Jerry's dead body. But I didn't want to believe the voice.

I stepped across the impatiens and knelt down beside the body, crushing more blossoms. I took a deep breath and forced myself to reach for his wrist to check his pulse. But my hand stopped before touching him. It jerked back as if it had a will of its own.

Then I noticed something moving on his head and neck. What were those black specks? I bent closer. Ants! Jerry was covered in ants!

I jumped up and staggered away, willing myself not to vomit. I came to a stop on the other side of the van. I leaned up against it, comforted by the cold metal against my forehead. Then it came to me. The killer might still be here.

I whirled around. I couldn't see anyone. I strained my ears. I couldn't hear anyone either. I told myself I had to call the police.

I ran to the front door and rang the bell. There was no answer. I tried the doorknob. Locked. I stood on my tiptoes and ran my hand along the top of the lintel, hoping for a key. Nothing. Frantically, I yanked the doormat up, dislodging a rock. There was nothing underneath the mat. But the rock felt strange when I picked it up to replace it. It was too light. Then I realized it wasn't a rock at all. It was plastic, molded to look like a rock. And there was a compartment on its flat bottom. I slid the cover open and found a key.

I felt a brief surge of triumph when the key opened the front door. It was enough to carry me through the dark house as I searched for a phone. I found one in the kitchen and called the police.

I was back outside, leaning against my car when I heard the police sirens. I didn't feel triumphant anymore. I just felt sick.

A car screeched to the curb and stopped behind my Toyota. A uniformed sheriff popped out and trotted toward me.

"Are you Kate Jasper?" he asked.

I nodded. It was all I could do. I heard more sirens, more cars stopping.

"Where's the body?" he demanded.

I led the sheriff back around the van to the flower bed and pointed a shaking finger. I glanced at Jerry, then turned away, only to come face to face with Sergeant Feiffer.

"What the hell are you doing here?" he hissed at me angrily.

"Finding . . . finding . . ." I faltered. I pointed at Jerry's body again. Feiffer's features softened.

"Just a few questions," he said gently.

"A few questions" turned out to mean a few dozen. And he repeated them over and over again. "Why were you in the neighborhood?" for example. "How come you stopped to talk to Jerry?" "Why did you walk around the van?" "Why did you break into the house?" And the big one: "Did you kill him?" He only asked me that once. But he was serious. When I answered "No," he told me I could go.

I drove home slowly, unable to focus on the implications of Jerry's murder. I had no doubt that it was murder. But my mind refused to stay with it. I turned on the radio and listened to some solid-gold hits. Diana Ross sang "Someday We'll Be Together" and I felt nostalgic tears pricking my eyelids. The Four Tops were next with "I Can't Help Myself" and I was transported back through the years, to my girlfriend Laurie's bedroom, where we were illicitly drinking rum and Coke. When "Eve of Destruction" came pouring out, I came back to the present with a shudder and turned off my radio.

Coming up my driveway, I realized my clothing was soaked with sweat. My mother's voice barged into my mind. "Horses sweat, people perspire," it corrected me. I parked, and pulled my sweaty body out of the Toyota. A searing pain shot up from the base of my spine. For a moment I thought that someone had actually shot me. Then I realized that I had once again popped my lower back out of alignment. I could just hear my chiropractor asking me if I'd been under any stress lately.

I limped my way into the house and checked the answering machine, hoping Jerry's message was still there. It wasn't. Once the machine was reset, any new calls recorded over the old ones. Jerry's message had been buried under a series of calls ending with a plea from the Marin Sheriff's Department for a donation to take a needy child to the circus.

I stood there and screened suspects in my mind. Jerry was out. That only left Linda, Ellen, Myra, Peter, Vivian—Vivian! She had been there this morning when I had played the message from Jerry. But then I remembered. She had been in the back room. Could she have overheard the call from the back room? I set the messages going at full volume on the answering machine and hobbled as fast as I could to the back room to listen. I could only hear a faint blur of noise. I certainly couldn't hear any distinct words.

I walked back down the hallway slowly, every step marked by pain. After I reset the machine, I lay down on the floor to do some back exercises. As I pulled my left knee across my body I wondered whether Jerry had confronted the killer. Or had the killer just figured out what Jerry knew? I pulled my right leg across. Maybe he hadn't been killed for his secret knowledge at all. Maybe his death was brought about by the same unascertained motive as Sarah's. Or maybe, just maybe, it didn't have anything to do with Sarah's death at all. That was an encouraging thought. I sat up quickly. My spine sent me a signal I couldn't ignore.

I called my chiropractor and made a late afternoon appointment. As I hung up the telephone, the doorbell rang. I groaned. The only person I wanted to see was Wayne. It rang again. I hobbled to the door and opened it. Wayne wasn't at the door. Sergeant Feiffer was.

"Well?" he demanded, marching into the living room.

"I told you, already," I muttered. He didn't respond. Wearily, I repeated the story I had given him earlier. "I was driving by when I saw his van. I walked around it because I knew he had to be there."

"You just happened to be driving by. On the same street where

Sarah Quinn was killed. Then you stopped and found another dead body," he summed up. He shook his head. "Tell me another one," he said, his voice loaded with sarcasm.

"I was out talking to some . . . some friends," I stammered.

His face told me that my faltering did not go unnoticed. Suddenly I took a mental leap into Feiffer's shoes. I was looking through his eyes and listening to my voice. And what I was hearing sounded very suspicious. In fact, what I was hearing sounded like someone guilty of murder.

"All right, all right," I gave in. "I was talking to Sarah's neighbors. I thought maybe I could come up with something. I didn't expect . . ." A picture of Jerry's body flashed in front of my eyes with sickening clarity. "I didn't kill anyone, honestly," I finished.

"You are in the interesting position of having known both of the victims," Feiffer said, his voice tense with anger. He fixed accusing eyes on me. "I could say that you are the link between the murders."

From the midst of my distress I realized Jerry had called me because I was a link, a link between him and Sarah. He had called me because I was the only person he knew who had been a friend of Sarah's.

"You know something you're not saying," Feiffer enunciated slowly and carefully. "You are hiding something. What you are hiding may get you killed." He was deadly serious.

"Jerry called me this morning," I confessed. Suddenly I wanted to tell Feiffer everything I knew. "He left a message on my machine."

"What did it say?" Feiffer asked eagerly. "Can we listen to it?"

"No, it was recorded over." Feiffer's face hardened. Damn. Now that I was telling the truth, he looked like he didn't believe me. I rattled on anyway. "He just said he wanted to talk to me about Sarah. But I couldn't get him on the phone. So when I saw his van—"

"What were Jerry's exact words on the machine?" Feiffer interrupted. "Do you remember?"

I stood there and tried to remember. "I think he just said 'this is Jerry' and 'I want to talk to you about Sarah' or 'it's about Sarah' or something." I threw my hands up. "It wasn't a long message."

"And you didn't talk to him?" Feiffer prodded.

"No, I was too late." I looked down into my lap. Poor Jerry. "Was he married?" I asked. "Did he have kids?"

"Yes, he had a wife. No, he didn't have kids," Feiffer rapped out. "Now let me ask *you* some. How well did you know him?"

"Hardly at all," I squeaked defensively. I took a breath and deepened my tone. "Sarah recommended Jerry to me. I barely spoke to him. He showed up twice a month to mow the lawn and keep things trimmed. Then he billed me through the mail."

"He knew you well enough to call you," Feiffer insisted.

"I wish he hadn't!" I burst out. "If he really knew something, why didn't he call you guys?"

"Right," said Feiffer. "I want you to keep that question in mind while you listen to me." He spoke in a tone of controlled fury. "If you know anything else about this business I want you to tell me. And I want you to stop your meddling in this as of now. Do you understand?"

I nodded yes.

"Is there anything else you have to tell me?" he asked.

I shook my head no. As far as I knew, I didn't know anything.

"I'm not even going to try to convince you to be more careful," Feiffer continued. "It would probably be useless. But I want you to think about Jerry Gold before you do anything foolish. And call us if you have any information at all. Or if there are any new phone threats. Or if you feel you're in danger in any way."

With those words he turned and marched out my door. It was a very effective exit. At that moment, I felt sure that my sleuthing days were over. I wanted no more part in murder.

I dutifully locked all my doors and windows. Then I sat down at my desk to do paperwork. I was negotiating with one of my suppliers on the telephone when the doorbell rang. I told the supplier that I'd get back to her. Then I crept to my office window. Felix was on my doorstep. I kept quiet, hoping he'd go away.

He pressed the doorbell again.

I gave up and opened the door.

"We need to talk," he said. His voice wasn't as demanding as usual. Trying to catch more flies with honey?

"About Jerry?" I guessed.

He nodded, then tried to step past me into the house. I held my ground, straining my back as I tensed. But Felix didn't get in.

"Who told you I was the one who found him?" I demanded.

The moment the words left my mouth I knew I shouldn't have said anything. Felix's eyes widened, then narrowed angrily. No one had told him. No one until me.

"You found his friggin' body!" Felix shouted in my face. "And you didn't call me!" So much for the soft-pedaling.

"Listen, Felix!" I shouted back. "I found a dead body. It was horrible. I need support now, not yelling. So be nice or leave!" I looked him in the eye.

He returned my angry gaze for a few heartbeats, then lowered his eyes.

"Okay," he capitulated. He patted my shoulder awkwardly.

I let him into my house. The shoulder-patting ended the moment he was in. He hounded me for details I didn't have. I threatened to throw him out. After fifteen minutes he decided to believe me. Then he started telling me about the book he wanted to write about the murders.

"It'd be a friggin' best seller," he told me. "People scarf up these kind of stories." His eyes glowed. "Man, I'd be in fat city for years. Just the movie rights alone . . ." He shook his head slowly and drifted off into a daydream. What was he dreaming about? The money? The fame?

As I watched him, a little chill went up my already agonized spine. Felix had a motive. Were a best seller and movie rights worth killing for? Are acupuncturists into needles? But if Felix had set up the murder for the story, how was he going to write it without implicating himself?

"Felix," I asked nonchalantly. "Can you write your book without a confessed murderer?" As soon as I had asked the question, I realized just how paranoid I had become. Felix as a murderer was too farfetched, I thought ruefully. But what about Linda Zatara?

"Maybe I could, though it wouldn't be as easy without a confession," Felix was answering me. He looked at me curiously.

"Anyway, back to Jerry Gold," I said briskly. "What did you find out through your friends at the Sheriff's office?"

"Wouldn't you like to know?" he answered snidely.

"Yes," I said evenly. "And if you don't tell me, I'll never speak to you again."

Felix opened his mouth as if to argue, then seemed to reconsider. "There isn't much," he assured me. "I know how Jerry bought it, though. The poor doof was whacked with a shovel. No fingerprints," he finished.

A shovel. I thought of Jerry's misshapen head and felt nausea rising again.

Felix went on. "There're a few angles besides the connection with Sarah Quinn. Jerry married that woman I told you about, the ex-client's wife—"

"The one he was playing 'hide-the-salami' with?" I asked.

His face pinkened as he nodded. He must have recognized the quotation. "But the client remarried anyway. He didn't seem uptight about Jerry," Felix said. "There's another angle too. It seems that old Jerry still kept some sweet stuff on the side after he was married. So they're checking the ladies out, and checking his wife out."

Felix was sharing. I decided to share too. I told him about Jerry's message on my machine.

Felix stood up from his chair. "Jeez-Louise, Kate!" he exploded. "Why didn't you tell me before?"

We were off and running again. I gave Felix the details. He wanted more. I escorted him outside to his car.

The rest of my afternoon was punctuated by incoming telephone calls, each timed to occur at crucial junctures in my paperwork. Tony called to confirm the seance date as I was about to total out my payroll deposits. Barbara called at the moment I glimpsed a possible reason why the bank was charging me for someone else's automatic teller withdrawals. She chuckled over my account of Felix's visit. Then, just as I found the IRS code section that might justify my tai chi fees as a business expense, Peter called.

"Sarah came to me in a dream," he told me.

"Oh," I said.

Peter spoke in a low, awed voice. "In my dream Sarah and I were sitting on this mountaintop and talking, and she said to me, 'You really do create your own reality.' And suddenly I understood, I mean really understood!"

"What did you understand, exactly?" I asked cautiously.

"That I am the one getting in my own way." His voice was gaining momentum. "That it's all good if I let it be. That everything is good and God and love at the core. It is only our own minds which limit us. That I can create exactly what I want!"

"Are you all right?" I asked. Perhaps it wasn't the most sensitive way to greet his revelations.

"Yes, of course I'm all right," he snapped. "Don't tell me you don't understand. You must understand."

"I think I understand what you're saying," I answered slowly. "I feel that way periodically myself. But it just doesn't sound like you, Peter."

"Damn it, listen to me!" he exploded. "I'm telling you that I understand now." So much for "good and God and love," I thought.

"All right," I soothed. "It sounds like a wonderfully positive dream. Then what happened?"

"Then Sarah floated up into the sky. Kate, I think it was really her," he said, his voice low and reverent again. "I think she contacted me in my dream."

"Did Sarah happen to tell you who murdered her?" I asked.

- Eighteen -

"Sarah contacts me in a dream and you want me to talk about her murder?" Peter demanded indignantly. "She came to me, Kate. She came to me to tell me about my life!"

"All right, calm down," I said.

"I am calm," he snapped. "I understood what Sarah meant. Can't you see how important that is?"

I told him how happy I was for him in about four different ways. Then I hung up.

Late that afternoon at the chiropractor's, I had plenty of time to ponder Peter's new behavior while I waited for my turn on the treatment table. Anything was better than thinking about Jerry's dead body.

Why had Peter suddenly come to understand Sarah's message? Sarah had told him that he created his own reality at least five times a month while she was alive, and only succeeded in irritating him. Now that she was dead, Peter believed her. Was this new belief akin to the posthumous increase in the value of an artist's work?

My chiropractor hauled me into the treatment room, laid me on a table, and popped my spine back into place. "What's new?" she asked when she was done.

I opened my mouth and shut it again. I climbed down from the table and said, "Nothing."

I was still thinking about Peter on the way home. If Tony or Barbara had told me about the same dream, I would have been comfortable with it. But I wasn't comfortable with the new Peter Stromberg.

* * *

I started fretting over the seance the minute I walked in my front door. It was almost six. A seance! I couldn't believe I had suggested such a thing. I moved the couch back against the wall and arranged five ladder-back kitchen chairs in a circle next to the pinball machines. The arrangement didn't look very occult. I reminded myself that whether or not Sarah emerged as a spirit this evening, it would be instructive to watch the group members react to the possibility. I closed the curtains and surveyed the effect. The room still didn't look otherworldly. It looked like a dark-beige and white living room with a bunch of chairs in a circle. I sighed and opened the curtains again.

C.C. sauntered in and lay in the exact center of the circle of chairs. She rolled over on her back and lectured me loudly and enthusiastically.

"Sarah, is that you?" I asked her, giggling.

The doorbell rang. I jumped half an inch into the air. C.C. bolted. That would teach me to joke with my cat. Damn, I was nervous about this seance. If the murderer was one of the invited participants, I just hoped that she or he was suffering worse anxiety than I was.

"Hey," Barbara greeted me as she came through the door. "Got any spare ectoplasm?" Her choice of clothing for a seance was a simple red-silk jumpsuit. She hugged me tight, then gazed into my face as she released me.

"Felix is really worried about you," she said. Felix worried? I kept forgetting he was a human being. "He told me how freaked you are over the murders and all."

I shrugged my shoulders.

"Should I come stay with you?" she asked softly.

It was tempting. I considered the offer for a moment. Would Barbara's presence protect me? Or would it just put her in danger, too?

"I appreciate it, but no thanks," I said finally. "I'll be all right."

"Are you sure?" she probed.

"I'm sure," I told her. I took a big breath. "Now about this seance," I said briskly. "What do I need to do? Should I go get a crystal ball or some colored lights or something?"

"Nope," she chuckled. "All I'm going to do is contact some of the spirits I work with and have them try to communicate with Sarah's spirit. I could do it in the hot tub." She paused for a moment and grinned. "In fact, I like that idea a lot. Hot tub seance, what about it?"

"Oh God, no," I groaned.

"Okay, no hot tub," she agreed. "But don't worry about any esoteric props. They aren't necessary."

"What's going to happen exactly?" I asked.

"Damned if I know," she answered cheerfully.

The bell rang before I could ask her for a more reassuring agenda. I let Peter in and offered him some tea. I stared at his tight face. Could this man have killed Jerry only hours before?

"You've met Barbara," I said and left them together. From the kitchen I could hear her asking him what he did for a living.

"I'm an attorney," he replied somberly.

"So, catch any ambulances lately?" she asked, laughing. Peter didn't join in her laughter.

I put the kettle on the stove and returned to the living room quickly. Barbara was already acting like Sarah, and we hadn't even started the seance yet. Barbara offered to do a psychic healing on Peter, but he declined hastily, then lifted an eyebrow at me. I ignored the eyebrow.

"Kate, I have some personal things I'd like to discuss with you," he announced.

"Fine," I said. "Go ahead."

"Privately," he whispered, rolling his eyes toward Barbara.

I shrugged my shoulders and followed him into the back room. He closed the door behind us.

"What are that woman's credentials?" he hissed.

"Credentials?" I asked. "I don't think psychics need credentials." Peter opened his mouth. I forged ahead quickly. "I'll say this for her. She's the only person I know who puts down experience from past-life incarnations on her resumé."

"That's appalling," he pronounced, affronted. If he ever did become a judge, I wouldn't want to plead *my* case before him, I thought as I watched his pinched face pinch even tighter.

"So, what's wrong with that?" I demanded.

"It's fraudulent," he told me.

"Oh, Peter," I sighed. I patted his arm. "Be open for once. Barbara isn't lying. She sincerely believes this stuff."

Peter wasn't impressed. "What are her qualifications to conduct a seance?" he pressed.

"Barbara's my friend," I said hotly. I told myself to calm down. "She's honest. And she's taken classes at the Marin Psychic Institute. Look, Peter," I said finally, "I'm not going to accept what she comes up with one hundred per cent. But we can consider it, can't we? In the proper perspective?"

Peter glared at me as he thought over my proposal. Was he looking for an excuse to avoid the seance?

"If Sarah were here, she'd tell you to lighten up," I said. Then I opened the door and led the way back to the living room before he had a chance to respond. It worked. He followed me without further comment.

Tony was sitting on one of the ladder-back chairs, talking to Barbara. They were sipping the tea I had forgotten and discussing punk hair as an art form. Peter and I sat down too.

"How about you, Barbara?" Tony was saying. "You'd be gorgeous in purple spikes."

"I might just do it," she said thoughtfully. I hoped Felix liked purple.

The bell rang again. I didn't have to open the door. Linda entered the house on her own, swiftly and silently. Now the group was complete. Barbara studied Linda intensely for a moment, then smiled and nodded her head as if they had actually conversed. Linda took a chair.

"Shall we begin?" Barbara asked, taking her own seat.

"Sure," I said. I scrutinized the faces in the circle.

"I'm ready," said Tony, his face now serious.

Peter nodded ponderously in the affirmative. He didn't seem particularly nervous.

Linda just stared, deadpan as usual.

"Okay," Barbara instructed. "If you guys will just sit and think of Sarah for a while, I'll ground myself."

She let her eyelids close slowly, then began breathing deeply. After a few minutes, her face relaxed and she seemed to sink into her chair. Suddenly, she looked like a Buddhist monk. A Buddhist monk who wore a lot of makeup, that is.

I pulled my eyes away from Barbara to watch the others. Tony had closed his eyes too and appeared tranquil. Peter was fidgeting in his chair. Linda continued to stare at Barbara without expression. Then Sarah's face came into my mind. She was laughing. I closed my own eyes to see her better.

"I'm asking the spirit guide I work with to communicate with Sarah," Barbara said, her voice thick now, unrecognizable.

I popped my eyes open. This was too spooky.

After a few more minutes Barbara spoke again in a deep, slow voice. "I'm not sure what it means," she said. "But I'm seeing orange everywhere."

Tony, Peter and I simultaneously leaned forward with interest. Even Linda blinked.

"There seems to be a peace and joy here, no pain," Barbara intoned in an even deeper voice. "Do you have a question for Sarah?"

"Ask her what the meaning of her death was," Tony requested softly.

"Whoops," said Barbara.

"What?" I asked.

"That's a quote, you guys," she explained, opening one eye. Her voice was back to normal. "Sarah's answer is 'Whoops.'"

"Ask her who killed her," I demanded.

Barbara closed both eyes again. But it didn't work. "I'm not getting anything more," she announced after a few deep breaths. "Nope, my guide says that's the end of transmission. 'Whoops' is all you get."

"Wait a minute—" Peter began.

"Sarah's a real kidder, isn't she?" Barbara interrupted easily as she opened both her eyes and stretched. "That's it, folks. You get to figure out what it means. What a kick!"

"But Sarah didn't say who killed her," I objected.

"Apparently that doesn't concern her anymore," Barbara said dryly.

Barbara rose to leave as Peter's mouth opened again.

"I would like to—" he started.

He never finished his sentence. Barbara grabbed her purse, gave me a quick kiss on the cheek, and was down the stairs to her Volkswagen, before he had a chance.

"I told you that woman wasn't qualified," said Peter. "And another thing—"

– Nineteen –

"IT'S OKAY, PETER," Tony interrupted gently. He rose from his chair and stood behind the agitated attorney. "No harm done," he soothed as his hands massaged Peter's shoulders. Linda watched them unblinkingly from her chair.

Peter allowed Tony to work his shoulders, and limited himself to scowling for a few moments. I was glad for the break. I needed time to think about the seance. And about Barbara. Why had I failed to notice the similarities between Barbara and Sarah before? They both shared the ability to drive Peter up a wall. They both managed to revel in whatever experience came their way. And then there was the way that Barbara had left. Actually, I had never noticed Barbara leaving so abruptly before. Was her uncharacteristic departure due to Sarah's influence? Damn. That was a spooky thought.

"Was that your friend's idea of a joke?" Peter asked. But his voice was calmer now.

"Actually—" Tony began thoughtfully. He stopped massaging Peter's shoulders. "I wonder if it might be *Sarah's* idea of a joke."

"You know, it does seem more like Sarah than Barbara," I said slowly. "And Barbara wouldn't pretend to get a message if she didn't. I'm sure of that. But Sarah, on the other hand—"

Peter stood up. "I've wasted enough time on this . . . this event," he declared ungraciously and marched to the door. He turned back for a moment to glare at me. "I'll talk to *you* later," he said. It sounded like a threat. He slammed the door on the way out.

I stared at the door and thought about Peter. How come he could accept Sarah telling him he created his own reality in a dream, but refused to accept a channeled "whoops"?

"Maybe 'whoops' really means something," Tony said eagerly, bringing me back to the present. I turned to look at him. His open face was lit with hope as he spoke. "Maybe she was trying to let us know that her death really was an accident."

"I hate to tell you this, Tony," I said softly. "But I don't think an accident's very likely." I paused. "Sarah's gardener was murdered today. There has to be a connection." I watched his face as I spoke. And Linda's. Tony's eyes widened and his mouth gaped for a moment. Linda didn't blink.

"I just don't understand what's going on here," Tony murmured miserably. "There must be a reason for all of this. Are you sure the poor guy was murdered?"

"He was hit over the head with a shovel," I answered.

"That's terrible," Tony whispered, shaking his head.

I wanted to ask Tony where he had been when Jerry had been killed. But when I looked into his worried face, I just couldn't. I turned to Linda instead.

"Where were *you* this morning?" I asked outright, no longer caring how she felt about my bluntness.

I thought I saw a smile flicker for an instant on her face. I wasn't sure, though.

"Around," she answered a beat later. Then she slithered out the door.

I turned back to Tony. He was staring at me, round-eyed and pale.

"Kate," he said somberly. "In case you want to know, I was at The Elegant Vegetable, working on the books this morning. Josie was cooking."

"Oh, Tony—" I began guiltily. How could I suspect him?

"It's okay," he assured me.

Then he helped me carry the chairs back to the kitchen. We moved the couch back where it had been and sat down, side by side. Maybe I shouldn't have invited Linda, I reflected. Maybe I should have warned people about her. But somehow the threat of journalistic exposure had seemed pretty lightweight after finding Jerry's ant-covered body. And after six months of talking freely in front of her, a warning that day would have been a case of locking the proverbial barn door once the horse had gone. I promised myself I would confront her soon, though.

Tony let out a long sigh. I squeezed his arm and told him that I was coming to The Elegant Vegetable the next day with a friend. He smiled, but his smile expressed more sadness than enthusiasm. He got up slowly from the couch, murmured "Take care" and shuffled out the door like an old man.

On the way to my ex-husband's office at eight-thirty I spotted a familiar bottle-green Jaguar in the rearview mirror. Good. Wayne was on the job again. But how would he feel seeing me with Craig, I wondered guiltily.

Craig greeted me at the door with a big smile. I dodged his attempted hug. I was there for information, not romance. And Wayne might be watching.

"Gee, you're working late," I said conversationally. "Did you spend your whole morning here, too?"

I watched the smile leave his face. The tone hadn't fooled him. "Why?" he demanded.

"You first," I insisted.

"Yes, I spent my whole morning here," he answered evenly. "You can ask my secretary if you need confirmation." He paused. "Now tell me why you're interested."

"I'll tell you in the car," I promised.

By the time my Toyota got to Mushrooms, Craig knew everything I did about Jerry's death. At first he had been noisily concerned over my involvement. But when I told him I didn't want to hear about it anymore, he had dutifully changed the subject. He was telling me about a new software contract he had landed as we walked into the restaurant.

Mushrooms may have been located in a windowless cavern, but it was a chic windowless cavern. Fish tanks were inserted into the pale blue walls with artistic randomness. The tanks glowed softly as did the rosy shell-shaped fixtures on the tables. There was just enough light to read the menus, but not enough to intrude on a romantic mood. I always felt like I was underwater when I ate at Mushrooms. The taped whales singing softly in the background helped the illusion.

Our host sat us in front of one of the glowing fish tanks. Craig did a noisy fish imitation, snorting and blowing out his cheeks. I tried to smile. Craig often reverted to humor in times of stress, usually mine. As I watched him, I remembered the years of intense conversations in which I had insisted desperately, "I'm serious," and he had replied, "I'm Roebuck, let's start a department store." Somehow in retrospect, it seemed pretty funny. It hadn't then. God,

I didn't want to be married again, even if Wayne was a different man than Craig.

I had forgotten how expensive Mushrooms was. And Craig insisted on ordering the works. Mushroom pâté, green salad and the mushroom platter for two, which included stuffed mushrooms, teriyaki mushrooms and lemon mushrooms. As I handed my menu back to the waiter, I vowed to split the bill down the middle with Craig.

I was pondering a subtle approach to interrogating Craig about Sarah's computer when the pâté and crackers came.

"Did Sarah have a modem?" I asked. I've never been very subtle.

"Yes, but why do you—?" His eyes came up, startled. "Oh, murder by modem," he said slowly. "I hadn't thought of that." He spread pâté on a cracker.

"How does a modem work, exactly?" I asked.

"It depends," he answered. He shoved the cracker in his mouth absently, chewed and swallowed. "In general, a modem enables you to access a computer over the telephone so you don't actually have to be there." He paused again, spreading pâté on all the crackers as he thought. "Sarah uploaded her software to Dave Yakamura by modem," he said finally.

My brain tingled. Dave Yakamura. But I wasn't limiting myself to one suspect. "Could someone else have dialed in?" I asked eagerly.

"Hypothetically, they could," he mumbled through a mouthful of crackers. "But they would need her password and account name to get in." He shook his head. "I doubt that she would have given anyone her password."

"But couldn't someone have figured it out?" I pressed.

"Well, there are ways." He sighed and looked at me, his eyes asking me to leave it alone. I kept my gaze level. He rattled off a few scenarios. "They could just dial in every possibility until they happened on one that worked, but that would take a few million years. Or they could tap the line and run it through a modem analyzer. Or they could look over her shoulder when she was working, but I don't think she let people do that." He shook his head and popped another cracker in his mouth.

"Anyhow," he mumbled dispiritedly. "As far as I know, those robots weren't even set up to be run remotely."

"But it is possible?"

"Just possible," he agreed. "But not probable." He shoved another cracker in and frowned at me as he chewed. He looked like a concerned chipmunk.

"All right," I said. "Say for the sake of argument that the robots could be run remotely, and that someone had her password and account name." I paused for a breath. "Could they have programmed her robot long-distance?"

He let out a long sigh before conceding, "Maybe, given a lot of conditions. The robot program was probably pretty simple, and a modem might give you access to the computer. But the line quality sucks and the graphics wouldn't be very good either."

"But it could be done?" I insisted.

"Conceivably, Kate," he gave in unhappily. "But it's not likely. You'd need a pretty clear map of the coordinates of the house in the first place. And you'd want to test it before you actually tried it."

I reached for a cracker. They were all gone. Maybe I wouldn't split the bill fifty-fifty with Craig.

The waiter brought us our salads. I took a bite before springing my next question.

"Could it have been done from New Jersey?" I asked.

"So that's what you're thinking," he said slowly. He looked through me for a moment as he considered the question. "Not likely," he concluded, shaking his head. "No map of the house, poor line quality, and how would she have picked up the password?" He paused. "Maybe it's not totally impossible . . ." He paused again.

"Yeah," I prompted eagerly.

". . . but it ranks up there with the longest long shots." His lips curled into a weak smile. "Like I'm the reincarnation of Cleopatra. Like Gore Vidal will win the next presidential election. Like you could go on the Ed Sullivan show—"

"But Ed Sullivan's dead," I objected.

"That's exactly what I mean," he told me. "A long shot as long as—"

"I get the idea," I said hastily.

We ate our salads in silence, while Craig's face grew more and more serious.

"Kate, I'm worried about you," he announced finally. He slid his empty salad plate to the side and leaned forward. "Please let me move back into the house," he whispered. "Just for the time being. Just until this is settled."

If only Wayne had made that offer, I thought with a surge of self-pity. I pushed the feeling away and turned my attention back to Craig. Craig had been cooperative. I owed him a gentle refusal.

"Thanks for the offer," I said softly. "But I'll be all right." I put some fun into my voice. "I know tai chi, remember?" I mimed a tai chi struggle with an invisible opponent. But he didn't smile.

He looked at me with big brown puppy-dog eyes. "Seriously, Kate," he said, reaching for my hand. "I miss you."

"Seriously?" I replied. "Does that make me Roebuckly of department store fame?" I pulled my hand out of reach. He looked so sad.

"You must have women swarming all over you," I said, trying to cheer him up. "I've been informed that intelligent, single, straight men are as rare around here as tofu burgers at the Cattlemen's Annual Barbecue."

"That's what everyone says, but it's not true!" Craig exploded. His puppy-dog eyes looked rabid now. "I cannot tell you the disastrous dates I've been on. Everyone keeps pushing me to go out with these *awful* women. Either they want to go to some bar, with smoke and booze, or they say 'Let's go out for ice cream,' like it's something healthy they're suggesting instead of poison—"

I couldn't help laughing. He was a worse food fanatic than I was.

He looked startled by my laughter for a moment; then slowly his face softened. He smiled sheepishly.

"Sorry about that," he said and went back to fish imitations as our waiter approached with our third course.

The mushroom platter was delicious. And Craig kept the conversation light. I stuffed my mouth as he amused me with comic tales of his various dates. He told me about one date who made her living selling powdered urine to drug-users who wanted to beat the urine tests. I wasn't sure if he was serious. He put on a falsetto voice and a dazed stare to imitate a woman he had gone out with who was "really into celibacy." He kept the comedy rolling until we left the restaurant.

I avoided an embarrassing goodbye hug by staying in the car when I dropped him back at his office. I rolled down my window and waved.

"I'm not going to let you go like this," Craig announced abruptly. He bent down to make eye contact. "I want to move back in. I care about you."

"Just consider me another funny date," I advised him. I kept my tone light, but my stomach contracted with pity. I reminded myself that it had been Craig who had left me and divorced me, not the other way around.

Craig let out a bark of laughter that sounded more bitter than amused.

I rolled up my window and drove away. A block later I glanced in my rearview mirror. Wayne was still on my tail.

– Twenty –

WAYNE'S CAR FOLLOWED me all the way home. I lingered at the front stairs, hoping to send a provocative message that would pull him from his Jaguar. I listened expectantly for the sound of the car door opening and eager footsteps . . . and heard nothing but a stray dog barking and the sound of distant traffic. I turned and looked out into the dark. Wayne was still in his car.

I'm not going to beg him, I thought angrily. He knows he's welcome. Men! I trudged up the stairs and opened the front door, feeling heavy with the emotional exhaustion that follows unfulfilled hopes. C.C. greeted me sleepily. Her eyes opened and closed as she meowed. I picked her up and leaned my face against her silky fur. At least my cat loved me, I told myself. C.C. squirmed and jumped out of my arms. So much for my cat's love. Cats! I wouldn't invite her to share my bed either.

I went to sleep aching with weariness. And loneliness. And fear.

I woke up the next morning with a racing heart. I had been dreaming about Jerry. Actually, about Jerry's corpse, which had risen to its feet, covered with writhing layers of ants, opened its arms wide to embrace me and stepped slowly forward. I had screamed myself awake. I didn't need Jungian analysis for that one. Death had almost given me a great big hug.

I lay in bed taking deep breaths to calm myself. As soon as my heart settled down, my mind began to race. Murder, arson, threats. And Dave Yakamura. His friendly face flickered in my mind. He had been linked to Sarah by modem. He had the means to program her robot remotely. Craig had said it wasn't likely. But it wasn't impossible.

A yowling sound from the other side of the bedroom door told me that C.C. knew I was awake. And, according to her own testimony, she was starving. I took one last deep breath, pulled myself out of bed and opened the door, all the time thinking about Dave Yakamura and Linda Zatara. What was their connection? C.C. danced around my feet, then jumped up to bat my leg impatiently with her outstretched paw.

"All right, all right," I mumbled and followed her down the hallway to the kitchen, tripping over her catnip mouse halfway there. I needed a refresher course in assertiveness training just to deal with my cat.

A scoop of KalKan, a shower and a few hours of Jest Gifts paperwork later, it was nine o'clock, time to tackle Dave Yakamura. I found his business card beneath a pile of invoices. I had forgotten the name of his company. There it was: 2020 Robotics.

I dialed the number on the card. Dave Yakamura's voice was so friendly when he came on the line that I almost faltered. But not quite. I introduced myself and began lying.

"I'm doing a short biography of Sarah Quinn," I rattled off, getting through the lies as quickly as possible. "I thought I might interview you."

"That's a wonderful idea," he replied seriously. "Sarah Quinn was an exceptional human being. Her life deserves a book."

He bought it! After a short conversation, he agreed to be interviewed, and I agreed to call him Dave. I put on my glasses and rushed out the door to my Toyota.

Dave Yakamura's business was housed in a barn of a building in San Rafael's industrial district. I parked my car and walked to the front door. I heard another car pull into the parking lot as I put my hand on the doorknob. I looked behind me. It was Wayne. I blew him a kiss and was rewarded by the flicker of a smile on his otherwise dour face.

I opened the door to 2020 Robotics. The interior of the building was spacious, intersected by cubicles whose walls reached only halfway to the ceiling. A well-groomed receptionist sat at the front desk. And next to her stood a robot. It looked just like one of Sarah's, a cousin to the one that had killed her.

I stopped breathing. If anyone could have murdered Sarah Quinn with a robot, Dave Yakamura could have.

"Cute, isn't he?" the receptionist was saying.

"He?" I preferred "it" for a robot. I resumed breathing and nodded. I forced my face into a smile.

"Ms. Jasper," a friendly voice boomed behind me. I swung around and watched Dave Yakamura limping toward me. I wondered once again what had happened to his leg.

"Kate," I corrected him.

"Kate, then," he agreed. "I see you've met Oscar," he said genially.

I nodded again and tried to look receptive. That was all it took to launch Dave into a demonstration. "Oscar, offer Kate some refreshment," he said, slowly and clearly. The robot came to life.

"What may I get you?" Oscar asked in the same choppy syllables I had heard from Sarah's robot.

I shrugged my shoulders. The robot was silent.

"Continue," Dave ordered.

"Coffee perhaps?" Oscar offered.

"No, thank you," I said gently. I realized I was trying not to hurt its feelings. I almost laughed out loud.

"A soft drink perhaps?" it tried again.

"No," I answered brusquely.

"Herb tea perhaps?" it soldiered on, undaunted.

"Well, all right," I gave in. "Herb tea would be just fine."

The robot was silent again. "Yes," Dave translated.

Oscar turned and whirred away, evidently in search of tea. The stairs didn't stop its progress. It climbed them easily.

"Hydraulic lifters," Dave explained proudly. "With the lifters and the three monster tires, Oscar can go almost anywhere you can."

Like into a hot tub, I thought. I reminded myself to keep breathing.

"Most people still think of robots as novelties," Dave continued, "but they can be very useful, very practical. Oscar can be programmed to vacuum, mow the lawn, even bark like a dog to scare prowlers." Oscar, I felt sure, would scare me more than any dog. I kept the feeling to myself.

"And they're great for the disabled. They can carry groceries, serve meals, you name it!" His enthusiasm couldn't be ignored. I smiled, genuinely this time. "It's all in the attachments," he added.

"But can it bake a cherry pie?" I wisecracked.

"Sure," said Dave, chuckling. "It can even boil water."

"How does it know if the water is boiling?" I asked. In spite of my fear, I was curious about the critters.

"It sticks its finger in the water," he answered.

I laughed. Dave laughed with me, insisting, "It really does, you know." He was an attractive man. There was no doubt about that. Handsome, bright, friendly. He even had a sense of humor. I reminded myself that Ted Bundy had been charming too.

"Who buys your robots?" I asked, keeping the conversation going.

Dave's face grew serious. "Mostly the very wealthy," he admitted. "These robots aren't cheap. It takes a lot of effort to build and program each one." His brows relaxed slightly. "But we're working on the funding to modify them for the disabled. I had polio when I was a kid. I know how important mechanical assistance can be."

I winced guiltily. I had suspected him because of that limp.

"And then there's the future," Dave went on. His eyes went out of focus, somewhere into the next century, I guessed. "It won't be too many more years when people will be buying domestic robots like they do microwave ovens. The best labor saving device around."

Oscar came whirring back with a cup of tea, a bowl of sugar cubes and a pitcher of cream, all on a tray clamped between its metal pincers. Dave grinned proudly. I was going to ask Dave if Oscar had made the tea itself, but then remembered I was here to talk about Sarah. The minute I said her name, the grin left Dave's face. His shoulders slumped.

"One of our robots was used to kill her," he said, his voice deepening. He gazed downward as he spoke. I looked down too. One of his hands was twitching, the fingers dancing as if he were playing a honky-tonk piano. "It could have been a radio or a toaster just as easily. But still, I feel so responsible." He massaged the twitching hand, then brought his eyes back to mine. "Let's talk in my office," he suggested.

Dave walked me toward his office with Oscar trailing behind, still clutching its tray. Dave pointed out an assembly area as we passed. Two women sat at a workbench putting together heads, torsos and limbs for this century's Frankenstein's monsters. Did Dave really think a radio could have killed Sarah as easily as a robot? You can't program a radio to hop into the hot tub. Was he painfully naive or just protecting the good name of his product? As we entered the cubicle that housed his office, I had another thought.

Maybe he was concerned about 2020's legal liability for the actions of Sarah's robot.

Oscar handed me my cup of herbal tea after I sat down in the visitor's chair in front of Dave's desk. The robot hadn't spilled a drop. I refused its offers of sugar and cream and turned back to Dave.

"Return to reception," Dave said to Oscar. The robot left us.

"I understand Sarah used a modem to send you her software," I prompted.

"Yes, she did," he said. He shook his head sadly. But my eyes were on his hands. Both of them were twitching now, playing piano in the air above his desk. "Sarah was an innovative woman," he told me. "Her latest idea was programming the robots to do promotions. Put one of our robots in a busy mall, and have it explain the advantages of your new product. You can bet people will remember." He looked into my eyes. "We'll miss her," he finished.

"Do you manufacture the robots here?" I asked.

"Oh, no," he answered, a smile on his face now that we had returned to a less troubling subject. He leaned back in his chair and his hands disappeared behind the desk. "The parts are manufactured in Japan. We assemble and program them here. It's one of the advantages of having Japanese relatives," he told me. "The Japanese know their robots."

I sipped my tea and thought about getting the conversation back to Sarah.

"In Japan," Dave was saying, "the people are so well-educated that there's a shortage of skilled workers for the factories. So they use robots to replace the humans." He leaned forward. His eyes were wide with excitement. "But they've neglected the domestic automation market. That's where 2020 comes in."

I nodded intelligently. He stood up. Damn. Was the interview over?

"Look out there," he directed, pointing out his open office door. I relaxed. It was just another demonstration.

I swiveled my head around in time to see five robots rolling by in military precision, followed by a bearded young man with a clipboard.

"Stop," he ordered.

They stopped obediently.

"Beautiful, aren't they?" Dave said enthusiastically. "A good percentage of our time is spent in testing. We always test them thoroughly before they leave 2020."

I looked away from the robots and back at Dave. Was he trying to convince me that his robot wasn't responsible for Sarah's death? He avoided my eyes as he sat back down, hands locked together on his desk.

"Beautiful," he repeated, looking at the space above my head. "We're completing two robots a day now. And selling them! Starting to pay back our investors. Most of the robots are selling through elite mail-order catalogues. Foreign sales—"

"Did you ever see Sarah's robots at her house?" I interrupted. I had a feeling Dave Yakamura could talk about his business all day if I let him. He was beginning to remind me of my ex-husband, Craig.

"I never went to Sarah's house," Dave told me, making eye contact again. Was he lying? There was no clue in his eyes. I looked at his hands. He was still holding them locked together, but a pinkie finger had wiggled free and was conducting a silent orchestra. So what? I said to myself. He's nervous. That doesn't mean he's lying. It doesn't mean he's a murderer.

"How do you know Linda Zatara?" I asked. I tried to keep my tone conversational, but I don't think I was fooling him.

Dave shoved his hands behind the desk before answering. "We were in a Recovery from Divorce support group together," he said. His voice wasn't quite hostile, but it certainly lacked the geniality of his earlier tone. "Linda's an awfully good listener," he added.

No kidding, I thought. I heard movement behind me. I turned my head to look. Five robots rolled by, each balancing a tray on one pincer and holding a vacuum attachment in the other. I couldn't tell if they were the same robots as before.

I turned back to Dave. "Beautiful," I said.

His face softened into its former friendly expression. Too bad I couldn't think of any more good questions for him. I thought of asking where he had been the morning before, but I didn't have the nerve to try to pass the question off as light conversation. So we talked a few moments longer and then I said goodbye. I would have pumped the receptionist on the way out, but she wasn't at her desk. Oscar was, though. He waved a pincer as I left. I waved back, then realized I was waving at a robot and jerked my hand down.

As I climbed into my Toyota, I scanned the parking lot for Wayne's Jaguar. It was nowhere in sight. I let out a long, sighing breath and turned the key in the ignition.

I pulled the slip of paper with Linda's address from my purse. Should I warn her I was coming? No, I decided. I might have a better chance of cracking her stone façade if I didn't.

Linda's house turned out to be a condominium. I got lucky. Linda was not only home, she buzzed me in.

She met me at the door with her usual deadpan expression. "Kate," she acknowledged curtly.

It was one word. Maybe I could get more out of her.

"I was in the neighborhood, so I thought—" I began babbling. There was something about Linda that made me go on like that. A good listener, indeed. I decided to get to the point, even if I hadn't been invited in.

"How do you know Sarah?" I demanded without further preamble.

Linda's grey eyes widened ever so slightly. But I couldn't tell what emotion the widening signified.

She silently motioned me into her living room. The room was as devoid of life as she was. There were no pictures on the white walls, no knickknacks anywhere. The only furnishings were two slate-grey couches and a teak coffee table. There were two thick stacks of paper on that table, though. I looked closer. The top sheet of one stack was typed and had scribbling between the lines and in the margin. Was this a manuscript?

"A W.I.B. support group," Linda said in a monotone. I jumped, startled. I had almost forgotten she was there.

"What?" I asked.

"Women In Business," she droned on. "That's where I met Sarah."

I didn't know what to do with the information. I was stunned. Linda had volunteered a full sentence. I kept on going.

"Did you visit Sarah's house very often?" I asked.

Again her eyes widened. "A few times," she answered.

A phone rang in the next room. Linda got up slowly and glided out of the living room to answer it.

I pounced on the manuscript. I scanned the top sheet. "—self-indulgence in hot tubs," was the first line, continued from the page before. Then, " 'You create your own reality,' was Sally's favorite phrase." And scribbled between the double-spaced lines, "Little did she know what reality she was creating . . . (see insert 42)." Was "Sally" Sarah? Plenty of people in Marin parrot "You create your own reality" at the first sight of anyone's problems except their own. But what about the hot tub?

I read on. Peter and Tony's words leapt up at me. And my own. The names were all changed, but the words were ours. Was Linda updating the chapter to include Sarah's death? I leafed through the pages quickly, searching for "insert 42." No luck. I turned over the other stack and saw the title page. "SUPPORT GROUPS, THE NEW ADDICTION, by Z.L. Harvard." Damn. Another best seller.

I heard a harsh chuckling sound behind me. I whirled around to face Linda. She was smiling widely now, the first smile I had ever seen on her face. But it wasn't a friendly smile. Her teeth were bared in triumph, her eyes narrow with something close to hatred. A sudden shudder jerked my shoulders.

"Satisfied?" Linda asked flatly.

I wasn't satisfied. "Did Sarah know you were writing this?" I demanded.

Linda took her time walking to one of the grey couches and sitting down. I had a feeling I was in for the silent treatment again. I sat down myself, determined to wait her out.

"No," she finally answered, surprising me. "I don't think so." She bared her teeth again. "That woman was so caught up in self-adoration, she didn't even think to ask me why I wanted to join your group."

Linda laughed. It took me a moment to place the sound as laughter, it was so slow and deep. My shoulders jerked involuntarily again. "Sarah," Linda hissed. "What an incredible bitch! She'd been to almost as many groups as I had, but I was doing research. Sarah had to have an audience every other minute for her incessant preening."

Linda settled back into the couch, her eyes alive with malice. "Support groups!" She sneered. The mask was gone from her face. "Alcoholics, Overeaters, Sex Addicts, Asexuals, Menopausals, Compulsive Shoppers. You wouldn't believe some of these groups."

"And ours," I prompted quietly.

"What a joke," she snarled. But she didn't laugh. "Human Potential. Bitch-and-crow sessions, that's all. Bitch about the people less advanced than your self-righteous selves. And crow about your success. What bullshit!"

She vented her spleen for a few long minutes more, her eyes no longer on me, her face mobile with long-suppressed malevolence. I almost wished she'd put the mask back on. I felt nausea rising as I listened to her.

Finally, she seemed to remember me. "So what have you found out about Sarah's murder?" she asked, her voice flat again. Her grey eyes were still alive though, intent on mine.

"Not much," I said, wondering if I was looking at the murderer.

The rage this woman had hidden could carry her through murder. I was sure of it. But what about motive?

"No more fires?" she asked.

"No," I said. I realized I was grinding my spine into the back of the couch, trying to get as far away from Linda as possible. I took a breath and slid forward, determined to take the advantage again.

"What's your relationship with Dave Yakamura?" I demanded.

She shrugged. I waited five tense minutes for an answer, but none came. She was apparently finished talking. But she wasn't finished smiling. She bared her teeth once more as she stared at me.

I left without saying goodbye.

I felt the sweat on my body chill as I walked out into the late-morning light. I hadn't realized just how much I had perspired in Linda's living room. I breathed in the cool air gratefully.

I reviewed Linda's words in my mind as I drove home. She was a spy, a particularly venomous one at that, but was she a murderer?

I hadn't come up with an answer to that question by the time I pulled into my driveway. All I had come up with was a bunch of new questions. I walked up my front stairs lost in thought, opened the door and stepped inside. Something grey squished beneath my foot.

– Twenty-one –

I JUMPED BACK, startled, then decided I must have stepped on C.C.'s catnip mouse. I shook my head affectionately and bent over to pick it up. Only the grey thing I had stepped on wasn't a toy. It was a real dead mouse. I gagged and turned away.

I was sweeping the mouse into a dustpan when the phone rang. I raced to the garbage can and gave the poor little thing a hasty burial before answering. C.C. yowled in protest, berating me for my cruel refusal of her gift. She tripped me as I lunged for the phone, then slunk off, her honor satisfied.

I regained my footing as the answering machine clicked on. I switched it off and grabbed the receiver, panting, "Hello, hello, I'm really here."

"Wanna buy some life insurance, lady?" the voice on the other end asked ominously.

"No, thank you," I replied cautiously. My shoulders tightened. Was this another death threat?

"Just kidding!" the voice assured me. "This is me, Ellen Quinn."

"Oh, hi," I said, relaxing.

"Listen, me and Nick were wondering if you'd like to come over for dinner tonight," Ellen went on blithely.

"You and Nick?" I repeated. I didn't understand.

"Yeah, we've been getting along pretty well, if you know what I mean." She cackled suggestively. "We wanted to pay you back for helping Nick out, and for giving me dinner. Nick says he can do something vegetarian, like he used to do for Sarah. How's about it?"

I agreed to dinner, wondering just how dangerous it might be. I hastily added that I might bring Barbara along. Even if Barbara couldn't come, I could tell her where I was going. No one was going to kill me at a well-publicized dinner, at least I hoped not.

I shook off the thoughts. I had some questions for Ellen.

"Where were you and Nick yesterday morning?" I asked. I didn't even try to sound casual this time. It never worked anyway.

"Why?" Ellen said, her voice suddenly serious. "What happened?"

"I'll tell you about it tonight," I promised. I didn't want to talk about Jerry now.

After a brief silence, Ellen answered my question. "I was in my motel room for most of the morning," she said. "Then I came over to visit Nick."

"Was he there?" I demanded eagerly.

"Of course he was," she snapped. Then she lightened her tone. "The kid doesn't go out much, you know."

But I could still hear a trace of anxiety in Ellen's voice. If she was "getting along" with Nick, she had to wonder if he had murdered her sister.

"Nick couldn't hurt anyone," she insisted, as if she'd heard my unspoken thoughts.

"Sure," I said uneasily. "See you tonight."

I hung up the phone and looked down at the carpet, pondering the wisdom of dinner with two murder suspects. Then I saw C.C. She had retrieved the mouse. She laid it at my feet and looked up expectantly. It's not everyone who gives you a second chance, I thought. I thanked her for the mouse graciously. But I wasn't going to eat the damn thing.

I was ten minutes late by the time I reached The Elegant Vegetable to meet my friend Ann for lunch. Luckily, she hadn't arrived yet. Tony was there, though. He greeted me with a warm hug and kept me company while I waited for Ann.

We sat at the front bar surrounded by massive ferns, and shared lemon-and-hibiscus tea. A colorful selection of young punkers served the tables quietly and efficiently against the background of Bach's Brandenburg Concertos as we sipped and talked. Tony's face looked lined to me that day. His eyes were pink and puffy. But he put on a cheerful voice and told me about his specials, vegetable pilaf and stuffed mushrooms.

He had just finished a description of the day's soups when Ann Rivera came through the door. Heads turned as she walked toward us. She was tall and elegantly dressed-for-success in a mauve wool suit with a maroon silk blouse. Her brown face had a big toothy smile that didn't usually go with that kind of outfit. I introduced her to Tony. He showed us to our table and left us to our menus.

Today's waitress had gold-tipped lavender hair. She set a basket of fresh-baked bread on the table and asked us for our orders. Ann followed my lead and ordered the potato-dill soup and garden vegetable salad.

"It's driving me crazy," Ann said once the waitress was gone. She pulled a slice of oatmeal-rye bread out of the basket.

"What's driving you crazy?" I asked.

"Tony." She frowned and tore the bread into bite-size pieces. "I know I've met him, or maybe just seen him before, but I can't think where."

"Have you ever been here before?" I asked. A new mystery to solve. Just what I needed.

"No." She shook her head. "Somehow there's something, oh, sleazy associated with him. Oh hell, I just can't place it."

"Sleazy? What's sleazy to you?" I probed. "Anything to do with gay bars or parties or something?"

She rolled her eyes upwards and thought for a moment. "No, I don't think that's it," she said slowly. "That doesn't compute as sleazy to me."

"Is it the punk help?" I asked, helping myself to bread. It was warm and sweet when I bit into it, delicious.

"No." She frowned even harder, deepening the grooves between her eyebrows.

"Stop thinking about it and it'll come to you," I advised. "That's how it usually works."

"You're right," she said and looked at me as if for the first time. "How've you been, Kate?" she asked.

My answer was postponed as our soup arrived. I slurped a couple of spoonfuls before telling her. Should I burden her with my problems? Yes, came the instantaneous answer from my brain.

"Have you read in the paper about the recent Mill Valley murders?" I asked her.

"Not 'Mysterious Hot-Tub Death' and 'Gardener Bludgeoned with Own Shovel'?" Ann said. She put her spoon down and leaned toward me, her interest evident.

I nodded.

"You're involved with those? How do you manage it, Kate? Every time someone gets murdered—" She must have seen something in my face. "Not so fun, huh?" she said softly. "Want to talk about it?"

I found that I did want to talk about it, at length. I told her about the murders, the death threats and the arson. Ann was a good friend. And a good audience: intelligent, attentive, and exempt from suspicion of murder. Our salads had been served and halfway consumed by the time I had finished my rundown.

"Have you looked at this thing from the psychological angle yet?" she asked, peering into my eyes. An appropriate question from the administrator of a mental health facility.

A sudden chill raised goose flesh on my arms. The last murderer I had met had been pathologically embittered. Was I up against that kind of hatred again? I thought of Linda Zatara and put down my fork, my appetite temporarily gone.

"Who has the requisite personality for murder?" Ann asked gravely. "I know theoretically anyone is capable of murder, given compelling enough circumstances. But two murders and arson! Somebody must have a real kink in them to do these things."

"So, 'who's crazy' is the question," I summed up. I tapped my fork on the table and thought. "The obvious one is Nick, the Rodin of the reproductive organs," I answered, trying to lighten the tone of the conversation.

"He doesn't seem the right type of crazy to me, though," Ann replied. Her tone was dead serious. She reached her hand into her hair and twirled a curl around her finger absently, lost in thought.

"No," I agreed, sighing. "Nick isn't right. The same goes for the accountant. He's screwy, but murderous? I don't think so."

"How about Sarah's attorney?" Ann asked.

"She's a beacon of normalcy in this crowd. And Dave Yakamura appears to be a nice guy, at least on the outside. Of course, there's Peter." I smiled for a moment, feeling an unexpected surge of affection for him. I tried to explain. "Peter's not crazy, just compulsive and perpetually irritated. He wants the world to be perfect and he's always disappointed when it's not."

"A neurotic, not a psychotic," Ann diagnosed.

That was one way to put it. I nodded and took a bite of my salad before continuing down the list.

"Ellen is certainly obnoxious, for what it's worth," I mumbled through the salad. "And Vivian is downright hostile at times."

"Hostile enough to murder?" Ann demanded.

I swallowed hard. "I just don't know," I answered slowly. I

thought about it, then shook my head. "I can't see Vivian as the murderer."

"Who, then?" Ann prompted. She found a new curl to twirl around her finger and went for it.

"Linda," I said in a low whisper. "God, that woman's full of hatred." I was chilled again just thinking about her. I moved on quickly. "On the other hand, Myra's pretty strange too. She's bitter, and she seems right on the edge of insanity." I paused to consider Myra seriously. "But she probably just sounds nuts because she's one of these people who's been in therapy so long that she tells complete strangers her innermost feelings. Anyone sounds like a lunatic if they do that."

Ann smiled her toothy smile. Too late I remembered her sharing the details of her therapy with me the first time we had met.

"Tony seems the most unlikely to me," I continued hastily. "He's so sweet, so good to people."

"But if he's that saintly, is he repressed?" asked Ann.

"He's not repressed sexually," I assured her.

"I didn't mean sexually," Ann said. "I meant anger. Someone that sweet and good has to be suppressing a lot of anger."

I thought about Tony and couldn't agree. "I think he really is one of these people who just doesn't feel that much anger," I said.

"That makes me suspicious," Ann insisted, frowning.

I chuckled. After years of therapy, Ann would suspect anyone who didn't express anger. Then I remembered how serious the question of Tony's repressed anger could be.

"He *is* the kind who's described as 'such a nice young man' after they dig up the bodies in the basement," I conceded. Then I shook my head. "No, I just can't buy him as a murderer."

"Who else?" prodded Ann.

"Craig," I said. "He used to know Sarah."

"I was wondering if you recognized him as a suspect," Ann commented with a smile.

"Oh yeah," I admitted. "But like Tony, it just doesn't fit. Craig rants and raves sometimes, but he never tries to hurt. He's like a great big friendly dog that'll knock you over by mistake and then stomp all over you licking your face to apologize." Ex-husband or not, I knew he wasn't murderer material.

I looked at Ann's thoughtful face and sighed. Talking to her had only served to expand my list of suspects. I wasn't any closer to narrowing it down to one person. Two murders and arson. She was right. Someone had to be pretty sick.

"How's Wayne doing?" she asked.

I jumped in my chair, startled out of my thoughts. "Still holding out for marriage," I muttered. I didn't want to talk about it.

"Why don't you want to marry him?" she asked. There was genuine curiosity in her tone.

"Because!" I cried angrily. I caught myself and modulated my tone. Ann wasn't the enemy. Even Wayne wasn't the enemy. "I liked our old relationship," I told her briefly. "No dirty laundry, no dishes in the sink, no lies." I sighed. "I just don't want to be married again."

"Then you shouldn't have to be," she agreed in the time-honored fashion of all good woman friends.

I reached across the table and squeezed her hand.

"Thanks," I said.

"Any time," she replied. "Now maybe you can help me with *my* love life." A blush tinted her brown skin. She reached up to twirl her hair again.

"Who, what?" I asked eagerly.

"I have a new sweetie," she blurted out. Suddenly she looked very young, despite her dress-for-success suit. Young and insecure.

"That's wonderful," I assured her. Ann had been single for a long time. She deserved a good man in her life. "What's he like?"

"He's kind and sweet and handsome and charming," she said uncertainly. "But he is a man."

I burst into laughter. Ann looked stunned for a second, then grinned and laughed with me.

"So what's he really like?" I asked finally.

"He's a Jungian therapist," she answered. Her eyes looked so vulnerable as she described him. *He'd better treat her right*, I thought fiercely. "It makes me a little nervous. But he really is kind and sweet. And he really is handsome and charming." She was twirling her hair furiously now. "The only friction, so far, is that he's a meat-eater and doesn't understand why I'm not."

"That's not insurmountable," I said. "Wayne—" I began, then stopped. Wayne and I weren't a good example right now.

"I know, I know," she said. "Every once in a while I sneak off to McDonald's myself for—" She stopped mid-sentence. "That's it!" she shouted suddenly. She slapped her palm on the table.

"That's what?" I asked, startled.

"That's where I've seen Tony!" Her voice was loud and carrying. I saw heads turn toward us.

"At McDonald's?" I asked incredulously.

"Yes," she said, bending forward across the table, her voice quieter now. "The reason I remembered him is because he looked so damned furtive. I could tell he was ashamed of what he was doing."

"What was he doing?" I asked, fearing the worst.

"He was buying two Big Macs and a milkshake!"

– Twenty-two –

"OH, NO, NOT Big Macs!" I protested.

A momentary hush fell over the restaurant. My voice must have carried through the whole room. I could feel a flush creep up my neck and into my cheeks as I turned to look for Tony. He stood staring at me, just through the swinging kitchen doors. He wasn't smiling. Lines of worry had sharpened his usually smooth face. I turned back to Ann hastily, wondering whether Tony had heard my outburst. And if he had, did he know it concerned him? Then another worry grabbed me.

"I hope the customers don't realize I was talking about Tony," I whispered urgently to Ann.

"It's not a crime to eat at McDonald's," she whispered back, her whisper belying her words.

"No, it's not," I agreed. "But to the people eating here, it might be an incentive to spend their money somewhere else."

Ann began twirling her hair again. "Sorry," she said.

"No problem," I assured her in a voice far more cheerful than I felt. "Anyway, it's not your fault." Tony at McDonald's? I was still reeling. "But back to your new sweetie," I said with what I hoped sounded like heartfelt interest.

We discussed Ann's new man through the rest of our meal and a pot of blackberry tea. He sounded wonderful, but my thoughts kept whirling back to Tony's guilty secret.

Tony thanked us graciously for the visit as we left. I pretended not to notice the tension in his face.

* * *

I called Barbara as soon as I got home. "I'm going over to Nick's for dinner tonight," I told her.

"The loony sculptor?" she said incredulously. Her voice was filled with concern. "Are you going alone?"

"No, not exactly," I mumbled defensively. "Do you remember Ellen, the graveside comedienne? She *and* Nick invited me."

"What's their connection?" Barbara demanded.

"Romantic, I think. Ellen seems to be taking over with Nick where her sister Sarah left off."

"Ah," Barbara murmured thoughtfully. "They might make a good couple. I wonder what their signs are. She's got to be a Taurus—"

I took a deep breath and interrupted her. "I told Ellen I might bring you with me."

"But I can't go tonight," Barbara objected. "I'm facilitating a Kundalini workshop."

"That's all right," I assured her, ignoring the way my stomach was tightening. "I just want them to know that someone else knows that I'm going to be there."

"I understand," she said. I couldn't see her, but I knew she was smiling. "Dinner for three, hold the blunt object."

"You've got it."

"Be careful anyway, kiddo," she warned. The concern in her tone scared me. When a psychic worries about you, there may be a good reason.

"So what else did you call about?" she asked.

"What makes you think there's something else?" I demanded.

"I can hear it in your voice," she explained. Some explanation. Psychics!

"Tony," I said, giving in.

"Tony is very centered, very well-grounded," Barbara responded quickly. "He'd probably be a dynamite healer." She paused. "So what's he done that you're so worried about?"

"A friend of mine saw him eating at McDonald's," I whispered. Laughter sang over the phone line. After fifteen minutes, Barbara had almost convinced me that eating Big Macs was not a secret to kill for, even if you did own a vegetarian restaurant.

A few hours of paperwork later, I stepped carefully up the overgrown pathway to Nick's house wondering for the four hundredth time if I should be going to dinner with two murder suspects. A big grey cat came tearing out of the undergrowth, ended up almost a my feet, gave me a startled look as I jumped, then turned and scrambled down the path. I reminded myself just what it was that killed the proverbial cat. I stifled a groan and finished the walk to Nick's front door.

"Hey, how's the detective lady?" Ellen greeted me as she opened the door. She gave me a bear hug, then released me. She was wearing a loose embroidered linen blouse over her jeans. Her hair was loose, too, and I thought I detected new makeup. She was looking far more attractive than she had the day of the funeral, living proof that big can be quite beautiful. She motioned me into the hall.

"I don't know how Miss Marple is," I answered flippantly, walking in. "She's the only 'detective lady' I know." I wanted to squelch the detective reputation, though it was probably too late. I noticed a new picture on the wall in the hallway, a blowup of the Golden Gate Bridge. Ellen's work, I guessed. "My friend Barbara couldn't make it, but she sends her regards," I added quickly.

"I suppose you've left her with a sealed letter, explaining your suspicions and conclusions, to be opened at the time of your untimely death," Ellen said. Her large body rippled with laughter.

I forced myself to smile. I wasn't about to tell her that I had considered doing just that.

Ellen was still chuckling when she asked, "So what was all the fuss about where Nick and I were Monday morning?"

"Someone else died," I explained brusquely.

Ellen stopped chuckling.

"Who?" she demanded.

"Jerry Gold, Sarah's gardener," I answered, watching her closely as I did.

The confidence seemed to drain from her body, leaving her looking stooped and old. She stared down at the space between us, unseeing.

"It's not over, is it?" she asked in a small voice.

"No," I told her. I hadn't expected this kind of reaction from Ellen. What was she thinking? Was she afraid that Nick was the murderer? Before I could ask her what was going on, she straightened her shoulders and came back to life. She even smiled again.

"Enough of death," she said, her tone a bit too hearty to believe. "I'm on vacation." She pointed a thumb toward the kitchen. "Nick's been really sweating to do you up a vegetarian meal," she said in a lowered voice. "He's really trying, right? He's a good kid."

"What's with you and—"

A loud clanging interrupted me. It was followed by some assorted thumps and bangs.

"Does he need to do all that to cook?" I asked.

"Oh, that's not Nick," Ellen told me. "That's Vivian, your crazy cleaning lady." Ellen tapped the side of her head with a finger. "Vivian called Nick and asked if he needed any cleaning done, right? So he agreed. She offered him some good rates."

"She did?" That didn't sound like Vivian at all.

"Cheaper than she charges you, I'll bet," Ellen said.

"Probably," I agreed. Something crashed in the next room. "Is Vivian mad or something?" I asked in a whisper.

"Maybe you oughta ask her," Ellen suggested.

Vivian stomped into the hallway on cue. "What are *you* doing here?" she snarled as she came toward us. Her eyes looked strange, wide and unfocused, more than just drunk. I could see why Ellen had called her "crazy."

"I'm here for dinner," I mumbled, feeling a surge of gratuitous guilt.

"I wanna talk to you. Alone," Vivian growled. She waved a bottle of Lysol bathroom cleaner pointedly in Ellen's direction.

Ellen took the hint. "Be my guest, so to speak," she said, bowing at the waist. She swept her hand toward Vivian grandly.

I followed Vivian down the hall and into a small, Spartan bedroom in the back. I sat down on the single, straight-backed chair. Vivian remained standing. She began to pace in her agitation.

"You know that woman's probably a murderess," she hissed, waving the fist that still held the bathroom cleaner. "And now she's got her big fat hands on Nick. She's old enough to be his mother. She's talking about them moving in together! Taking him to New Jersey, slime capital of the United States!" Vivian's eyes moistened.

"Are you interested in Nick?" I asked with sudden comprehension.

"So what if I am!" Vivian burst out. She dropped the cleaner and wiped her eyes angrily with the back of her hand. "I'm a lot younger than that bitch out there. You wouldn't believe her. Jokes about everything. It's enough to drive you nuts." She sat down on top of the narrow bed and crossed her arms. "And the bitch doesn't invite *me* to dinner. No, not me, not the hired help—"

"How about lunch with me again, tomorrow?" I interrupted softly. "We could go out if you want to."

"What?" she asked, looking up at me, confused by the change in subject.

"Lunch tomorrow," I repeated.

She stood up again. "Thanks for asking," she muttered. "But I probably can't. I'm squeezing in a quick once-over for the Kornbergs at lunchtime tomorrow. Twelve to two. They've been outa town for the week, but they're coming back tomorrow night." The anger had gone out of her voice. "Their daughter got engaged to this Born Again Christian, so they went back East to talk her outa it. I'll bet they come back converted." She chuckled at the thought.

"At least you've got your sense of humor back," I said. I stood up and put my hand on Vivian's shoulder. "Listen, I really would like to go to lunch with you soon. When you come on Monday, let's arrange it."

"Okay," Vivian mumbled. Then she looked me in the eye. "You don't have to, you know," she said with a touch of hostility.

"I know, I'd just like to," I tried to reassure her. She looked unconvinced. "I've been doing more socializing lately," I insisted. "And you're not just hired help to me, all right?"

"All right," she repeated hesitantly.

I gave her shoulder a squeeze.

"I'll see you Monday," she said brusquely. Then she picked up the bathroom cleaner and shook it menacingly. "Watch out for Ellen," she growled. "I don't trust her."

I followed Vivian as she stomped back down the hallway into the living room, where she gathered up her cleaning accouterments. She was out the door a few moments later. I wandered into the kitchen to find my hosts.

"Whoooee!" Ellen was singing to Nick, one hand on her jutting hip. "Does that girl have a crush on you."

Then it hit me. Vivian had a motive for murder. I was looking at him.

"I didn't do anything!" Nick bawled. A new-looking powder-blue jogging suit hugged his muscular body nicely. But his handsome face was flushed a beet-red. Was this man worth killing for? Could his gorgeous body make a woman forgive that trombone of a voice?

"You don't have to *do* anything, honey," Ellen drawled. "You just have to stand there for women to go nuts over you." Apparently his body was worth his voice as far as she was concerned.

"I'm sorry," Nick boomed. He hung his head.

"Hey, don't be sorry," Ellen said. "You're gorgeous, like a work of art, you know." Her tone was amazingly gentle.

He brightened at the mention of art. "It's okay?" he asked at top volume. I heard the tinkle of glass vibrating on the shelves.

"It sure is, honey," she said and playfully punched his bulging biceps. "Tell Kate what you've cooked."

He turned to me. "I made brown rice," he announced proudly. His voice wasn't quite as loud as before. I wondered if the volume was stress-related. "Sarah always said there was no way to mess up brown rice. And I made a salad. And I made guacamole dip," he said, reciting the list like a child. Like a large, loud child, actually. "And Ellen bought some of those brown-rice crackers. You can eat those, can't you?" he asked anxiously.

"I love brown-rice crackers," I assured him. "I appreciate the trouble you've gone to."

"Oh, good," he boomed. I winced.

"Let's eat," Ellen suggested.

Nick helped us into our chairs at the table. Had Ellen taught him this new behavior? He poured us tea and brought out the guacamole and crackers. Only then did he sit down himself.

"The Lord helps those who help themselves. So help yourselves," Ellen wisecracked. Nick gave her a lopsided grin. Ellen gazed back at him fondly.

I took a sip of tea, then dipped my cracker into the guacamole. Nick eyed me anxiously as I tasted his creation.

"Great guacamole, Nick," I pronounced. He relaxed into his chair. He dipped a cracker himself and took a huge bite. Guacamole dribbled onto his jogging suit.

"Do you stay here at home most of the time?" I asked him once he had swallowed. I knew he did, but I needed a lead-in to the more specific question.

I saw Ellen stiffen. But Nick nodded without a sign of concern and fixed himself another overflowing cracker.

"Yesterday morning?" I probed.

"Oh, I worked real hard yesterday," he said, his voice rising to its customary level. I was getting used to his volume. It was no longer painful, just annoying. "On my new sculpture, all day."

Ellen relaxed visibly after his answer.

"Wanna hear a new joke?" she asked.

"Sure," I said.

"This koala bear goes to a house of ill repute . . ." she began. After that joke she told another. And another. Nick laughed dutifully at all the right places. So did I. After a few more, Nick cleared the empty guacamole bowl and brought the salad and brown rice to the table.

"Nick is quite a find," Ellen said, watching him serve up our meals.

"A real house-spouse," I agreed.

"He wants to go back to New Jersey with me," she said. Her eyes were sparkling. "He'll be able to make a new start. I'm teaching him to drive."

"And we're going shopping tomorrow," Nick bellowed happily.

"You know, some people shop by computer modem these days," I said casually, accepting a full plate from Nick. I followed up with the punch line quickly. "I wonder if Sarah had a modem."

"What's a modem?" asked Nick. So much for the casual approach.

"It's a device that lets you run someone else's computer over the phone from your computer," Ellen explained absently. Her brows were pinched together in thought. "I don't know if Sarah had one," she said slowly. "But it makes sense that she would. She would've just loved having a state-of-the-art toy like that at her fingertips, right?"

"You mean you can type on the computer without being there?" asked Nick.

"Yeah, by phone," confirmed Ellen. "You know this could mean that anyone might—" Her face tightened. "Kate," she said urgently. "Do you know if Myra ever had a modem link with Sarah for their old business?"

"I don't know," I answered slowly. "But she still would have had to have known the setup of the robots and the house," I thought out loud.

"You mean to kill Sarah?" asked Nick, his voice rising to a volume that shook the room like an earthquake. Glass and metal banged together on the shelves. A colander crashed into the sink.

Ellen and I exchanged glances. She changed the subject. "Nick's working on a new theme for his sculptures," she said cheerily. "Tell Kate about it, honey."

"Feet," he announced, smiling broadly. He seemed to have forgotten his earlier question.

"Feet?" I repeated.

His eyes lost focus as he spoke. "Beautiful feet, ugly feet, feet of saints, feet of criminals, rich feet, poor feet, all kinds of feet in all kinds of mediums. The subtle variations could be infinite."

His voice lowered and matured as he spoke. The man clearly had a vision. It was not an appealing vision to me, but it was a vision nonetheless.

"That sounds like a step in the right direction," I said and dug into the salad.

"That's a good one, a 'step in the right direction,' " guffawed Ellen. "I told him it was certainly a well-grounded theme. Starting at the bottom up, so to speak."

Nick grinned and joined in Ellen's laughter.

We ate our salads and brown rice. We never did get back to the subject of Sarah's death.

At the end of the meal Nick brought out some sliced melon for me and Oreos and Cool Whip for Ellen and himself. They dipped their cookies into the topping and munched companionably. They were a good couple. I felt warmed by their company.

"Don't take any wooden turnips," Ellen wisecracked as I left.

Back home, my answering machine was filled with calls. A singles club had left an invitation to join other singles interested in personal growth, at a lecture on "creating a comfortable relationship with a less than perfect person." I tried not to think of Wayne. A water purifier company had provided me with information regarding exactly what was in my drinking water. I wished they hadn't. I was dared to succeed by a corporation offering a home study course in arbitrage and crisis investing. Peter had left a terse order to return his call. And Tony's gentle tones had asked for a chance to "really talk."

I called Tony first.

"I don't feel right about keeping secrets anymore," he sighed. I could hear the clanging of pots and pans in the background. "I need to have a real talk with you, Kate. I could come to your house tonight. Or you could come up to The Elegant Vegetable for breakfast tomorrow."

I thought about my choices. An isolated nighttime tête-à-tête with a potential murderer, or a gourmet breakfast in the company of witnesses. I tugged at the tight waistband of my pants thoughtfully. All this eating out was beginning to show.

"What do you serve for breakfast?" I asked.

"I usually have three kinds of homemade bread," he answered. "I'm making millet-raisin and banana-apricot bread tonight, and I'll do cashew-oatmeal muffins tomorrow. I've got all kinds of fruit

or fruit-smoothies. Then there's scrambled tofu and polenta pan-
akes with fresh blueberry sauce—"

"That's enough," I gave in. So what if my pants were tight. "I'll
be there for breakfast. Are you sure you can take the time to eat
with me?"

"I can always make time for a friend," he replied, his tone warm
with affection. At least I hoped it was affection.

I tackled Peter next.

"Are we having a study group this Sunday or not?" he demanded.

"Damn, I forgot all about it," I replied.

"Well, you shouldn't have," he lectured disapprovingly.
"You've taken on the responsibility for hosting these groups. It's
up to you to arrange them."

I took a deep breath before answering. I didn't want to scream at
him. "I didn't take the responsibility," I explained slowly and
clearly. "Sarah just decided she wanted them at my house, and that
was that."

"It's up to you in any case," Peter insisted.

I decided it wasn't the time to tell Peter what a pain in the rear he
was. "All right," I said. "We can meet at the regular time. It doesn't
seem the same without Sarah, though."

"I know," said Peter, his tone softened. "But we need to carry on
or the group will just fall apart. Your house at ten, then?"

"Sounds good," I agreed. "I'll talk to Tony."

"I'll call Linda," Peter offered.

"No, don't call Linda!" I burst out.

There was a silence on the other end of the line, then an appre-
hensive, "Why not?"

– Twenty-three –

I BROKE THE news to Peter in stages. First I told him about Linda's profession. He groaned. Then I told him her pen name. I heard his sudden intake of breath clearly over the telephone line. Finally, I told him about the manuscript.

Peter's reply wasn't fit for a judicial aspirant, especially one who has found God recently. But I was glad to have told him as I hung up the telephone, glad to share the burden of worry.

I sat down to my neglected paperwork and reminded myself that I was a businesswoman, not a detective. But even as my pencil added figures, my mind totted up suspects.

I woke up the next morning determined to talk to Myra Klein. The combination of Ann's psychological angle and Ellen's question about a Word Inc. modem had catapulted Myra to the top of my suspect list. Well, almost the top. There was still Linda Zatara to consider.

I waited until nine o'clock, then called Word Inc. and asked for Myra. Her greeting was polite but cool when I reminded her who I was.

"I wanted to make sure you were all right after the funeral," I said. Just a little deceit in a greater cause, I told myself.

"Oh, I guess I am," Myra replied. Her breathy voice grew warmer. "I apologize for not participating in the ceremony, but I just wasn't clear in my feelings then." She paused for a moment before rushing through an explanation. "There's a part of me that's ashamed of not doing my part. And a part of me that's still angry with Sarah. But there's a growing part that has finally learned to accept things as they are."

"It sounds like you've done some thinking about Sarah," I said quickly.

"Oh, a lot." She let out a long sigh. "And a lot of difficult emotional work too." I could just imagine. Getting a room big enough for all of her warring parts would be difficult to begin with. "I really think that if the funeral were today, I could find something meaningful to say about Sarah," she declared.

"I'm sure you could," I agreed heartily. "Listen, Myra, I had thought about using your services. I have a modem on my computer. Could I link up to your computers and send my correspondence over for word processing?"

"A modem?" she asked. She sounded genuinely ignorant.

"You know," I prodded. "A phone line to your computers."

"Oh, I think I know what you mean," she said slowly. "But we don't use them here."

I tried another tactic. "I thought I remembered Sarah saying she communicated to Word Inc. from her house by modem."

"Maybe she did," Myra said, her voice cooling again. "But we just do glorified typing here, no complicated computer functions."

"I mainly called to say hello anyway," I said as soothingly as I could. Just a tad more deceit, I promised myself. "I tried to get you Monday morning, but you were out."

"No, I wasn't," Myra objected. I thought I detected new suspicion in her tone. "Did the receptionist tell you that?"

"Well," I temporized. I didn't want to get the receptionist in trouble. "Maybe it was Sunday," I said finally.

"We're not open Sunday," Myra said, pronouncing her words very carefully.

I hung up the phone a few moments later, feeling very foolish. Did Myra really believe I couldn't tell the difference between Sunday and Monday?

More important, was she telling the truth when she said she didn't use a modem, when she said she hadn't been out Monday morning?

I stared at the phone and sighed. There was no way I could know for sure. I rose from my comfy chair unhappily. It was time to tackle the next in line on my list, my friend Tony Olberti.

The Wednesday morning crowd was dense at The Elegant Vegetable when I arrived. As I pushed my way up to the front where the woman was taking names, I was struck by how successful Tony's restaurant was. In an era of billion-dollar drug and defense industries, it was gratifying to see Tony making money cooking health food good enough to line up for.

Tony came up behind me and whispered, "I've fixed up a private table for us in back."

He took my arm and steered me through the dining area and down the short hallway to his private office. When he opened the door I saw a small table that had been placed in front of his desk. It was covered with a linen tablecloth and topped with a setting for two and a vase of flowers.

Tony ushered me in and shut the door behind us. So much for witnesses. I took a quick surreptitious look over my shoulder and saw anxiety in the new sharp lines of his face. I couldn't tell what other emotions remained hidden. Tony pulled out my chair and sat me down at the table without his usual hug, then stood staring at me.

"Aren't *you* going to sit down?" I asked.

"Oh, yes, of course," he said, hastily slipping into his own chair. "I thought we could eat in here away from the crowd. Is that okay with you?" He peered into my eyes.

"Sure," I answered, after a moment's hesitation that I hoped went unnoticed.

"I wanted to talk in private," he explained solemnly. "I have some confessions to make." He turned his eyes away from me. "I've taken the liberty of ordering for us."

A knock on the office door startled Tony. He jumped slightly, then called out, "Come in."

A waitress brought in a teapot and a cloth-covered tray. Her maroon hair stuck straight out around her white face. She reminded me of a Raggedy Ann doll. After she left, Tony poured tea and uncovered the tray to reveal assorted home-baked breads. I exhaled gratefully. My imagination had produced guns, knives, any number of lethal objects under that tasteful cover.

"Remember the last study group, the one where Sarah said, 'I know your secret'?" Tony began hesitantly.

I nodded eagerly.

"I think she could smell my breath," he continued, talking faster now. "Or maybe it was her intuition but . . ." His words trailed off as he stared at his lap.

"But what?" I urged.

"It all boils down to . . ." He faltered again and turned moist eyes on me. "Kate, this is really hard."

I reached over and squeezed his hand. "Tony, does this have to do with meat?" I asked gently.

"You do know!" he yelped. "I thought that's what you and your friend were talking about. I'm almost glad," he said. "Living with this in secrecy has been very hard to handle."

"What exactly have you been doing?" I pressed. I picked up a slice of bread and began nibbling nervously.

"Eating junk food, and worse, meat!" he cried. "I've eaten hamburgers and doughnuts and pepperoni pizza and fried chicken." He paused and looked at me anxiously.

"So?" I challenged him.

He looked at me for a moment without comprehension. "But I've eaten *meat*, Kate," he insisted. Then he put his head in his hands and moaned. "Oh God, every time I do it I tell myself it will never happen again, but it does. I'm so ashamed. I don't even like the food! I don't know why I do it."

"Maybe just so no one mistakes you for a saint," I said in a sudden leap of intuition.

"But nobody could ever mistake me for a saint," he objected, pulling his head out of his hands to look at me again.

"Tony, I've never heard you say a nasty word to anyone," I shot back. "You spend an hour a day meditating. You donate time to Hospice every week. You share your space with ants. You're even nice to Peter. That alone should qualify you for sainthood!" I realized I was shouting, and lowered my voice. "I think somewhere inside you, someone just wants to rebel a little."

"Maybe," he murmured, considering. He looked through me for a moment, his eyes unfocused. "But hamburgers," he said, shaking his head.

"Who are you hurting with hamburgers?" I asked. "You're probably not even hurting yourself, at least not permanently." All that cholesterol, I thought to myself. I hurried on. "As rebellion goes, hamburgers are pretty mild. You don't get drunk. You don't do drugs. You don't make a public disgrace of yourself."

"But they kill animals to make hamburgers," Tony whispered. There were actual tears in his eyes. Damn.

"Have you eaten enough hamburgers in the last year to make up a whole steer?" I demanded brusquely.

He stopped to consider. "I've probably had six or seven."

"Maybe a leg," I said. "All right, so you've crippled one steer."

I looked him in the eye. "Do you think you can burn off that much karma in this lifetime?"

"Well—" He was cut off by the arrival of our fruit-smoothies. The tension level in the room must have been uncomfortably high. Raggedy Ann took one look at us, dropped the glasses unceremoniously on the table, and left.

"Drink your smoothie," I ordered. I resisted the urge to hug him. He needed some tough talk. "You ought to just go for it, without guilt," I advised. "Then it wouldn't work as a rebellion anymore."

He didn't look convinced as he sipped his drink.

"Maybe you need to find some other way to rebel," I suggested. I tasted my own smoothie. It was thick and sweet with bananas, coconut and berries.

"Well, I have been thinking about a rainbow Mohawk," Tony confided diffidently.

"But you'd look ghastly!" I protested.

"I know," he murmured wistfully.

"Isn't it enough to be a gay man in a straight society?" I asked, suddenly anxious about what I might have unleashed with my talk of alternate rebellions.

"Oh, I got over feeling defiant about that years ago," he answered with a dismissive shrug.

Raggedy Ann came back in, carrying more food. The dish she set before me contained a mini-smorgasbord of fruit crêpe, scrambled tofu and soy sausage. As I smelled the mixture of aromas, I decided to heed my own advice to Tony and go for it without guilt.

"In any case, Tony, you're a helluva cook," I told him. "If you want to feel guilty, feel guilty about the inches you've added to my measurements."

Tony smiled his first big smile of the morning. Then we dug into the food. After I had sopped up the last of my scrambled tofu with a slice of banana-apricot bread, I told him about Linda.

"Oh, so that's what she was doing in the group," he commented mildly. "I always wondered."

The idea of being in her next book didn't seem to upset him. Probably because he was the only member of the group who had comported himself with dignity at our meetings.

Tony didn't hold back when he hugged me goodbye. I left The Elegant Vegetable with a lighter heart and a heavier stomach.

The lighter heart didn't last long. Driving home, the wheels in my mind began to turn again. First I began to wonder if the act of murder might be the ultimate rebellion for a person who needed to rebel. No, that didn't really fit, I decided. But was meat-eating really "the" secret? What if Tony had told me about his carnivorous leanings in order to lead me away from a more heinous guilty secret, one worth murder to hide?

My legs felt like they weighed a hundred pounds apiece as I climbed my front stairs. I was dead tired. As I opened the door the telephone rang. I spurred my leaden body on and caught the phone on the second ring, before the answering machine kicked in.

"Hello," I said.

"That's our last warning," a gangster's voice snarled in my ear. I slammed the phone down and flopped into my comfy chair, blood rushing too fast through my veins.

Oh God, I thought, *recycled death threats.* I was sure that the words were the same as the last one. What was I going to do? The police couldn't do anything about this threat. They hadn't done anything about the last two. I was at a dead end. Even if I wanted to investigate, I couldn't see any further avenues to pursue. I didn't know who the murderer was.

But the murderer knew who I was. I wanted to scream, but I settled for deep breathing. After five minutes my body had almost stopped shaking.

Then a clear, reasonable thought rose out of the ashes of my panic. When Jerry Gold had left a message on my answering machine, he had been talking to someone else at the same time. And he might have been talking about whatever it was that had precipitated his murder.

But who had he been talking to? The murderer? Not likely, I decided. If Jerry had been talking to the murderer, he probably would have been killed right there as soon as he hung up the phone. Who then? Sergeant Feiffer had mentioned a wife. Jerry talking to his wife made more sense. The wheels in my mind were turning again.

I dug through the piles on my desk and found Jerry's business card. I dialed his number.

"Hello," answered a lifeless voice. I realized that I would be intruding on a recent widow and hesitated.

"Hello," the voice said again, tinged with fear this time.

"Is this Mrs. Gold?" I asked, keeping my voice soft and unthreatening.

"Yes, who's this?" she demanded, the fear still in her voice.

"This is Kate Jasper, one of Jerry's customers," I said.

There was a long silence at the other end of the line.

"My husband's dead," Mrs. Gold said finally, her voice flat again. I asked myself whether I could really go through with this.

"I know, Mrs. Gold," I offered gently. "And I'm so sorry."

There was no response. I took a breath and continued.

"I wanted to ask you some questions about Jerry's last day," I said quickly. "It's possible that the answers might help find the person who killed him. Do you feel up to talking to me?"

"Who are you, again?" she asked.

"Kate Jasper."

"Yes, I think Jerry'd mentioned you," she said slowly. "He liked you. Said you always paid your bills on time." She paused. "He called you that day. Said he wanted to talk to you."

Mrs. Gold's voice became more lifelike as she went on. I listened to her speak about Jerry's last day without interruption. After she had finished, I offered my condolences. She thanked me for listening and hung up.

Then I just sat, rooted in my chair by a mass of conflicting emotions. Pity for Mrs. Gold weighed me down. And I was afraid that I might be wrong about the murderer, but even more afraid that I might be right. Should I tell someone my new theory? It would only be an unverifiable opinion to the police. And telling anyone else might be slander.

I dialed Barbara's telephone number. When I heard her answering machine I slammed the receiver down with a force that shocked me. I told myself to relax. Then I reached for my good stationery. A sealed letter no longer seemed silly. I outlined my ideas on an embossed sheet of paper and stuck it in a matching envelope addressed to Barbara. With what felt like an enormous effort, I walked the few blocks to the corner mailbox and dropped the letter in.

Walking back, I decided I needed more information. I needed to talk to Vivian, a.k.a. Information Central.

Twenty-four

I GLANCED AT my watch anxiously and accelerated my pace toward home. It was twelve thirty. That meant Vivian would be cleaning for the unhappy parents of the bride-to-be that she had mentioned yesterday. I could probably catch her there. But what was their name? I stopped for a minute to remember, but my brain refused to cooperate. My brain could tell me the name of the woman who played Beaver Cleaver's mother in another decade, but it had forgotten a name uttered less than twenty-four hours ago. I cursed to myself and stomped the rest of the way home in disgust.

I was climbing the front stairs when the name surfaced. Kornberg, that was it! I hurried into the house and grabbed my phone book. There was only one listing for Kornberg in Marin. Barring the chance of unlisted Kornbergs, these had to be the ones. I briefly wondered whether I should intrude on Vivian while she was working, but only briefly. My need to know had overwhelmed my sense of courtesy. I put on my glasses, got in the car, and drove in search of the Kornberg residence.

The address from the phone book was in the upscale end of Marin. I drove through miles of sparsely populated rolling hills until I reached the black wrought-iron gates that guarded the Kornberg residence. My heart did an anticipatory leap when I saw Vivian's Datsun in the driveway. Information Central was in. The iron gates were open a few feet. I climbed out of my car, pushed them open further, and drove up the long driveway to park behind Vivian's car.

As I rang the doorbell of the impressive three-story glass-and-redwood structure, I realized I was going to feel pretty foolish if anyone but Vivian answered. I figured I could always pretend I was collecting for charity. But it was indeed Vivian who greeted me at the door, holding a bottle of Windex in one hand and the working end of a vacuum cleaner in the other. I breathed a sigh of relief. My relief was short-lived.

"What the hell are you doing here?" Vivian snarled.

I decided to skip the pleasantries and get straight to the point. I pushed my way past her into the house. She turned to glare at me.

"Vivian, I talked to Jerry's wife," I said carefully, watching her face. "She told me what he called about."

Vivian's tan skin paled to a sickly yellow. Her pupils contracted. I was still watching her face, fascinated, when she jerked the Windex bottle up to my eye level and squeezed the trigger.

I saw the blur of spray and smelled the ammonia in the same instant. A millisecond later the cold spray hit my face. But it didn't reach my eyes. I had my new glasses on.

I could taste ammonia, though. I spit it out and wiped my face with the back of my hand frantically. Then I yanked my wet glasses off, clearing my vision just in time to see Vivian drop the Windex bottle and grasp the long neck of the vacuum cleaner with both hands.

I turned and stepped to the side without thinking. The beater brush crashed down in front of me.

"Vivian, I've written it all down—" I began.

She wasn't listening. She lunged at me, muscled arms outstretched. I backstepped quickly. She tripped over the vacuum cleaner cord and hurtled to the ground. A sound of startled pain and rage erupted from her lips.

"—in a letter," I finished. "They'll know what happened. They know I was coming here. It's no good," I told her.

"You and your goddamn tai chi!" she screamed. Her eyes looked strange again as she looked up at me, wide and unfocused like they'd been at Nick's house. But now I recognized the expression. It was pure hatred.

"Vivian . . ." I said gently, then faltered. What words could help her now?

"Why didn't you just keep your nose out of it!" she screeched. "I left you three messages."

"It'll be all right," I lied softly.

"SHIT!" she roared.

"Oh, Vivian, I still can't believe it was you," I burst out. "I really do like you, for God's sake!"

It might have been the sincerity of my last words, or maybe just the knowledge that her mistakes were irrevocable. Vivian bent her head and exploded into loud and wrenching sobs. I sat down next to her on the carpeted floor. My own eyes were watering profusely. I told myself it was just the ammonia fumes. The skin on my face was beginning to burn too. I pulled an old wadded-up Kleenex out of my pocket to wipe my face. Vivian wordlessly handed me a damp cloth to better do the job.

We sat on the floor, side by side, for some time. I wiped my face and she massaged her hurt knees. I could smell her acrid sweat over the tang of ammonia.

"Why?" I asked finally.

"That bitch couldn't even keep her fuckin' house clean!" Vivian bawled. Her face tightened as she turned toward me.

I kept quiet and waited for more.

"Prosperity consciousness. Bullshit!" Vivian shouted. She turned her head away from me again. But I could still see the angry sneer that twisted her face as she stared across the room.

"All the time telling me to 'just open up to the universe.' Asking me why I was blocking my own success. And then, finally, she got disgusted with me because I *chose* to be poor." Vivian pounded her fist on the thick carpet. "She turned her back on me, goddammit! No more pep talks. Just 'Clean my house and shut up.' I was the fuckin' hired help again."

Vivian turned her head toward me once more. Her eyes were glazed, her face distorted by rage.

"Prosperity consciousness, when I can barely afford to live in Marin!" she cried. "My whole apartment is smaller than Sarah's living room."

Then suddenly all the anger, all the spirit, seemed to drain from her. Her body slumped, deflated. She dropped her gaze to the floor.

"It was the same thing when I was in high school," Vivian explained in a subdued voice. I wasn't sure if she was explaining to me or to herself. "I went to Woodside with all the rich kids. Only I wasn't rich. They all lived in nice houses, like this one." She waved her hand. I noticed the well-appointed living room for the first time.

"There were only a few of us from across the tracks," Vivian droned on. "I remember inviting one of the rich kids over to my parents' apartment. She couldn't believe our whole family lived in an apartment. Apartments were for when you moved out from home, for fun, not for families."

As she continued, her speech grew more slow and monotonous, her eyes unfocused, rounded and shining. She was seeing something I wasn't. I couldn't control the shudder that came with the realization that I was no longer watching my friend Vivian, but a murderer.

"I could steal the clothes to keep up, but it still wasn't the same," she said quietly. "They still had the cars. And the dates."

Her torso spasmed suddenly, as if someone had grabbed her shoulders and given her a quick shake. Anger came back into her voice. "And then Sarah with her new investment program," she snarled. "Do you know how much money you can make off of something like that? And she was already rich. She didn't deserve it. *I* deserved it. I know computers backwards and forwards. But nobody will hire me 'cause I'm self-taught, a hacker. I have a right to just one break, don't I? Just one good program?" She looked into my face, searching for something, maybe approval, then turned away again, disappointed.

"It should have been mine," she insisted sullenly. "So I took it." The spirit seemed to have left her voice again. It was flat as she continued her story. "Sarah noticed somehow. She asked me if I'd been at her computer. I told her I hadn't, but she didn't believe me. She just smiled that weird-ass smile of hers and told me to be careful what reality I created. Said she'd take legal steps if I tried to sell her program."

"It's worthless, you know," Vivian sighed, turning to face me again. She looked tired, haggard even. But at least her eyes were seeing me. "Totally worthless without channels of distribution. That's what my brother-in-law said when I took the program to him. He said it was too dependent on the intuition of the average investor." She shook her head. "No software house would touch it. He said if someone had already established channels of distribution, it might make some money. But for me, nothing."

"Worthless, all worthless. I thought maybe Nick and me . . ." she trailed off, her face softening a little as she spoke of Nick. She stroked her own cheek with one hand absently. "But, no, not even Nick. All worthless."

"So you programmed her robot to kill her?"

"Yeah, I did," she answered, her eyes narrowing. "But I warned her first. I sent her a message. I taped it from an old Bette Davis movie." Vivian laughed bitterly. "Sarah ignored the message. She never even mentioned it. So I decided to kill her with her own fuckin' robot."

Vivian's eyes searched mine again. I couldn't approve, but I was beginning to understand. It's all too easy to insist that success is a matter of will when you're successful. The concept must have felt like salt on an open wound to Vivian. She was the outsider looking in, gazing at the lush fruits of success from the vantage point of poverty. Relative poverty, I corrected myself. Vivian wasn't poor except by Marin's standards. I stroked her shoulder gently, wondering what had drawn her to a place where she would always be relatively poor.

"I wasn't really sure the robot would kill her," Vivian said softly. "It was kinda like flipping a coin. If it did, I thought maybe it would mean I deserved the program, deserved success." She shrugged her shoulders. "If it didn't, I thought maybe it'd be sorta a joke, you know." She shook her head sadly. "But it worked. The one thing I do right in my life, and it's wrong. God, when I found her body I was so sorry, but it was too late."

She clapped one hand over her face and began to sob again, more quietly this time. I put my arm around her shoulders.

"What about Jerry?" I asked after her tears had subsided.

Vivian jerked her head up. "I heard his message on your tape," she explained, her husky voice full of mucus. She stared out across the room, unseeing. "You never rewound it before you left. So I did it for you after I finished cleaning. I had to listen to the old messages to make sure I didn't erase anything important."

She sniffled loudly. I handed her my Kleenex. She paused to blow her nose, then went on in a near whisper.

"Once I heard Jerry, I knew he must have seen me working at Sarah's computer while she was gone. I spent a lot of time at her computer, copying her stuff and programming the robot. I even copied her will. Nobody from the outside ever would have noticed me in there. But Jerry was working inside the hedges.

"I went to talk to him. I knew where to find him. He always did Bolinas Avenue on Mondays." Her body tensed as she remembered. "He said no problem, he wouldn't tell anyone about seeing me if . . . if I'd sleep with him. I don't think he knew I killed Sarah. He just thought I stole from her. And he was an ugly toad!" Her hands clenched into fists, bunching up the muscles on her arms. "I climbed onto the bed of the truck and hit him with his own shovel. The fucker deserved it!"

Her eyes were wide and unfocused again. I was frightened. I took my arm away from her shoulders carefully.

"I'm going to call the police now," I said as calmly as I could.

"Yeah, I guess you have to," she responded lifelessly.

I called the Marin County Sheriff's Department and told them I was sitting with the murderer of Sarah Quinn and Jerry Gold.

I could hear excited voices and sounds of scurrying in the background. As police cars were dispatched I was advised to leave the house and leave the house fast. The voice on the line assured me that they would take care of things from here on out. I thanked the voice politely for the advice, hung up, and went back to sit with Vivian.

"Did you set my woodpile on fire?" I asked as I sat back down a few yards away from her. I kept my tone easy, friendly.

"Yeah," she answered sullenly. "I had to. You wouldn't stop nosing around."

"But I could have been burned alive!" I protested, my tone no longer easy.

"No," Vivian said, shaking her head. Her eyes filled with hurt. "I knocked on your door and made sure you were awake before I left." She extended a hand toward me, but I was sitting too far away for her to touch. She drew her hand back and sighed.

"You're my friend," she said softly. "I wouldn't have killed you. I just wanted you to stop."

I heard the truth in her sad voice. I scooted closer and reached out to her. She grasped my hand for a moment, then let it go.

"Did you try to kill me with a potted plant?" I asked. I had to know.

"What the hell are you talking about?" she demanded irritably. I was relieved by her tone. She sounded like her old self again. Then I heard the police sirens.

"Did you shred my macrame?" I pressed her.

"Jesus, ain't it bad enough that I've killed two people?" Vivian drawled. "Now you wanna blame me for your macrame." She even managed a wan smile.

Vivian and I stood up together. I put my arms around her and hugged her tight as the police cars sirened up the driveway. She was shaking in my arms. I heard the sound of running footsteps and released her gently. Vivian's eyes looked like a child's as they widened with fear and uncertainty. My insides knotted.

In no more than an instant, the Kornbergs' house was filled with the noisy activity of police and Sheriff's personnel. A couple of uniformed sheriffs separated me from Vivian and took me into the shining stainless steel, glass-and-ceramic kitchen. I could smell the herbs and garlic that were artistically festooned on one wall and the cleanser from the recently scrubbed sink. Poor Vivian.

Exhaustion tugged at me then. I sank into a steel-and-leather chair and lay my face down on the table. The tabletop was made of glass. I could see my own chair-flattened thighs through it. That seemed grossly unfair. One of the sheriffs, a good-hearted Oriental man, asked me if I was okay and offered to get me a cup of coffee.

I was explaining my viewpoint on coffee as a form of poison when I heard a commotion outside. I looked through the kitchen window and saw two sheriffs escorting Vivian to a waiting car. Her muscular body looked small and vulnerable between the two six-footers. The sudden gush of tears that flowed from my eyes seemed unconnected to me. But I knew then that I would mourn the loss of Vivian even longer than the loss of Sarah.

As I watched the Sheriff's car carry Vivian away, I noticed someone else. Wayne. He was standing in front of a burly uniformed policeman at the end of the driveway. The policeman had one hand on his gun and the other hand held out, palm forward. Wayne's face was unreadable at that distance. But the hunch of his shoulders told me that he was angry.

I stood up and walked to the window quickly. I waved both my arms at Wayne, semaphore fashion. His shoulders relaxed. His wave back was exuberant.

I heard new voices behind me. I turned and saw Sergeant Feiffer and his dog-faced sidekick. Feiffer pointed toward the chair I'd been sitting in. I blew Wayne a kiss, then sat back down.

Sergeant Feiffer looked tense. I wondered whether he was going to yell at me some more. But he didn't. He just asked me to tell my story in my own words. When I explained why I had suspected Vivian he kept nodding as if to say, "I know, I know." Then I wondered if he had known, or had at least guessed, that it was Vivian all along. Hadn't he said that he had ideas, but no proof, from the beginning? When I got to the part where Vivian flung herself over the vacuum cleaner cord, the sergeant's sidekick cleared his throat.

"I guess her karma just caught up with her, huh?" he said in a low and sincere voice.

Sergeant Feiffer groaned and walked out of the room.

He never came back. Another less friendly Sheriff's sergeant marched in with a tape recorder. Then the real interrogation began. It was almost two hours later when he finally let me go. I promised to sign a written transcript of my statement the next day.

Wayne was waiting for me outside.

He held me for a long time. When I finally drew back, he bent over and looked into my eyes.

"I'll be there whenever you're ready," he growled softly.

He climbed into his Jaguar and rolled out past the iron gates before I could say I was already ready.

– Twenty-five –

"HEAVY," TONY MURMURED. His voice was barely audible over the whoosh and gurgle of the circulating water in the hot tub.

So far that Sunday afternoon, "heavy" had been his only comment on my account of Wednesday's confrontation with Vivian. Tony was listening, though. His sincere face declared his attention and concern without words. Unfortunately, his new rainbow Mohawk was sending another message. I pulled my gaze away from his hair and slid deeper into the hot water of the tub. Maybe in time I would get used to the multicolored fan of spikes that divided his otherwise shaved skull. But I wouldn't bet on it.

Peter bent forward in a posture of impending interrogation. Drops of sweat shimmied down his nose and into the water. Peter hadn't limited himself to one comment. Objections, arguments and questions had spouted from his mouth concerning each and every piece of my story.

"I can't believe you were foolish enough to go alone to confront a woman whom you believed to be a murderer," he lectured peevishly. "What is wrong with you, Kate?"

"Vivian was my friend," I answered sullenly, wondering why I had said "was" instead of "is." I hadn't really believed Vivian was a murderer until the Windex had hit me in the face. "Anyway," I told him, "Wayne was there."

"That's another thing," he pressed. "What was Wayne doing there?"

"He was following me in his car," I explained. "When he heard the police cars he thought . . ."

I faltered. What had Wayne thought? We had spoken by telephone four or five times since Wednesday, but our conversations had been superficial—chitchat on my side, monosyllables on his. Neither of us had mentioned either of the two "M" words, marriage or murder. I hadn't invited him to see me in person yet. I wasn't prepared to handle the possibility of his refusal.

Peter's sour voice tugged me back to Sunday once more. "I still don't understand her motive—"

"Vivian didn't kill for only one reason," I interrupted sharply. "Not just for the investment program. Not just for Nick. There were a lot of reasons." I sank deeper into the tub, letting the hot water flow over my shoulders. "Sarah wounded Vivian deeply. Sarah told Vivian she was entitled, then threatened her entitlement."

I paused, remembering the hatred in Vivian's face when she had talked about Sarah. I shivered, wondering how I could still feel so cold while immersed in the steaming water of a hot tub.

"Sarah preached the doctrine of prosperity consciousness," I said softly, looking down at the swirling water. "Over and over again, she said that everyone was entitled to wealth and success. All they had to do was develop a positive attitude. To create their own reality." I looked up at Tony and Peter.

Tony nodded. Peter opened his mouth to object. I pressed on quickly.

"Vivian believed in the idea of entitlement literally, like a child believes in fairy tales. So when the magic that Sarah promised didn't work, Vivian blamed her." I could almost see Sarah's grinning face in the steam. She must have driven Vivian crazy. "Then Sarah gave up on Vivian. You know how Sarah acted when she decided someone wasn't on her path."

"Like they were invisible," Peter said softly. Was he beginning to understand?

I nodded and went on. "Vivian was hurting, emotionally and financially. Then she saw a way to get her share of the goodies, by copying Sarah's investment program and selling it. But Sarah caught her. Vivian wanted that program. And she wanted revenge."

"But she *had* to know she might be caught," Peter argued.

"Vivian isn't big on long-range planning," I explained, thinking of her disastrous spur-of-the-moment marriages. "The alcohol didn't help either." I didn't want to talk anymore. I felt so tired. I wondered if I was coming down with something.

Tony reached over to give my shoulder a squeeze. I looked up to thank him, but the sight of his Mohawk stopped me before I got my mouth open. I had forgotten about it again.

"What did Jerry want to talk to you about?" Peter probed. "What did he tell his wife exactly?"

"He told his wife he wanted to let me know that he saw 'the cleaning lady at the computer,' " I answered. "He didn't say *what* cleaning lady, or *whose* computer. And Mrs. Gold didn't connect the comment with Sarah's death. She never told the police what Jerry had said." I shook my head slowly. Jerry shouldn't have died. Or Sarah. I might have prevented both their deaths if I had been quicker off the mark.

"It wasn't your fault," murmured Tony. Was I that transparent? Or had he received psychic powers along with his Mohawk?

I squinted at him. His hair looked better that way. "Thank you," I said.

"I never considered Vivian as a suspect," Peter admitted. So that was why he kept arguing with me!

"I didn't think of Vivian right away either," I told him. "Though I should have. Programming that robot took time and access, and she was the only one who had plenty of both. Remember Sarah told us that Vivian 'fancies herself a computer programmer'? Not to mention the fact that Vivian told me the contents of Sarah's will. The will that was stored on the computer." I shook my head. I had missed so many clues. Maybe I had missed them on purpose. I hadn't wanted to believe it was Vivian.

"What'll happen to her now?" asked Tony.

"I don't know. I didn't ask," I sighed. I hadn't really wanted to know. "Prison or a mental hospital, I guess." I closed my eyes. Fatigue was settling down on me again.

"You know, Vivian is going to have one great advantage in either institution," said Peter in an unusually gentle tone.

"What advantage?" I demanded, opening one eye.

He sat up straight in the tub and smiled. The smile looked good on his sweating face. "I predict she will become the queen of gossip," he pronounced. "Closed institutions thrive on gossip. She'll have plenty of subjects."

"Yeah, really?" I asked, wanting to believe.

"Really," he assured me. He even reached and patted my knee, then flushed and drew his hand back, probably embarrassed to be caught in an act of kindness.

"Thanks, Peter," I whispered. My cold hands grew a little warmer as I imagined Vivian regaling rows of inmates with her tales.

Peter cleared his throat. "I have a theory about the seance," he announced.

"Yeah, what?" I asked.

He steepled his fingertips before beginning his lecture. "Much of New Age conjecture is insensitive to the needs of those who are truly less fortunate," he elucidated. "If Sarah finally realized this basic concept, she might have realized that she had made a mistake with Vivian, as well as with others."

"So, she said, 'whoops,' " I concluded for him. It was an interesting theory, but I had my doubts. It didn't sound like a concept that Sarah would understand, even in death.

"I've been thinking, too," began Tony diffidently. The spikes of his Mohawk were beginning to wilt in the steam. "Sarah was an immortalist. She believed she could live forever. And her will was so strong she probably would have, too."

"Perhaps," Peter granted impatiently.

"But isn't immortality in this lifetime the ultimate limitation?" Tony argued. His eyes were wide and moist with emotion. It felt good to be able to trust his sincerity again. "Maybe it was important for her to go on to the next stage—"

"But—" Peter began.

"I think that's what she realized when she sent us 'whoops,' " Tony finished quickly.

Peter opened his mouth to object again, but apparently thought better of it. He let his mouth close and leaned back against the tub's wall, his face pinched in thought. I leaned back too and considered Tony's theory. I didn't really buy it. It supposed a message from the dead in the first place, and insight from Sarah in the second place. Before I could get to the third place, Sarah's voice came into my mind reminding me that nothing was impossible. All right, all right, I told myself. Maybe it's true.

Peter's face began to relax, the flesh loosening around his jaw and cheekbones, hints of a smile at the corners of his mouth. Tony's Mohawk was even more relaxed. It looked less like a fan now, more like a row of colorful spider chrysanthemums. I smiled, then noticed the crisp blue sky for the first time, and the smells and sounds of October that were lazily floating around us. A radio was playing rock'n' roll somewhere; someone was barbecuing, and C.C. was meowing.

She came racing around the side of the house, her eyes blinking with pleasure. The object of her excitement was shuffling close behind: Wayne.

I gazed at his battered face. I couldn't remember a lovelier sight since I had retrieved my teddy bear from premature burial in the garbage can some thirty years ago.

Wayne kept his eyes on the ground as he walked toward us, lifting them only for a quick nod at Peter and Tony, then lowering them again.

"Brought you something," he growled softly.

He moved close enough to the tub to touch me. But he didn't take advantage of the opportunity. He stuck his hand in his pocket instead and pulled out a small purple velvet box.

He brought his eyes up from the ground again briefly. I saw the uncertainty in them; then they were obscured by his brows as he looked back down.

"Here," he said. He held the box out to me on his open palm like a tourist feeding a wild animal.

I reached a wet hand through the steam and plucked the box from his palm. I examined it cautiously. It looked like a jewelry box. Wayne rubbed his empty hands together anxiously.

"For God's sake, open the thing!" Peter snapped.

I opened it. A ring was nestled inside, a ring with an unusual setting. Small sapphires sketched a rod and a circle. The circle was filled with tiny sparkling diamonds. Damn. What did it mean?

I looked up at Wayne. His gaze remained fastened on the ground. "An award for the best sleuth I know," he explained in a low rumble.

Finally, I recognized the shape. It was a detective's magnifying glass. I leaned my head back and laughed.

A magnifying glass set into a ring. What a great present! Then my stomach lurched. Was this an engagement ring?

"No," Wayne said, as if he had heard me. Was everyone psychic now? He lifted his head and gazed at me with an intensity that could have fried eggs.

"It's a living-together ring," he said, his rough voice stronger now. "I'm offering to make you a dishonest woman." He paused. "Okay?" he asked softly.

"Okay!" I agreed and launched myself out of the water and into Wayne's arms, triggering a small tidal wave which soaked everyone.

C.C. and Peter howled in unison. Tony yelped, "My hair!"

But Wayne didn't complain a bit.